A Dream Untold

MICHAEL BERG

In memory of
Marianne Jacoby (1908–2005)

RQ

Published by Rafael Q Publishers
5 Brookside Road London NW11 9NH
www.adreamuntold.com

© Michael Berg, 2008

All rights reserved. No part of this publication may be reproduced, stored in a retrieval system, or transmitted, in any form or by any means, electronic, mechanical, photocopying, recording or otherwise, without prior permission, in writing, from the publisher.

Project Management by the Cambridge Editorial Partnership Ltd
www.camedit.com
Designed by Paul Barrett Book Production, Cambridge
Printed by the MPG Books Group

A copy of this book is held at the British Library.

The diagram of The Ten Sefirot on page 107 is by Tsila Schwartz and used by permission of the artist.

ISBN: 978-1-901017-01-4

For Ros, who has always been there

"A dream uninterpreted is like a letter unread"
Babylonian Talmud

Author's note

The core elements of *A Dream Untold* have been drawn from my own experience, namely that of having the dream in 1978, its effect on me, my obsessive research and the revelation of it being a dream shared with Hayyim Vital. I was filmed in Safed for a TV documentary, but the experience did not result in a psychotic episode. However, this is a work of fiction and all present-day characters are fictitious. Any resemblance to real persons is purely coincidental.

The historical episodes are my own extrapolations of the thoughts, feelings and lives of Isaac Luria, Hayyim Vital et al. based on well-documented stories and legends. I give full credit to the sources in the Acknowledgements. A Glossary is included at the end of the book, with brief definitions of the Hebrew and Kabbalistic terms used in the text.

THEN

PROLOGUE

Damascus 1610

There is a table. The faded wood is knurled and an old man sits and stares at the shadows cast by the flickering candle that stands above these ridges of time. He looks at the wall in front of him and is drawn to the powdered whiteness and decay of the crumbling plaster.

His breathing slows and his body stills as he enters a meditation. Patterns emerge in the peeling flakes. Faces of women that speak silently, of men in puzzlement, of himself reflected in his mind. And through this mirror of his existence, the wall swells and becomes the infinite expanse of the heavens.

Immersed in this fullness, white becomes black and through this emptiness his life materialises. Soniadora, the wise woman of his past, beckons and he follows her as he once followed her prophecies. They float and drift above the cobbled streets of the place that was home to them, looking down upon the synagogues and study houses of his youth. Prayers rise and the words adhere to his soul, leaving their meaning within. They connect him to the mysteries revealed by the sage from Egypt.

And in this trance, his eyes moisten with a vision of his master's death bed. And his thoughts turned to unaccomplished deeds. Of how the year of *tikkun olam*, the healing of the world, had passed and the greatness his master had assumed was not enough.

A DREAM UNTOLD

So he watches his departure from the town on the mountain and the wanderings of these past 30 years between the three great cities of Safed, Jerusalem and, finally, Damascus. And now, in his evening, he sits expecting his illustriousness to be acknowledged. Soniadora whispers in his dulled reverie:

"Hayyim, tell them of your life. Tell them of your dreams. And your visions. Tell them of your master and what he revealed to you."

The rabbi reaches out to this voice, touches the sound, grasps it and takes the clenched hand to his heart. And he remains thus while Soniadora sweeps the heavens for his story. She gathers his dreams, and those of others who had dreamt of him.

And Hayyim wrote of these things. To tell who he was and what his purpose in the world was. And this *Book of Visions* told of events in his life in the first part, which were numerous and selected to explain the great merit of his existence.

And then he recorded his dreams by month and year, and how he came to each dream. But he did not record their meaning. Those to come would interpret them in their own way.

Many had come to him in his life and told him of their dreams. These he also transcribed, and gave prominence to those in which he featured.

In the final part he wrote of the things his teacher, the Ari, had told him about his soul. And how the Ari had instructed him in the practice of *yihudim*, the unification with the souls of righteous men.

The old man drew back from the page and thought of the time he was sent to the cave where the revered rabbis Abbaye and Rava were interred.

A DREAM UNTOLD

"For 1200 years their debates on the *Talmud* have informed us. Hayyim, go and commune with their souls. Perfect the unification and much will be revealed." This his master had told him.

Some 40 years later the memory of this visit was as clear as the experience itself. Burnished on his being, absorbed into his core.

Of how he had been instructed to lay prostrate on the grave of Abbaye until the stillness in his body reflected that of the corpse. And then to perform invocations as if guided by an inner voice until he was overcome by a great trembling and heard from a strange voice perched on his tongue.

"*Wisdom and knowledge will be given to you from heaven like the knowledge obtained by Rabbi Akiva.*" Then it repeated. "*And more than that of Rabbi Akiva. Like that attained by the illustrious Rabbi Yeiva Sabba.*" And then it repeated. "*And more than all these rabbis.*" And then it said "*Greetings to you. They send you greetings formed from heaven.*"

And it was all said many times while he was in a waking state.

And the knowledge revealed to him was a confirmation of the exalted status of his soul.

His soul; he could trace its history back to Adam. His master had told him at length about all those who were its source. More than 100 names. After Adam there was Cain and the transmigrations went through many others mentioned in the Bible. Jethro, Samsom, Rahab the prostitute, Jesse the father of David, Elijah the prophet, Uriah the priest, and many illustrious rabbis including the Abbaye and those who had revealed themselves during the unification.

But what of the future and his soul? How was he to maintain his greatness?

The Ari had told him that he was required to favour sinners for his transmigration. Like him, the majority of them were from the source of Cain and had inherited his sin. Such was the status of his own soul, it could overcome this evil and it was his mission, so his master said, to repair those souls from that source through his deeds.

Was this the destiny of his transmigration? To reside in the body of transgressors and guide them to redemption?

NOW

1

Two little dicky birds sitting on a wall
One named Peter, one named Paul
Fly away Peter, fly away Paul
Come back Peter, come back Paul

London 1996

I am Peter. I am Paul. Fly away Peter, come back Paul. I am Peter Paul Levi. I am fifty. I am five hundred. I am five thousand. Body. Mind. Spirit. The wholeness of being, each with its own temporal sense. Physical and mental age diverge from conception, but they have this common starting point. When is the birth of our soul?

All souls emanate from Adam Kadmon, the primordial man. This is the belief of Hayyim Vital. That name, that 500-year-old Kabbalist, has haunted me for nearly 20 years. He has guided me and taken me on a journey of intrigue, enlightenment, despair and redemption. His *Book of Visions*, a mystical autobiography, transcends the period between us. It has forged a link that has pierced my psyche and stripped bare my defence mechanisms. For half my life, that link has prodded, probed, exposed, clarified, mystified and energised the me. The I. The Thou.

There are key moments in anyone's life when a chink appears in a closed edifice of personality. A moment when there is an unperceived heightened awareness – an unknown feeling that something will become known.

A DREAM UNTOLD

I was an unassuming vessel and the dream came unexpectedly. In retrospect, perhaps it didn't. Fate had taken me to the area where Vital lived, walked, studied and became the disseminator of Kabbalistic wisdom.

Looking back, I suppose I was in a position to receive.

I had always been drawn to hostile environments. Not hostile in a life-threatening way, but in a way that created an edginess to affect your stability and sense of being. They were my challenge. I needed the test. I needed the fates to decide.

My India trip was seminal. In 1967 the path between London and the sub-continent was a Magical Mystery Tour. For an aimless 20-year-old it was a rite of passage. No planning, just an urge to follow the trail, born out my natural inquisitiveness. Whoever looked into my steely blue eyes admired their wonderment and searching gaze, before being confused by my accompanying doleful expression.

Some found my silence uncomfortable, rude even, as I drifted within the interaction, assessing the situation and whether it was worth expending any energy in dialogue. Minimising effort was also a physical trait and my lean, angular body gave rise to a loping, fast-paced stride that did not seem to tire me whatever distance I covered.

Organisation for the journey was perfunctory and consisted of undergoing some necessary inoculations and obtaining visas to Persia and Afghanistan. As regards transport, a knowledge that a coach would be in Dover Docks, en route to my mythic destination, was sufficient. Minimal luggage and a semi-convincing story was enough to get me a ride. I had my Pentax and a pen, a starter in photo-journalism.

A DREAM UNTOLD

Three dope-ridden months later I was back in London with mind-encrusted notebooks and an Afghan bag full of exposed black-and-white film. An article or two burgeoned into a book. No passion of authorship, just a sense of inevitability that it had to be written. And then came the documentary. Apparently I had insight into the psychology of the hippy trail. I had tapped into a Zeitgeist and was commissioned to direct a film capturing the essence of this sixties' voyage of discovery. The producer had vision, an *enfant sauvage* approach to film-making, and had supplied me with a VW campervan, cameraman and sound engineer. I was no Ken Kesey and it wasn't a Hieronymous Bosch bus full of Merry Pranksters, but our film had the flavour of his trans-America trip. I was a sort of Donovan to his Dylan and it was enough to launch me into a career making off-beat travelogues.

So that was how, ten years later, I found myself in Safed. That phrase now resonates – a physical transport, a mental uplifting. It was to be the fourth in a series of films on mystical places of the world. The only brief given to me by the producer were the locations – the Inca site of Macchu Picchu, Ayers Rock, the spiritual place of the Australian aborigines, the Hindu temples of Khajuraho and Safed, a town in the Galilean hills of Northern Israel.

Arriving in Safed I was surprised by its vibrancy. The other three places had been desolate, unoccupied and they exuded presence by their physical being and relationship to the ground on which they stood. But this place was alive and was a home to a population that seemed to absorb its lingering energy.

I had read no books, done no research; the history and nature of the place was a mystery to me. That was the way I worked, serendipitously. I just let the spirit, the aura, the vibe of the location get to me. It was an established pattern, otherwise George my cameraman would have been driven mad. We had worked together for five years. Our styles suited each other. He enjoyed the independence I gave him and was able to experiment and enjoy the creativity required to support my idiosyncratic approach to film-making. We worked without a sound engineer. Ambient noise was all that I required. We never interviewed. Voices over and music were added in the edit suite.

George, like me, was unmarried, with no current partner or relationship. He was older, solid, mature, dependable. Perhaps he *was* a father figure. It was an oft-quoted remark, especially by those who knew that I'd lost both my parents by the time I was in my early twenties.

He cut a shambolic figure, bulky with red hair and a ginger beard that obscured a pock-marked, seasoned face. Unusual for a cameraman, his thick, stubby hands protruded from an ancient Harris Tweed jacket that was worn as a second skin. I don't think I ever saw him take it off and I suspect he even slept in it.

The harshness of the material belied a softer interior. A manner that was slow, reasoning and thoughtful to the point of ponderousness. But he used it to display great empathy and understanding – especially towards me.

There was, though, an emptiness about him, a lack of fulfilment in his own life that exuded an element of vicariousness in living through other people's experiences. It was strangely supportive, a sort of sado-altruism that left him in despair if his attempts at helping out did not work.

Over the years our symbiotic relationship developed into a rhythm and routine of working. On the first day he would shoot stock location material – people, buildings, landmarks. I would wander alone, letting my senses guide me. Safed seemed to have an extra dimension. The streets were narrow, the arches low. Buildings oppressed the passer-by with their history, each stone with its own message, a watchword from 2000 years of observation.

By late afternoon, I was still wandering. In other locations, other places, I would have developed a theme for filming but my process of osmotic inspiration would not metamorphose into a storyboard. I was still in chaos. I could not grasp this place. It did not want to relinquish its secrets.

Dusk descended and men appeared on the flat rooftops of the Jewish Quarter. Their prayer shawls billowed in the evening breeze like wings of devotion. Ritual voices sent centuries-old stanzas ringing to the heavens in a chorus of the devout. The scene had a brooding strangeness, a foreboding that I felt was directed at me. Hebraic words of unknown meaning, but inner familiarity, filled my mind and I marched to the pace of their repetition. Without knowing it I found myself at the house where we were to stay the night.

"Great place," George said as I came through a wrought-iron gate and onto the patio where he was sitting. The house, which was owned by an Israeli cousin of our producer, was used as a holiday retreat. It had the feel of temporary stays.

"Did you get its history?" I was curious to know what George had gleaned when he had picked up the key.

"Some of it is from the sixteenth century. Bits have been added since then. Basically it's Ottoman style."

From the courtyard I looked down at a walled, terraced garden full of wild undergrowth. The main room, kitchen and bathroom were all accessed from the patio. A path led to bedrooms at lower levels, their entrances shielded by the foliage. No corridors of interconnection – each room had its independence, giving me a sense of unease and disorientation as the dark closed in around us.

We entered the main room. It had the arched ceiling, thick walls and alcoves of a typical house from the Ottoman period. George repeated the instructions he had received from Adera.

"This is where we sleep. We can put our sleeping bags on the seat under the window and on the floor."

"I'll take the window. I need to be able to breathe. I've never felt so oppressed by a place before." I used the word oppressed because it was a sensation I could articulate. That's the problem with language. Words are used as labels to display our ideas, to enable us to interact, to portray emotions, to communicate. We are dependent on the inventory gathered from our own experience. There are some feelings, some sensations, some internally directed lines of consciousness that are beyond words – an entry into the realm of the senses. I was unsure, uncertain, hesitant.

"What are your thoughts about tomorrow? I've got a good feel for the place now. I'm ready to hit its soul!" George was his usual keen self and his discrete and gentle prodding was typical.

"I'm not ready." The phrase came out involuntarily. I wasn't sure what I meant by it.

"How do you mean?"

"I don't know. I seem to be lacking inspiration. It's as if I need to know more of something."

"More of what?" George was intrigued. He hadn't seen me like this before.

"I wish I knew. Tell me more about the house."

"It seems Adera bought it from a hundred-year-old witch!"

"What!"

"A white witch. Legend has it that she made up love potions for the local Arabs. Her other job was to wash the bodies of the dead in preparation for burial. Not sure if you noticed, but the house overlooks a cemetery."

"I feel like she's still around."

"I think we should eat. Falafel and pitta bread?"

"Any wine?"

"No. You need a clear head for tomorrow."

"OK! Maybe I'll have an early night. Things might be clearer tomorrow."

We squatted on the floor and ate our food from a low beaten copper table. Candles lit the room – flicking a light switch would have transported us back to our own time. The glow from the flames illuminated the centre of the room with unseen alcoves surrounding us, their blackness nudging our imagination. The wooden door that opened onto the patio was cast in George's shadow, which twitched and turned from the flicker caused by our shallow breathing. Indentations and markings were revealed in the weathered timber: a formless shape, a face, a letter, a word. A creative and receptive imagination could see all these things in the wood, beckoning.

We finished eating and moved the table from the centre of the floor to make room for George's sleeping bag. It was left unsaid, but neither of us felt like taking the plates outside to the kitchen. We were cocooned in this chamber, an unknown force directing us to take our sleeping positions.

The window seat was covered in large velvet cushions, which formed a comfortable mattress. I stretched out in my sleeping bag. George blew out the candles. Blackness. I floated into sleep.

And the dream came.

I was in Safed at the bottom of a long flight of steps. At the top were figures of men. One was prominent, his arms outstretched, reaching to the heavens. Their backs were towards me, the sun behind them, high in the sky. They wore round hats, robes and white stockings. Suddenly the sun disappeared and darkness fell.

There was confusion and despair in the crowd of people surrounding me. And then a chanting started, mostly of a word I could not recognise. Dispor? Yizkor? One man noticed me and I asked what was happening.

"They are trying to bring the light back," he replied.

And then there was light.

And then there was turmoil. And chaos. The scene vanished to be replaced by flashing lights and a circular red and green symbol that spun in front of my eyes. It was constantly moving towards and away from me.

It transported me to that state between sleeping and consciousness.

Unsure of being awake, I lay in the darkness in a state of anxiety and foreboding. I felt a presence. I sensed them – a number of them – on the patio, outside the door, waiting. Dressed in black. Bearded. Black beards. Were they waiting for me? Had they come for me?

They didn't come in. Not physically. But they entered my mind and secreted themselves in my being, laying dormant and waiting for an opportunity to arise.

They induced panic, anxiety and a desire to rid myself of this place.

Too terrified to move, I lay in that room until George awoke and I scrambled out of my sleeping bag.

"We have to leave," I cried, "I can't stay here. We've got to go. Now!"

"What! Why?" came a bleary response.

"I can't explain. Just pack your things. Quickly."

I threw on my clothes, picked up my camera and obsessively took photos of the room from every angle, needing to capture the source of my distress.

"George, open the door," was my next panicked command.

"Can't you open it yourself? I'm still packing," he grumbled, "are you scared of what you might find out there?"

An abrupt "Yes" shook him and he did as I asked.

Tentatively I ventured outside and captured the rest of the house on film. George was now ready to go. I grabbed my bag and ran to the car. George struggled to keep up, weighed down with his equipment cases, needing a second trip to collect his bag and lock up the house. I paced nervously around the car and watched the early morning mist rising to reveal the cemetery below. Was that where my apparitions had come from? A crazy thought, but I was in a crazed state. A state of alarm … of nervousness … of wonderment.

We drove back to Tel Aviv in silence. I needed to collect myself, to consolidate the experience and ponder on its significance. George drove, needing to occupy himself as I obviously wasn't going to give him an explanation. Not yet at least. I would have to tell him soon to make it real, give it a life. Make it shared, this dream. A dream with its own existence. It was alive. It was prescient. It was inside me: it nagged at me, demanded.

I kept replaying the dream in my mind. The images were still clear, vibrant, possessive and I still felt the presence of the bearded ones. I got out my notebook. Its original purpose was to plan the filming, write the storyboard, and outline the script. It became the carrier of another source document. One that was to transform my life. I wrote down the dream.

Trees, bushes, rocks drifted past. I was detached from this outside world. Inside the car was like being in another dimension. Of space. Of time. I reflected on the dream, its meaning, its content, its significance. Its mystery. There was so much I didn't know, but that there was a Jewish and religious connection was evident.

Most of it seemed to have a symbolic content. The steps. The sun disappearing. An eclipse? The return of light. The people. And *I* was in the dream. I interacted with one of them. Who was he? There was recognition, not personal knowing, but an intuitive contact. For an instant he drew me into their world. Until the turmoil. He had left me on the edge of an abyss in a strange country. Alone. Anxious. Terrified. The dream state became my reality on wakening, or so I rationalised. I was in limbo in timeless despair. My past engulfed me. The totality of events, actions, feelings, emotions overwhelmed me. A near-death experience of life flashing before me.

I looked across to George as we drove along the coast road south of Haifa. My left eye moistened and a single tear emerged and traced a damp trail on my cheek. Not wanting to rub it away, I remained motionless. My body had a soft rigidity; it was a vessel, a frame, for mind and spirit to reside. I was transfixed, transcendent and George's face blurred as I gazed across the Mediterranean to infinity. A second tear followed the path of the first as I recollected how we had met. How he had restored my equilibrium, my self-confidence, my belief as a creative artist.

I had been using the edit suite of the independent film company where George worked. As usual, I was behind schedule and under pressure. My client was a chain of holiday resorts that had camps in "exotic" locations. The commission was to produce a film that portrayed the company's concern for the environmental and the cultural impact of its business. The reality on the ground was that local managers had perceived it as an opportunity for furthering their own ambitions and lining their pockets. Funds earmarked for indigenous projects, such as restoration of water rights for neighbouring villages, had a habit of disappearing. I became more interested in capturing the corruption than idealising the company. The client was seeing the first results in the edit suite.

It was not what they wanted. It was not what they were paying me for. I had been expecting them to be shocked and horrified by what they saw, but they berated me, belittled me. They said that if I couldn't provide what they wanted, then I could go to hell. I argued in vain. I was still a shallow youth, they said. I didn't understand how the world worked, they said. Get real, they said. They left me drained, wrought with emotion, tearful and full of self-doubt.

"You look like you need a drink," George said as he entered the edit suite after the others had left.

"They knew. They knew. And they wanted me to portray something different." I fought back tears. It was the first time my work had so severely been questioned. It hurt – a hurt that pierced my outer core of belief and drained my integrity, leaving it limp on the floor.

"It's an old saying, but he who pays the piper …."

"… calls the tune. I know, but I felt compelled to film it the way I saw it."

"Tell me about it in the pub. Is this yours?" He helped me on with my worn and cracked black leather jacket. A single-breasted design, not the fur-lined bomber jacket favoured by my contemporaries. I had owned it for 10 years. A symbol that my physical growth had stopped at 18, an image of out-réness for university. I felt its comfort as George held it out to me.

That action forged a link between us. Empathy and caring came through in a single moment. Just that, no sense of a pick-up or a come-on in his asking me for a drink. Not much was said as we walked to the nearest pub, the Queen's Head.

"This do you?" George asked, not expecting a "no".

I nodded and we found a table in the corner, away from the cigarette machines and jukebox. Quiet enough to enable talking, but still sufficiently part of the ambience to cover any pregnant pauses. Not that there were any.

We had never talked, just passed by a few times in the corridor. A half-smiled nod of recognition was our only contact. After taking a few sips of his pint, George started by telling me of his early days in the industry – of failed projects, tough clients, producing to demand, taking the crap and surviving. I listened. He talked more. Somehow he knew of my work, knew of my philosophy, my potential. Don't let it all go, he said. They're just a stupid bunch of fat arses, he said. I smiled. It wasn't the last time George had that affect on me, knew the right bon mot. My hands cradled a second Guinness, felt its chill through the glass. Emerging from my self-pity I began to take in his appearance. I hadn't really noticed his red beard, round face, soulful eyes. A shabby sports jacket accentuated a figure that was slightly overweight and lent a kindly bulkiness to his mien. I put his age at early forties, maybe less, maybe more. It was hard to tell and in a way he was ageless.

What was his secret? How had he managed to survive and be so calm in our over-stressed industry? George didn't have the answers, or if he did he wasn't going to divulge them. Instead he sat there, on the other side of the table, listening to my questions. And then he began to draw me out. He wanted to know how I worked – if I had a particular approach, a style. He wanted to know who I had worked with, how I got on with them, if I had a preferred crew. All done with a controlled voice and softness of manner. His movements were slow, stroking palms and cheek as he listened. I relaxed. Alcohol and amateur therapy remedied the afternoon's trauma. As if seeing that his work was done, George got up.

"I've got to go. Let's keep in touch."

We did.

The wind blew. Crested waves ruffled the smooth surface of the sea and jarred me into the present. Sprinkles of sand drifted across the road to be swept up by the traffic. I became aware of the rumble of tyres, the noise of trucks, the presence of George.

"I had a dream," I said, breaking the silence between us. "It disturbed me, I panicked."

George glanced at me. The contact relaxed the furrowed strain on his face, but only slightly. There was still concern, still a sublimated anger that we weren't fulfilling our assignment.

"Are you going to tell me?"

I noted the sarcasm in his voice. He was demanding the right to know.

"Yes, but I'd prefer to do it when we're not driving. Let's take a break, I could do with some coffee and food."

I looked at my watch. We had been driving for over two hours. We left the road at the next turnoff, which led to an Arab village. It was mid-morning and the place still had a sleepiness about it. We drove slowly around a few dusty streets, found a small café and sat down at one of the two outside tables. George found the disinterested waiter, ordered some coffee and cake then sat down and waited.

"I've never had a dream like that before," I started and described the experience in a rushed, terse manner, wanting it to be over with quickly. There was too much in it that required an explanation I could not give.

"It's a weird dream, I'll say that, but how come it affected you like that? Why did we have to leave?" George was still a bit prickly, not used to this sort of irrational behaviour.

"I can't explain. Something took me over. It was if I'd been possessed and had no control of my actions. I was terrified."

George sat back, raised his arms, put his hands behind his head and ruffled his hair. His eyes gazed heavenward and then dropped to look into mine, to see through me, to find the source of my agitation. It seemed an age before he spoke.

"So what are you going to do now?"

"Get back to London. I couldn't focus on anything until then, till I'm out of this country."

"What about the film? We can't just abandon it."

"Right now I'm not sure I could make it. I really need to take stock of whatever it is that has affected me."

"I suppose you want me to placate Robin?" George was referring to our client, our producer at Myriad Productions.

Since teaming up with him, George always picked up the flak from our assignments. He felt the need to protect me. Well us, the team, really. He knew that I couldn't cope with being hassled, being put under pressure. Not creative pressure – I could thrive on that. Lose myself. Become immersed in what George called my "vision thing". No, it was people pressure. Dealing with them, reacting to demands, being responsible. Until I met George I would sublimate the fears and anxieties, as the greater desire to get work and produce a film overcame my internal terrors. George recognised that and became my front man. An interlocutor. A negotiator. A shield. I was happy to relinquish the role to him. But it meant I retreated into myself. It was something I hadn't done since adolescence. Since my first crisis.

"Of course. He prefers to speak to you." I said it with a wry smile that hid the knowingness of what had occurred.

"What's our story then? When can we tell him that we'll complete the filming?"

"I'm not sure. I need some space. Time to get some answers, do some research, I can't think about anything else. It's consuming me." Topics streamed into my brain for investigation, Safed, the house, Judaism. An immediate obsessiveness overcame me that was to continue at a greater or lesser intensity for over twenty years.

"Not sure how he'll react. It's not like it's the first time on this job." George was referring to the Australian leg of the film. The three-day walkabout with the Aborigines to their "camp of creation" had blurred into two weeks. I was on Dream Time.

That was my problem. Once I became fascinated with a subject all sense of reality disappeared. Compounded by my lack of planning, I suppose. George had tried to instil some discipline into me, with partial success. We would agree a timetable in principle. I would defy it in practice. What mattered to me was the end result. It was elemental. The essence of a place was to be revealed and contextualised. If I really thought about my "osmotic approach", I found that it drew on an intuitive framework. The reference point was a subconscious set of attributes that lent themselves to analysis, to a deepening within a holistic structure. That's why George and I worked well together. He had a logical mind and had delved into systems theory. It enabled him to perceive the fundamental basis to my approach and to appreciate it in analytical terms. Once I had articulated my ideas to him of the way I envisaged a place should be depicted, he could translate it into shots and sequences.

It was a highly efficient process. Editing time was minimised and invariably we could catch up with our schedule. It was how George could satisfy our clients.

"Robin will understand. We've got Peru, Australia and India in the can. Buy some time with Israel. Tell him that we expect something really different, but we need to work on it." I was trying to convince myself that once I'd resolved whatever it was I needed to resolve with the dream, I could go back to Safed.

"I'll try." George remained unmoved.

Those last words at the café were a turning point in our relationship. George was right. Robin's patience was exhausted and he stuck with the three completed films.

George and I communicated by phone in London. It was easier. There could have been something in our body language in face-to-face meetings that would have undermined our relationship. Voice contact kept things at a business level. Let me know when you are ready to work again, were his final words.

That was it. I had conjured the space. How much time? At that point I didn't anticipate the timeless nature of what I was undertaking.

I cut myself off from my friends. I was manic, devouring books on any related topic and went off in seeming tangents that turned into active streams of relevance. For three months I could not focus on anything else. I was restless in my researches. I travelled. Wherever I found myself, I sought out a bookshop, a library. I had a serendipity approach. Something might turn up, something new, something pertinent.

Of prime significance was Safed in the sixteenth century as the centre of Jewish mysticism and development of the Kabbalah. The foremost practitioner Isaac Luria, known as the Ari, had lived in Safed for two years before his early death. It was an intense period and he had imparted details of his Lurianic system to his chief disciple Hayyim Vital. I read more on the Kabbalah, becoming intrigued with its intellectual and structural side – the view of creation, of God's manifestation, of man's role, of universal redemption.

There were other Jewish mystics, in Safed and in other places. Abulafia, Karo, Cordevero – but Luria and Vital haunted me. The names seemed to have a special resonance.

I needed to read more about them, know them. But London seemed constraining, the bookshops and libraries having revealed all they knew. I needed to distance myself from my home environment and provide the mental space to further my enquiries. New York had the largest Jewish population outside Israel and seemed the logical place to go.

My hotel was near Central Park on the Upper West Side, close to the migratory community of Jews who aspired to leave the immigrant homes in the opposite corner of Manhattan. The combination of being in a cultural but secular neighbourhood and its proximity to open space suited my state of being.

After sleeping off my jetlag I took an evening stroll towards Columbus Circle, where the ever-open bookshops loomed. I entered the first one. Like most bookshops in New York they catered for its large Jewish population and had a substantial Judaism section.

My senses were invaded as I walked between the rows of shelves. Music played, fluorescent lights glared, books reached out to brush against me and I was consumed with a prickly awareness until I found my destination. Familiar titles were scanned and rejected, others spurned in their irrelevance until one leapt at me and seared my eyes. *Jewish Mystical Testimonies* dared me to select it and open it. There was his name, Hayyim Vital. There were the dreams from his *Book of Visions*.

Reading it I began to sway in imitation of prayer movement. Anticipation raised my heartbeat as Vital's account revealed to me what I already knew. Words from the sixteenth century spoke of his dream in Safed. Of steps. Of crowds. Of darkness at noon. Of singing. Of meeting a stranger described by Vital as dervish in appearance. Of the light returning. This is what I had dreamt. What had entered me in that Ottoman house and possessed me.

Alone in this place, with no-one to share my discovery, I stood stunned and silent in a bewilderment of confirmation. I returned the book to its resting place, paused, withdrew it and looked again. The dream was still there, still proclaiming that I had a shared experience with this famous mystic.

A DREAM UNTOLD

    I closed the book again and let it merge with the others on the bookshelf. I was unable to purchase it. Ownership would make it an actuality that I wasn't prepared for. Walking out of the bookshop in a daze, I looked into the eyes of passing strangers. "I have a secret", I wanted to shout at them, "I am in a state of disbelief". But they hurried past, not wishing for contact, propelling me back into the dream and into a state of suspended reality that clung to me as I made my way back to the hotel.

THEN

2

Safed 1570

Sabbath was upon Safed, a crescent moon casting shadows on its cobbled streets. Crowds of men jostled, gesticulated and gossiped in the confined alleyways that led from their communal synagogues, making their way home after the evening service.

Congregations of Musta'rabs, those longest in Safed, intermingled with the Maghrebis from North Africa, the Ashkenazim from Germany and the Sefardim from Spain. The *conversos*, however, remained apart from the other groups. Even though many had been here for three generations since fleeing Portugal, their enforced Christianity and practising of Judaism in secret was still regarded as a sin.

One, Caleb Pinto, had been accepted. He was tall and good looking, with an Iberian duskiness and olive complexion, his long strides denoting an athleticism unusual in his community. He had a charisma that attracted the youths of Safed, who joined him in long hikes over the surrounding hilly countryside.

Two figures strode ahead of the throng, Caleb and Judah Halevi, a Maghrebi boy who was slight of build and small for his twelve years. They emerged from an alleyway and quickened their step, needing to be home to join their families for the weekly celebration. Caleb led the way through the enclosed streets where he felt an ownership, a belonging.

His family had arrived two generations earlier and it was fifteen years since his barmitzvah in the synagogue of Joseph Karo, where many of his community had their sons blessed by the revered teacher. Caleb had been an avid, quick-learning disciple and put into practice all the rituals and observances he had been taught.

"Please tell me more stories of the Inquisition, Caleb," implored Judah, struggling to keep up, "they're much more exciting than the stuff I'm learning for my barmitzvah."

"Only if you remember not to tell your parents. Those tales are not meant to be discussed," teased Caleb, delighting in the opportunity.

"What was that one about being burnt alive?"

"You mean the auto-da-fé? That came after torture if you didn't agree to convert."

Judah felt his bones creak as he remembered being told of the rack. Caleb continued with excited breath, captivating the youth with the sound of his voice and visions of blood.

"They would tie you to a stake on top of a pile of wood that was then set alight. My grandfather told me you could hear the screams for miles."

As he spoke, Caleb welled inside with a force that caused his heart to flutter and beat with a new resonance, pumping fiery blood through his body. Quivering with the potency of the rush of energy to his limbs, his form assumed a new physicality and his mind became enraged.

Judah, unaware of the change in Caleb, shivered with the heat of the flames from the pyre in his friend's tale. Raising his head, he suddenly looked around and was smitten with anxiety.

"Where are we going?" he stuttered, "This isn't the way to my home. That's the cemetery down there!"

"We'll take a short cut, then." Caleb's voice was suddenly unrecognisable as the staccato words spurted out in a deep roar.

A flash of unease crossed Judah's face. He looked up at Caleb. Concerned. Questioning. Caleb ignored his worry, grasped Judah's arm and pulled him through a narrow archway into a darkened alleyway. His eyes turned to fire, blazing with the flame of primordial man, Adam Kadmon. Judah struggled as Caleb's outstretched fingers encircled his throat. A thumb pressed on the larynx, the pressure increasing as unyielding hands tightened their hold. The boy was wide-eyed with terror, fixed on Caleb's rictal face, his body gasping, flailing, kicking. But Caleb had a supernal strength and remained unmoved. Silently Judah sagged and grew limp as the last breath was extracted from his being. Caleb kept his grip. The soul could not escape. Not yet.

The streets were empty now. Sabbath peace reigned and the Jews of Safed were at one. Caleb dragged the body to the cemetery, down the path to the graves of the *tzaddiks* and laid the warm corpse on the nearest tombstone. While the body was still malleable and the coldness of death had not stiffened its sinews, he stretched the limbs and placed them in the symbolic shape of Adam Kadmon, the arrangement of the four letters of God's name YHVH, the *Tetragrammaton*. Now the soul could depart. It would join those of the righteous ones on their nightly journey heavenwards. Caleb was satisfied. He had tainted the boy's spirit with murder and the world was further from its final redemption.

A DREAM UNTOLD

On Jazirat al-Rawda, a small island on the Nile near Cairo, stood a man some eight years older than the murderer Caleb. A light evening breeze from the north chilled him as he gazed towards Israel, his spiritual home. This nightly ritual was a necessary adjunct to the intensity of his daily studies, calming and preparing him for the next stage of his life. But tonight he was troubled and felt a disturbance in the air. Isaac sensed it emanated from Safed, the place where he was to fulfil his destiny and impart the interpretation of Kabbalah he had developed during his years of solitude on the island. And with his system, the scholars of Safed would raise the levels of their souls to such a purity that the heralded age of the Messiah would arrive and the world would be redeemed.

A perturbation had taken place, an infringement of the law that was beyond penitence. I must leave, thought Isaac, before the anger in their hearts taints their souls. All must remain pure.

His thoughts were disrupted by the sound of his Uncle Mordechai's servant coming to collect him. Samuel, a young Arab boy, tied his small dhow to the jetty of the island and approached Isaac's hut.

"We must go, master," Samuel whispered. "Your family awaits your presence at the Sabbath table." Isaac nodded and went into the hut to collect the few things he needed for the two days away from his retreat.

He never exchanged words with Samuel. It was not an attitude born out of rudeness. That was not Isaac's nature, for he was gentle, compassionate and had a love for all living things. For him language was sacred and was the root stuff of Creation. While on the island, its use was internal and focused on unravelling the deep mysteries. Here Isaac studied, contemplated and meditated. Here he received Divine guidance. And it was here that Elijah revealed himself. Here his long immersion into the *Zohar*, the classical work of the Kabbalah, became intense and drove him to a clarity of interpretation. Chatting to Samuel would hamper his absorption.

Sitting in the boat, with the northerly breeze filling the sails, Isaac beheld the rippling water. The reflected light of the nearing city flickered on the surface as the encroaching dusk descended. Isaac peered deeper into the river. Images floated upward and one face became clear and replied to his stare. No name could be given, but he knew that this person was to be his disciple and would help resolve the trauma being enacted in Safed.

Samuel moored the boat and Isaac made his way to his uncle's house across the fields to the south of the city with thoughts of how he was to inform him of his leaving.

Mordechai Franses, his mother's elder brother, had taken the family in when Isaac's father died. Solomon Luria, an Ashkenazi, had passed away when Isaac was just eleven, leaving his wife destitute. It was many generations since her family had come from Spain, but the mix of German rigour and Sefardic Mediterranean flair coursed through Isaac's veins and was intrinsic to his being. It was manifest in the charismatic leader that he was to become and was the latent force behind the development of rituals and practices that were to be undertaken by his pious followers.

Mordechai was affluent and, like many Jews under the Ottomans, had a position of high responsibility in the collection of taxes and custom duties. Living in Cairo was very different to life in Jerusalem, where Isaac had been born in 1534. By the time he was eight he was recognised as a wonder child. In the community of 1500 Jews he was considered to be a marvel of rabbinical learning and none of Jerusalem's scholars could compete with him in Talmudic discussion. Now, local sages and rabbis gathered in Mordechai's opulent home to debate the finer points of the *Talmud* and *halakah*, the Law. Isaac would listen to often heated arguments and would make a succinct contribution to the discourse.

Often, at night, after all had left, he would sit in the courtyard of the *cortijo*, built by Mordechai to reflect his Spanish heritage. His family would be sleeping in the surrounding rooms as he replayed the day's discussions. Different viewpoints had been taken in interpreting the sacred writings. Some took them literally, while others insisted that they were allegorical and that the stories were moral illustrations. But Isaac was most interested in the views of those who perceived them as underpinning a philosophical basis to their beliefs. Somehow, even this perspective did not satisfy him. Something deeper lay within the writings, a hidden meaning to be revealed. Of this he was certain.

Isaac continued his rabbinical studies at the famed academy of David ibn Zimra, the chief Rabbi of the Jewish community in Cairo. Ibn Zimra brought tales of his travels to

Isaac, of Spain where his family had been expelled in 1492 when he was twelve and of his times in Safed, Jerusalem and Alexandria.

Safed stirred his imagination – its hilltop location, the mixture of its inhabitants, but mostly the community of scholars. "I will visit this place one day when I am ready," Isaac thought.

That day was not to be for many years, but the stimulus for his journey arrived sooner, at an age when physical and mental maturity are beginning to peak and the questioning that is inside takes on a deeper significance.

Worshipping in the synagogue as a man, four years past his barmitzvah, Isaac noticed a stranger in the seat opposite, muttering and mumbling from an unfamiliar text. His curiosity was roused and he spoke with the newcomer after the service.

"I did not recognise the text you were reading from," Isaac remarked. "Can you tell me about it?"

"I do not know what it is. I cannot read Hebrew." The old man bowed, slightly ashamed. "I wanted to be part of the community and needed a book. I bought this manuscript at random to bring to the synagogue."

Isaac read the title, *Zohar, The Book of Splendour*. He had heard his teacher speak of this, the prime Kabbalistic text. This ancient wisdom had been kept from him as he was considered too young to be introduced to the secrets of the Kabbalah. Years of study and maturity were thought necessary before the mysteries could be revealed – mysteries so deep and profound that they could disturb the mind of the unprepared.

"Please sell me this manuscript," urged Isaac. "It has meaning for me where it has none for you."

"I do not wish to part with it," replied the stranger. "Although I cannot read it, possession of it may bring me luck in my affairs."

"That is not the virtue of this book," replied an aghast Isaac. "But of what affairs do you speak?"

"I have brought wares to Cairo to sell. Unfortunately the import duties I have to pay means I will make no profit. My prayers are that the tax collector will pity me and forgo them."

"My uncle is the tax-farmer," Isaac revealed, even though he was taken aback by this abuse of devotion.

"If you were to introduce me to him, then I will sell you the manuscript," bargained the stranger.

And so Isaac encountered the ways of men in a transaction that was to change his life.

It was a short walk from the synagogue to the place that he now doubly called home, for he had married his cousin, Mordechai's daughter, and they shared two rooms in the *cortijo*. One, their bedroom, opened onto the courtyard, with access at the rear to the room that Isaac used as his study. Through the window above his desk, Isaac could look across the fields to the river and meditate on the beauty of the natural world as a complement to the intensity of his studies.

That night he began to read his newly acquired volume. It was unlike any other book he had studied. Here were the mystical passages he had dreamt of in the form of commentaries on the *Torah*. But such commentaries, the analysis and interpretation were combined with stories of fiction and fantasy that transcended all forms of writing he had known. Each word seemed to have its own secret, its own way of revering the text.

A few pages in he read the passages relating to the first chapter of Genesis, *"In the beginning God created heaven and earth."* The exegesis was ineffable. It considered the events before creation, the making of something from nothing. Isaac stood in awe at these words for they spoke at a level that was beyond reading, beyond literal meaning. Understanding was intuitive; it needed to tap into an inner resource that was hidden.

As he continued to read, a quotation from the Book of Daniel jumped out at him.

"The enlightened will shine like the zohar of the sky, and those who make the masses righteous will shine like the stars forever and ever."

Isaac raised his eyes from the manuscript and gazed at the night sky through the window of his study. It was *rosh hodesh*, the time of a new moon. The silvery crescent was reflected in the ripples of the Nile. Isaac needed the presence of the space above him and around him to fill his body with wonderment. He rose and silent feet ushered him outside to the nearby fields.

Even its partial form, the moon revealed the trees and buildings on the far bank. They were cast in shadow – shapes without substance. Isaac saw through the shapes, his eyes focused on an infinite point. His mind emptied of thought and images began to flow. The trees became form. The contours of their trunks became a landscape, the quivering palms were pointers, indicators of direction. The houses opened. Doors revealed rooms lit with unseen flames. Isaac could travel no further. The suffused red and yellow light cast a haze on grey stone blocks, which were impenetrable.

Isaac stood. His legs quivered. His body twitched. He became aware of his corporeal being. His mind drifted back to the words of Daniel. He would become enlightened. He would shine like the *zohar* of the sky. He would make the masses righteous. He would shine like the stars for ever and ever. At 17 he had found his destiny and he leapt from the bonds of youth.

"So Isaac, you are to achieve fame." David ibn Zimra smiled as his young pupil told him of his providence.

"There are three Isaacs in the academy, teacher. Each of us will become noted scholars." Isaac Luria spoke of himself, Isaac Apomado and Isaac Fasi, all members of ibn Zimra's prestigious rabbinical school in Cairo.

"And how will you fulfil your greatness?" David said this with a hint of irony. It was unusual for the young Ashkenazi to be so presumptuous. His scholastic achievements and intellect were renowned. They spoke for him in silence.

"I will study the Kabbalah and engage in the wisdom of the *Zohar*, teacher. I must find the path to redemption."

"That will take many years, Isaac. You must be prepared and ready for this. It is very different to *Midrash*." David spoke of the rigorous and methodical approach to interpretation of the *Torah*, where the intention of the text is in the words themselves.

"With Kabbalah you must be inspired," David went on. "You must have insight and see into the minds of the authors. You must understand the systems of interpretation, the *gematria* and the *sefirot*."

"Tell me of these systems, master."

"It is for you to find out, Isaac. I have written of the *gematria* in my essay Magen David. I can show you this. It is but an introduction to the mystical art of assigning numerical values to letters for the purpose of giving the hidden meaning of words and names."

"And the *sefirot*?"

"They are the ten stages in the process of divine emanation at the time of Creation. Each of them is connected to the other in a symbolic diagram which many call the Tree of Life, as they represent the divine attributes that can be found in us all. The *Zohar* has much to say about these vessels."

"I have the *Zohar*, master."

"But how have you acquired this text, Isaac? It is only available to the few that are ready to devote themselves to its complexities."

Isaac told of his encounter in the synagogue and of his first readings.

"I have looked with my eyes but know that I must see it with my soul," he concluded.

"That is the way, Isaac. I am amazed and heartened that you have begun your studies, but it will be difficult for you to pursue your rabbinical course here if you devote yourself to the Kabbalah."

"I will seclude myself, teacher. My Uncle Mordechai owns an island on the Nile. It has a small hut where I can live. I am prepared for many years of study and solitude."

"Very good, Isaac. I wish you well. We have some Kabbalistic manuscripts in our library which you are welcome to use. I would refer you to the work of Moses Cordevero of Safed. He has written a very systematic study called the *Pardes Rimmonim*, which brings together and analyses Kabbalistic thought of the past thousand years. You will find it of great use and guidance."

Isaac left the synagogue, clutching the books given to him by his teacher, in a mixture of anxiety and excitement. He did not notice their weight, but felt a lightness, an uplifting from the wisdom they contained. "How long will my studies take?" he thought, and then quickly banished the notion. "I must not be driven by any temporal sense, but let the pace be dictated by my understanding. I must prepare myself for many years of solitude."

A low morning sun cast a shadow across the courtyard as his family gathered to say farewell to Isaac. He spoke first to Mordechai.

"Uncle, I must thank you for providing me with a home for my seclusion."

"You are welcome, Isaac, it is a *mitzvah* for me. I remember the correspondence I had with your father that until now I have kept secret from you." Mordechai paused as Isaac struggled to contain himself with the mention of his father. Mordechai continued.

"He told me that Elijah had come to him in a dream, telling him that his wife was to bear him a son and that he should name him Isaac."

"The great prophet spoke to my father!" Isaac cried in excitement, exchanging rapturous glances with his mother and young wife.

"Yes Isaac, but more than that."

"What! Tell me. What did he say of me?" effused Isaac in a youthful exuberance not demonstrated for some time.

"I am only telling you this as you have come to it yourself. Elijah told your father that you were to deliver the people of Israel from evil and redeem many souls. And that you were to reveal the teaching of the Kabbalah to the world."

Isaac suddenly felt the greatness of the obligation he was assuming and was humbled by it.

"I must waste no time, Uncle, and should hasten to the island. My family is in your trust."

"You are not to forget them, Isaac. I will send Samuel for you each Friday so that you can spend the Sabbath with us."

"Thank you, Uncle. Now I must go."

Isaac was silent as they neared the island. Samuel brought the oars into the boat ready for mooring it to the jetty.

"Your uncle thought that the north of the island would be best for you."

Isaac's mood of anticipation was disturbed. There were many things to think about. He had set no time limit for the task. How could he when he was about to embrace the infinite. Samuel's comment took him back to his parting conversation with Uncle Mordechai. He still called him Uncle, even though he was now his father-in-law. His wife seemed to recognise the greatness in him and was prepared for a marriage that satisfied a ritual need. Isaac had told her of the saying in the *Zohar* "a human being is only called Adam when male and female are as one". On returning each Sabbath they would rejoice in union to honour the oneness of God. It was her role to satisfy this religious obligation. Isaac would not miss her. For six days he would be married to his studies.

He responded to Samuel. "Yes, he said that the south is busy with many visitors to the Nilometer. It is strange how the waters of the river help my uncle calculate the taxes."

"The Nilometer has been on this island since the time of the Pharoahs to measure the flood levels, for if they are too high it foretells of disaster. Too low there will be hunger as the crops will not be irrigated," explained Samuel, proud of this knowledge.

Isaac had visited the Nilometer with his uncle soon after he came to Cairo. It was exciting for the young boy to view the large pit that descended below the level of the Nile and the marks on the marble measuring column that ran down the centre. His uncle interpreted them in a simple way.

"The 16-cubit mark denotes an ideal flood. At this level the farmers will have abundant crops and I can set the most taxes. Any higher is troublesome and 18 cubits is a disaster, for the fields will be flooded. 15 cubits denotes security and 14 is happiness. Anything below is not good. At 13 cubits there will be suffering as there will be virtually no irrigation. When the water mark is 12 there will be hunger as the crops cannot grow. It will not be possible to set taxes when the water is this low."

Mordechai also told Isaac stories of how the island had previously been a retreat. Some fifty years earlier the Islamic scholar Jalau'd-din as–Suyuti had settled here to write his celebrated books on the Koran. Like Isaac, he had lost his father early in life. Solitude was now their common guide.

Stepping ashore, Isaac thought about these tales. They made the island appropriate for the years ahead, a congruence of spirituality and a signpost for human survival. He was pleased with his new home. Its simplicity reflected his requirement, a minimum of comfort and no concern for material needs. A single room with one corner set aside for his ablutions. Other bodily needs were satisfied by a pallet against the back wall and a store cupboard for the dried food that Samuel brought him, as he could spare no time for cooking. Under a window that allowed him to view the Nile was the rough table that would serve as his desk. From here he could raise his eyes from the text and gaze at the heavens, transporting the words upward so that they could descend with their meaning.

His days soon fell into a pattern of prayer, study and contemplation, the latter often during a morning stroll along the bank of the Nile. As he walked he noticed the reeds on the opposite shore waving in the water. From this distance he could not determine what may be concealed within the clumps. But the more he gazed the more he saw.
And a verse of Exodus entered him.

> "A man of the house of Levi went and married a daughter of Levi. The woman conceived and bore a son; she saw how good he was, and she hid him for three months."

He saw the ark of bulrushes that contained the three-month-old Moses and watched Moses' mother Jochabed turn and walk briskly away. He heard the cries of a baby, alone and drifting in the current. He saw Princess Hatshepsut come to bathe in the river, react to the cries and so instruct her maid to fetch the ark.

"What images are these?" Isaac thought. "I see before me the son of the house of Levi. It is this place. It links me in time to the Great Patriarch."

A power surged through his body. It brought a realisation, a knowingness, an understanding of the *Zohar* passage relating to the birth of Moses that he had read the previous day.

> "Rabbi Yose said:
> This verse in Exodus reads 'she saw how good he was'.
> And the verse in Genesis states 'God saw how good the light was'. That is how good he was; he was everything."

Isaac had been mystified by this analogy of Moses' goodness. But standing there, in his trance-like state, Isaac was able to receive the insight. God's light was the primordial light of Creation and it represented the totality of cosmic consciousness. The light now shone through Moses and his awareness was unbounded; he was everything.

Isaac walked on in awe of his new-found acuity. By emptying his mind and allowing images to flow, the enigmatic tracts of the *Zohar* could reveal their meaning.

And so began his journey. Each night, when even the quiet noises of the day wrapped themselves in darkness to provide an empty silence, Isaac read.

The same passage, twice, thrice, until the repetition had taken the words deep within. Until the words became image. His gaze was directed on the page until he saw through the page. Nothing existed for him except that verse.

He saw the gaps between the words, the space between the lines. And then the void was filled. A supernal power directed him. At first a glimmer, a shaded interpretation. Next an unveiling that led to clarity. Isaac was in awe. His mind filled. He had tremors; his body shook as he pondered on the enormity of it all. At how all things are interrelated. In eternity. In reflecting and absorbing the light of the divine. The light of awareness. The emanations from creation. God's purpose. Man's purpose.

He was the vessel. A physical body as containment for an infinity of wisdom. He could not write down these thoughts. Parchment could not absorb the flood as he opened his mind. The rush of ideas swamped his ability to write.

Isaac thought of his destiny. Of making the masses righteous that would lead to redemption. A universal healing. He was alone, isolated, unable to communicate these ideas.

For many years Isaac studied. In his seclusion he meditated and prayed, unconcerned with the passage of time. Specific events punctuated his life and gave some structure to his existence: each week the Sabbath, each month a new moon. The observance of many festivals throughout the year connected him to the masses – their sorrow, joy and celebration – and heightened his awareness of the necessity of his work.

But it was Yom Kippur, the Day of Atonement, the holiest day of the year, that stirred him most of all. All individuals would atone for sins committed against God, the religious offences, but for offences against a neighbour there is no reparation on Yom Kippur until the neighbour has been appeased and the wrongdoing righted, the soul guided on its path to purity.

And with this dwelling on reparation, two things troubled Isaac. When would he be ready to leave for Safed and join the community of mystics to fulfil his mission? The task of making the masses righteous filled him with awe and concern as to how it was to be enacted.

As he read more of the *Zohar*, a passage leapt out as guidance on the timing of his departure.

> "*It has been taught:*
> *When a human being is created,*
> *On the day he comes into the world,*
> *Simultaneously, all the days of his life are arranged above.*
> *One by one, they come flying down into the world*
> *To alert that human being, day by day.*"

If I am alerted, Isaac thought, if I am given a sign then I will know of the day. He reflected on the rest of that *Zohar* passage, which was a commentary on Jacob's deathbed scene in the Book of Genesis. There was much he could draw from it. Jacob wished to leave Egypt and be buried in the land of his fathers, the Promised Land. Isaac too would leave Egypt with the knowledge that he would not return. It was the debate in the text that stirred him. Jacob was pure of soul; his life was the culmination of the days and lives of the patriarchs Abraham and Isaac. The *Zohar* described his life as a Garment of Days. Each day that *"came flying down into the world"* would *"climb up in shame"* if its owner sinned before God. But how was he to attain this absolute purity and not miss the day of his destiny?

Isaac was convinced that this would be attained through his day-to-day ethical, devotional and ritual practices. And if he could promulgate these to others, then the second of his concerns would be addressed.

And so Isaac began to formalise his Pious Customs.

Far in the distance, through the haze of the day, the Great Pyramids exerted their influence on the hermit of Jazaret Al-Rawda. Isaac felt the presence of the long-deceased occupants. He could sense their power, their arrogance, their ostentation. Their fear was death, their need was for immortality, their majesty entombed in the stone blocks in anticipation of rebirth.

As with all things, Isaac absorbed this message from the past, and then rejected its implication. This was a transgression: the pharaohs had put themselves above their fellow men and considered their righteousness to be divinely proclaimed. And so was born the first custom:

> *"The most important of all worthy traits consists in an individual's behaving with humility, modesty and with the fear of sin to the greatest possible degree ...."*

And the second custom?

It was night. Isaac lay sleeping on the straw pallet in his hut after a difficult day. He dreamt of his wife and family and the business affairs he had neglected. In the dream he questioned the life he was leading and the journey it had determined. He felt in awe and belittled by the expectation he had put on himself. And he saw himself at his desk, unable to concentrate, unable to complete his work. Isaac woke sweating, in panic, in a darkened mood. His anxiety deepened. He attempted to focus, to meditate, to enter the upper realm. But it was not to be. He lay in despair and felt an impotence of purpose and with it a momentary loss of belief. Isaac's will was challenged. He rose and lit a candle, the flickering flame illuminating the manuscripts he had been studying. Scrolls were piled on the floor next to his table. He touched the parchment, ran his fingers across the words, communed with the authors. They gave him strength. He breathed deeply and slowly till his body ceased the quivering that had convulsed it since his waking and calmness traced its way to his mind. Panic dissipated and softened to an uplifting. Isaac went outside and looked up at the stars. He was clear in his mind; he must overcome these feelings. The second custom was plain in its avoidance:

> "Melancolia is, by itself, an exceedingly unpleasant quality of personality ...... There is nothing which impedes mystical inspiration as the quality of sadness."

Another custom came from observing Mordechai. Isaac was having a break from his studies to help his uncle and watched him confront the farmers, demanding the taxes. Angry scenes developed.

"We have no money," the farmers cried. "It has been a poor crop, we have barely enough to feed ourselves."

"You attempt to mislead me," was his uncle's response. "The Nilometer indicates that the yield would be good this year." Mordechai became inflamed. The Governor of Egypt would punish him if he brought in too little money. The farmers shook their fists and Mordechai left in a fury. He would need support from the Governor, perhaps some soldiers to quell the mob. He trembled with anger. It possessed him and could think of nothing but the course of action to take.

Isaac noted the impact later, during the evening service. Mordechai could not concentrate, often losing his place in the prayer book, and was unable to perform the ritual movements properly during the Eighteen Benedictions. It disturbed Isaac to see his pious uncle act in this way, still full of searing emotion. This was not good. Isaac thought of the verse from the Book of Job:

> "Thou that tearest thyself in thine anger ...."

And so Isaac conceived that anger was the worst of all behavioural transgressions.

> "... this is because all other transgressions 'injure' only a single limb of the body whereas the quality of anger 'injures' the soul in its entirety, altering its character completely. This is the issue: when an individual loses his temper, his holy soul deserts him altogether; in its place a spirit of an evil nature enters."

Isaac was pleased. In following these customs he had found a way, a method to remain pure.

Over the coming years Isaac devised many more Pious Customs. He dealt with how people behaved and interacted, methods of contemplation and study and devotional practices at the synagogue and during the Sabbath and festivals.

This mix of the methodical and mystical defined his character, their balance enabling him to keep his sanity while contemplating the infinite. And always he thought of his destiny.

> "The enlightened will shine like the zohar of the sky, and those who make the masses righteous will shine like the stars forever and ever."

But to make the masses righteous, Isaac thought, I need to understand them so that they will be able to undertake my practices. And this troubled him, as he spent most of his time in isolation. At the Sabbath and Festivals he was with his family and a closed circle of devotees. He had occasional dealings with local merchants through his Uncle Mordechai but now he needed a closer involvement with the multitude, to know them and how they fought the battle between good and evil.

He asked his uncle, who was wise in his dealings with men. Become a trader, Mordechai advised, and then you will learn of man's deviousness and cunning. It will teach you of their character. You will encounter souls of many colours. You will enter the realm of the apostate and non-Jew. You will meet people from other countries and absorb their cultures. And then you will know the masses.

And so Isaac went into the world. At first he watched. Mordechai was also responsible for collecting the customs duties at the ports of Alexandria and Rashid in the mouth of the Nile Delta and arranged for Isaac to observe and audit the amount of cargo being unloaded from the dhows that plied their trade between Egypt, Turkey and Italy.

Seated at a desk in the corner of the port office, Isaac was intrigued by the interactions of all those involved in trading. The ships' captains, the customs officers, the merchants who came to collect their goods, the agents who acted as intermediaries, the organisers of transport, the dockworkers who unloaded the cargo, the financiers waiting to collect their dues – Isaac scrutinised each element of their exchanges. He noted how they influenced each other and who took a dominant role in the interchange. He registered their emotions, their body language. He made distinctions between the Jews, the Muslims, the Christians, the *conversos*.

And Isaac entered into their world. He dealt in diverse goods so that he could gain a wide experience. He involved himself in the buying, selling and transport of pepper, wine, cucumbers and leather. He established links with local agents trading goods between Egypt, Turkey and Italy. He bought and sold pepper from India. He borrowed money to invest in his business schemes and collected debts owed to him for the goods he supplied. He dealt with many people and learnt many things, using the knowledge gained during his time in the port office to influence his negotiations. All this experience built up to the prime thing he wanted to accomplish – to find out how the minds of the masses worked. What were their concerns, their worries? How did these trials influence their daily life and, more importantly, their spiritual life?

As with all things, he drew on his source of enlightenment, the *Zohar*. In the Book of Exodus, Jethro tells Moses:

"You shall seek out from among all the people capable men who fear God, trustworthy men who spurn ill-gotten gain."

The commentary in the *Zohar* indicated how physical characteristics such as hair, the shape of the forehead or eyes, the contours of the face, the lips, the ears and lines on the hands could signify certain moral and spiritual qualities.

But, Isaac thought, how could the state of a person's soul be determined? Did not the ancient mystics believe that visions of letters appear on the forehead as manifestations of the soul? This is how I will find the capable men, the trustworthy men, Isaac surmised. The light from inside will shine through the skin. Those who are sinful will have the light concealed.

Isaac developed the skill for these readings. As he had looked through the void between the words of the *Zohar* to determine their meaning, so he would look through the body of man. He would gaze upon an individual's shadow, the aura that exists outside his body – the bridge between his physical form and the soul. From that he would recognise the good or evil inclination that constantly accompanied an individual. In this transcendent state, Isaac saw through the skin of the brow.

And so Isaac looked into the minds of all men. And there were few who were capable, and few who were trustworthy. Could those who gathered at the synagogue be considered righteous? Isaac became dispirited as he saw through the rote rituals of the congregants. They could not ascend to the upper realm during prayer. He despaired as they broke off from their chants to discuss a business transaction. The behaviour was not according to the Pious Customs he had devised.

Isaac withdrew to his island undeterred. The way forward was clear. He was to select a group of disciples as suggested in the *Zohar* and make this group committed to the mending and purification of their souls. The power and intensity of their piety would bring the redemption of the cosmos on behalf of all mankind.

More years passed unnoticed in the intensity of study as Isaac prepared himself and awaited the day of his destiny. At long last he felt that he was in a state of readiness.

His meditations had taken him to the uppermost realms. He had convened with Elijah and absorbed God's intent in Creation.

He had profound understanding of the *Zohar's* depiction of the manifestation of God's attributes in the *sefirot*.

He was cognizant of the symbolic systems of the *sefirot*, as the Tree of Life, as metaphors for the spiritual and physical worlds, as a representation of all in the cosmos.

He perceived the flaws in Creation that depicted itself in a rupturing of the *sefirot*. He called this the Breaking of the Vessels and the release of evil.

He conceived that the most fundamental and ultimate goal of all human existence was *tikkun*, the repair and restoration of the cosmos.

He was sure that he could gather sufficient disciples and bring their souls to the purity that was a necessary condition for *tikkun*.

All this was within him. All this made him sensitive to all things, even to a pulse. The pulse of the smallest creature, the pulse of the universe.

To the emotion in the eye of a new-born and the collective fervour of the multitude.

To the anguish of a tormented soul and the cry of the sinner.

He felt the pain of the cosmos and wept.

The anguish from Safed carried on the wind and pursued Isaac as he walked back to his uncle's house. Each gust was the barb of the demon that was afflicting the community. Each flurry carried the frenzy of the crowd. Isaac determined to exorcise the evil that tormented them.

This was the auspice for his departure. Now he would leave for Safed.

NOW

3

New York 1978

Peter Paul Levi wept. I wept. Alone in my Manhattan hotel room. A weeping of despair, as all Israel had despaired in Vital's dream. A weeping of uncertainty, of not knowing who I was – of what I was.

The past three months had been blinkered. I had shut out all feelings, all emotion, all thoughts other than uncovering the symbolism of the dream. My self was sublimated to an internal force that was incessant.

Now I was no longer alone. Hayyim Vital had put a wedge in my psyche and confronted the inner me, questioning, exposing. Revealing?

My dream had been a game, a project. I could maintain an objectivity as it was somehow detached from the person I thought I was. The fear and anxiety I felt at the time belonged to someone else.

But no longer. I had a shared experience with one of the most prominent Jewish mystics and Kabbalists. It had been visited on me, a secular Jew, an ignorant Jew. Ignorant of rituals, practices, observances. Certainly ignorant of the esoteric side of Judaism, the mystical side.

Was that why I wept? I was being questioned, driven to search for my core. And I couldn't cope. I had no answers. I had never rejected being Jewish, but it was always something in my background, something I had been born with. In my despair I reflected on my past.

A DREAM UNTOLD

When did I realise I was Jewish? Or rather, when did I realise that being Jewish was somehow different? Our household was secular, but Jewish influences touched the life of my family. I was born just after the end of Hitler's War and raised in London's East End – well, almost. It was the better side of Victoria Park, the Hackney side. The lakes and fields were a physical enlightenment in the journey from the ghetto of Whitechapel and Stepney through the no-man's-land of Bethnal Green to the aspirational areas of North London.

My grandparents had made a longer journey west, arriving in England from Russia and Germany at the birth of the 20th century to set up home in Stepney. They died when I was about five, so I only have a distant memory of a short dumpy couple who could only speak the strange, sing-song language of Yiddish. My parents, both born in England, spoke this expressive tongue and continued to use it long after its prime use had disappeared with the death of my grandparents. Its emotive vocabulary was used to escape from the frustration of an English language that did not provide for the feelings and desires of people whose genes were fermented elsewhere.

I suppose the defining moment when I had to confront my Jewishness was when I was about nine. It was certainly before I went to Grammar School. My Junior School was a five-minute bus ride from home. I normally took the bus, but one fine summer's day I had just missed one and decided to walk. It was a twenty-minute stroll through a mixed residential area that had suffered bomb damage during the war, where once-elegant Victorian houses were separated by fenced-off plots of waste land. The plots were given names by the various local gangs of kids who frequented the area, each gang claiming ownership of a particular plot and using it as their base and private playground. Their aggressive reputations were common knowledge. It was not that I was courting danger; I probably did not know what that meant at that age, but it was more of a sense of adventure, of placing myself in an unknown situation. It was not the last time I would do that.

I passed "Blackie's Apple Tree". I had been told that if you got caught there then "you're a dead man". A shattered fence opened up a view of "Stoney's Grave Land", so called from the tombstone-like blocks of masonry that littered the overgrown garden of what was once number 24.

"Pssst, you a Jew?" A voice from nowhere.

A face appeared round one of the jagged wooden stanchions that kept the fence together. The face was joined by two others, leering in unison with the boldness of youthful bigotry. I ignored the question and walked a little quicker. Fear prevented me from breaking into a run.

The faces were behind me now. I hoped I had escaped. My heart trembled as I heard the rustle of footsteps on the other side of the fence. The pacing was uneven as the ground was littered with holes and lumps of stone and the irregular sound of their movement heightened my fear. There was another gap in the fence about ten yards further along where the faces emerged, bodies following, and the three formed a barrier across the pavement.

"You didn't answer us."

"Tell us or we'll knife ya."

"Well, my mum and dad are Jewish." I had to admit my ancestry as denial would have provoked them further.

"Say sumfink Jewish then," shouted the smallest of the three.

I stopped a couple of yards from them. They advanced and surrounded me.

"C'mon, you must know sumfink," said the little one, accompanying his demand with a push.

"Who d'ya fink you're shuvvin'," growled another of my captors as I rebounded off him.

My mind went blank. What was a Jewish word? I knew that some of my friends went to Sunday school to learn Hebrew. Could that be what they wanted? But that was no use, I didn't know any Hebrew.

"Kneidlach!" Saved by the thought of Saturday lunch.

"Can-aid-luck, what's that?"

"It's what you have in chicken soup. It's like a dumpling," I stammered, relieved to have found a word that was strange to them.

"Say sumfink else, more food, we like food."

"Bagel, latke, gefilte fish...."

"Fish, that's not Jewish." The English word earned another shove.

"Ah, let's leave him alone, he don't know nuffink." A voice from heaven through the mouth of a devil.

They disappeared through the fence. I ran home with relief and without sign of any physical damage. It meant I would be able to avoid having to tell my parents about the incident. I would keep it inside. I suppose I thought that talking about it would somehow give it a reality that I didn't want to consider. It was enough that I was confronted with this difference, this being Jewish, this excuse for being a target. It took a long time before I recognised that the depth of culture that permeated my being, that helped define my persona, was an intrinsic part of my makeup. A "Jewishness" informed me and provided a touchstone for my future creative life.

The story made me smile. As it made others when I told it. I had continued to keep it from my parents and family, though. It was a necessary protection for them and for me. A protection and concealment of my identity.

Barriers.

"Room service!" A repeated banging and a shrieking Bronx voice shook me from my reverie. "Jeez, I'd never thought you'ze answer."

A perky woman in her thirties appeared as I opened the door. "Where'd ya want it? Over here do ya?" and she almost dropped the tray with my coffee and bagel onto a low table by the window.

"That's fine," I said, fumbling for some small change to give her.

"Tanks, seez ya around." And she left before any more contact could be established.

I ate and drank standing up, looking through the window at the frenetic New York cityscape. Noises that I had blocked out now filled the room with a cacophony of existence. Texture, taste, smell – those senses of reality were delivered by the food, impinging on my detachment.

Barriers.

A dream from my childhood came back to me. How old had I been? Six, seven, eight? It was certainly an age before intellectual curiosity and awareness gave it any significance. But it kept recurring, was disturbing and left an embedded image. A wall ...

"*.... an unending faceless, smooth wall. It has finite height, but I cannot see over it. I cannot imagine what is on the other side. Whenever I try and think about the other side, my mind reacts and implodes into a fuzzy state.*"

Mostly I remember that fuzziness, a sort of mind-churning blockage. A way of coping with an inability to understand. At that young age all that I was aware of was a fluffiness, a frustration and a sense of a brain that was made of cotton wool. But cotton wool that had its own energy that swelled to the task, an anima. A bloating that led to pressure inside my skull, a pressure that said stop, think no more. And I slept as best I could.

It had been some time since I had thought of that dream or what it might signify. Perhaps the wall was an obstacle that I couldn't overcome as a child. A barrier to my unconscious as my "self" was immature.

This notion generated a half-smile of wryness and caused me to reflect on my physical self. Photographs at that age showed me with a haunted look. My eyes were deep-set and drew in the viewer with their darkness. When I look at them now it takes me into my early soul, bonds me with another being that is me separated by time. Some photos are cherub-like, curly blond hair, winsome smile. It was evident that the brooding pervasiveness of my early years, which I felt was total, did have some enlightenment within my feeling of loneliness.

But it was those eyes that I conjured up – their knowingness, their prescience. It was a look that spanned the years between the captured image and an immured mind.

I stood at the window for some time, cradling the coffee, simultaneously feeling its warmth and insulating the heat, looking into the blackness through those early images. Through the tormented youth and into late teenage sophistication, frequenting coffee bars, smoking Gauloises and discussing Colin Wilson's book *The Outsider*. And swapping quotes in a competition of who could feel the most angst.

Oh God, Eva. Tears. Memories of a first meeting in 1963.

"The Outsider is not sure who he is. 'He has found an *I*, but it is not his true *I*'...."

"His main business is to find his way back to himself." A blonde, blue-eyed girl on the other side of the table finished my quote.

"Hey, what d'ya think you're doing, that's my line," I responded in mock indignation, "but if only I knew what it meant."

"Stay cool, Peter. You'll work it out. I'm Eva, by the way," grinning as she introduced herself.

"You're new here, aren't you – and how'd you know my name?" I replied, trying to be cool and not overreact to an attractive girl showing an interest in me.

"David's my cousin." She grabbed the arm of the boy sitting next to her. He was one of "the crowd", the coterie of fellow sixth-formers who gathered in a basement coffee bar in Soho most Saturday nights listening to folk and blues as a backdrop to testing out our philosophy.

"So your fucking outsider knows about our Outsider!" I laughed, aiming a weak joke at Dave.

"You stroppy bastard! I didn't realise it was a fucking select club." At that, Eva glared at me, pushed the table as leverage to stand up and focus her anger and stormed off.

"God, I didn't mean to give her the hump."

"I'd better go after her. She's always been a bit spiky. Don't worry about it." Dave reluctantly left us in search of this wayward girl who had left me intrigued. Something in her lit a spark in me, enflamed my youthful passion. I sensed the challenge of a dangerous relationship and desperately wanted to see her again.

The next time we met it was just the two of us. I'd suggested a local coffee bar in Hampstead, quieter and somewhere that had a more intellectual feel. We met outside, late afternoon on a school day, both wearing black polo-neck sweaters and jeans. At least that broke the ice after my phone call, when she grudgingly agreed to the date.

"Don't get the wrong fucking idea. I've only come 'cos David tells me you're a smart guy and got some interesting things to say."

What an acceptance speech, I thought.

"OK, OK. I get the picture. This place all right for you?"

"It'll do. As long as it's quiet."

The café looked like it hadn't changed for 30 years, dark tables scattered around, the wood worn smooth by an eternity of gesticulating arms in debate. Benches upholstered in black leather lined the walls, with randomly placed wooden wing chairs providing for flexible numbers at each table.

We sat in an alcove at the rear, both of us grateful for its security and seclusion.

"Coffee OK for you?" I asked.

"Black, no sugar." The same as me, I thought.

"Want anything else?"

"No … thanks."

"They make a great apple pie here. I'm famished after school."

I ordered and wondered how to start the conversation, but Eva jumped in.

"David tells me you're a bit of a loner. Why?"

"That's a bit bloody direct!"

"So sorry! I don't want to waste time with flippant chat. You don't have to answer, you know."

"That's OK, like you took me by surprise. I don't think about it. Did Dave say anything else about me?"

"Jeez, I can't get used to him being called Dave. Must be his rebellion. His mother, my aunt, always insists on him being called David."

"So, what did David say? Better not use Dave in case his mother has her spies here!"

Eva laughed, her shoulder-length hair swaying as she did so.

"OK. Like it's not so much what he told me about you but what he said about your crowd. He did say you were a bit of a loner, though."

"What!"

"Come on, he didn't give me any shit about you, he just said that you were always a bit apart. He reckoned you were the brightest of the bunch and knew exactly what was going on."

"Who wants the apple pie?" The question from the waitress gave Eva a respite she seemed to welcome.

"That's for me. Do you want to try some?" Eva nodded and I asked for an extra spoon.

There was a pause as we sipped our coffee, exchanging glances.

"So did Dave …. David think I was a bit stuck up?"

"No. He respects you too much. I don't think he really understands you."

"I don't understand myself!"

"Funny! Maybe you need to find your way back."

"Like the *Outsider* quote?"

"Yeah, I suppose that's it. Did reading that book get to you?"

"It made me feel alienated."

"Me too."

For the first time Eva looked vulnerable, admitting this dark feeling. Suppressing the desire to come up with a smart quip, I reached out and touched her hand. It initially retracted, then it was turned over, inviting our palms to meet.

The sensation of that first contact still prickles after 14 years. It said more than words, bridging the isolation we both felt.

Isolation.

The coffee was cold now. I had been by that window for an age. God, I needed Eva now, that touch again that brought us together. And the look in those blue eyes that said so much in their moistness. Such a portent of our relationship. Desire, despair and most of all an expression of pleading.

Love, fun, excitement – these I was able to provide. But her need, her unstated imploring for stability and security, for me to be her rock – this was not within me to give. Others, like George, provided me with security, but not enough for me to share. Somehow I didn't want to dilute my resources and Eva was excluded.

Would more attention have kept her alive? Pain and guilt continually push this question to the front of my mind. Friends consoled me: "You couldn't have prevented it," they said, "for her it was an inevitable release." I suppose the signs were there almost from the start.

It was probably the third or fourth time we met. Always at the same coffee bar, same seat in the alcove. Our deepening relationship was going beyond common interests in books, music and teenage non-conformism and began to touch on the personal.

"So what do your parents do?" I asked, now curious to find out more of Eva's background.

"Don't fucking talk to me about them!" came out in a vituperative flurry.

"Jeez, I'm sorry. I just wanted to get to know you. So how was school today?"

"They're bloody away again."

"Who?"

"My parents, stupid."

"I thought you didn't want to talk about them."

"What I say and what I do can be different, you know."

"OK, OK. So do you want to tell me about them?"

Eva paused, cradled her coffee and looked up at the ceiling, revealing a taut white neck no longer obscured by a black sweater. Our mutual statement had been made and we no longer changed out of what passed for school uniform for our meetings. Her larynx quivered as she directed her words heavenwards.

"My mum's off on a bloody concert tour. Fucking again. And I never see my dad. He's always at the hospital or at meetings."

"Concert tour?" I immediately knew it was the wrong question.

"Come on. I thought you wanted to know how I felt."

"Abandoned?"

"Too bloody right. They think that if they buy me things it makes up for it."

"I'm sorry."

"Like, is that all you can say?"

I could have withdrawn then, into the protective shell, and remained silent. Brooding. But that might have meant the end of our burgeoning affair. A yearning and genuine fondness for Eva was building up inside me and I didn't want it to end like this.

"I can listen." No more questions. Leave it up to her, I thought.

"Peter, you're really sweet." Our palms touched again as a softening Eva reached out to me. This time she clasped my hand, not relinquishing it as she spoke, transmitting her emotion through the tautness of her grip.

"They're both quite famous in their fields. Mum's a pianist and gives recitals all over the world. Dad's a heart surgeon. Suppose that's why he spends a lot of time at the hospital. They're always long operations. They think I'm old enough to be independent, not that I saw much of them when I was younger."

Eva stopped talking and looked away, stifling emotion. It was my turn to squeeze her hand and it brought her back.

"When I do see them, we always go out. To the theatre, opera – that sort of thing. And we only talk over meals at posh restaurants. And then it's always about school and studying and what I should be doing with my life. They're so bloody pushy. Never want to know how I feel about it. The only person I can talk to is Coleen."

"Who's she?"

"Our Irish maid. She lives in. A bit bloody matronly but I can tell her anything. She gets a bit horrified about my love life, but won't say anything to my parents. See this ring? It's probably worth a fortune."

Eva let go of my hand and thrust a silver and jewel-encircled finger at me.

"I've had enough talking about them. Let's go."

"I'll catch you up. I've got to pay for our drinks," I called out as Eva rushed out of the café.

Despair and loneliness. That's what she felt, what we both felt. Except that hers was driven externally, by her parents. Mine was internal, a companionless soul. It was dark now and I saw my reflection in that New York window, framed by the lights of the surrounding skyscrapers. The face stared back accusingly with memories of the first time Eva and I had been alone together.

My parents were away for the weekend and I had the place to myself. I bought some condoms in anticipation and asked Eva round. We now lived in a maisonette above a shop in Finchley Road, near Swiss Cottage, moving west from Hackney so that I could go to a "better" secondary school, according to my mother. It had a comfortable, worn feel for such a new building and it was easy to call this place home. Traffic noise was my lullaby, the droning of cars heading north homewards to the suburbs or south for a night in the West End.

On a Saturday afternoon the sounds drifting upwards were more pedestrian, the pavement thronging with the buzz of shoppers.

"Is it always this noisy?" Eva remarked as we sat over the inevitable coffee in the front room.

"You get used to it. Sort of comforting after a while. It's quite eerie sometimes when there's no traffic and you can actually hear the birds."

Eva smiled and even looked relaxed. She was wearing her usual jeans but with a pretty white broderie anglaise blouse. Not that I knew the fashion term then, it's only with more experienced hindsight that I could name something that was so vivid in my recollection.

"You look nice."

"Thanks."

"Like some music on?"
"OK."
"Beatles?"
"Fine."
"Please Please Me?"
"Love it!"
"Love Me Do!"

Eva giggled at the joke relating to a track on the album as we hovered and verbally fenced in anticipation.

"You'll have to wait till Side Two for that," I continued, "I'm a stickler for playing the songs in order."

Music was important in our household and my father had invested in state-of-the-art hi-fi equipment – Bang and Olufsen amplifier, turntable and speakers that had to be used with care and deference.

"Sit there," I said, indicating the sofa. "It's the best place for listening. You get the full stereo effect."

Eva moved from the table where we were drinking and sprawled herself on the settee. As the strains of "I Saw Her Standing There" filled the room, I picked up on the lyrics …

"Well, she was just seventeen …"

"Like me!"

Laughing, I leapt beside her in an inept lunge and attempt at intimacy.

"You're crushing my legs."

"Sorry, I got carried away 'when I saw you sitting there'."

"Funny! I suppose I'll have to make room for you."

"It is my couch."

Track by track, the intensity of our contact increased. An arm round her neck, a peck on the cheek, a kiss and a stroking of white cotton until I felt the sensation of an erect nipple, synchronising with the last chords of "Please Please Me" wafting towards us. End of side one.

Eva adjusted her position and spoke, "Let's hear the other side."

"OK," I replied, getting up awkwardly, aware of another erect organ in the room.

Afternoon turned to dusk as "Twist and Shout" died away. Music had performed its function and lowered our inhibitions.

"My room is upstairs," I offered, aiming the words at her neck.

Eva stood up and took my hand. "This way?"

Our summer of love, some four years before its global proclamation, was one of extremes. Plaintive episodes of passion, melancholy gripped with lust, a darkness underpinning our youthful experimentation in lovemaking. Weekend walks in the countryside, seeking furtive spots for coitus and guilt-ridden pleasures. And Eva's guilt that she could not give herself entirely to our yearnings. Not that I was too aware of it then. At 18, the joy of sexual discovery blocked the empathy required to see into her darkness.

Now I was seeing into her darkness, in the ark of my hotel room, and it was an accusing face that stared back from the window. The intensity of that glare brought me out into palpitations as the memory of our last teenage embrace came flooding back. A cycle completed in my Finchley Road home.

"Oh Peter, I'm so desperate." I turned to see a quivering face that moments earlier had shone with the satisfaction of youthful passion as we lay together in cosy post-coital warmth.

"What is it?"

"My parents, they're off again. Dad's got a conference and Mum's on a concert tour. I can't bear being alone again."

"What about Coleen?"

"You don't understand, do you?"

"Try me." Words said with a pretend seriousness. Said without any accumulated experience that could lend itself to insight. How can you counsel at 18 when your heart is full of rebellion? Eva picked up my tone.

"If you loved me, you'd do more than try." A sob. A tear. She rejected my reaching out to her. Pushed away the hand that tried to caress her cheek.

"Eva, please." I struggled for words. I hadn't acquired the vocabulary of caring.

"I'm going. Back to that empty house where no-one wants me." She jumped out of bed and thrust her clothes on. "Don't try and follow me, just don't."

I let her go. How could I have known that it was really a request, a cry for help? My limited reaction was more of a "sod you then, if that's what you want".

I didn't try to contact her for a couple of days, giving her some time to think. I phoned and Coleen answered.

"You'd better speak to her mother," she said. "Eva's in hospital."

"What's wrong?"

"I can't tell you. All I can say is she's very ill."

"Can I see her?"

"No."
"Why not?"
"She doesn't want to see you."
"Did she say that?"
"Yes."
"Why?"
"I'm sorry, Peter, I have to go now."

I learnt later that she had ransacked her parents' bedroom, found some sleeping pills and taken an overdose. Coleen found her comatose on their bed, a place where she knew she could be found.

I was shaken. It was the first time I had been confronted with the frailty of our existence. That it was someone I had been so close to, but had rejected, was a double blow. I became withdrawn. Empty. I began to question myself and my relevance as a human being. I suffered from Eva's reflected hopelessness.

4

We strode the lonely fields
With daisies in our hair
And fucked in ancient woods
As Lawrence made us dare

We sheltered in the trees
'neath branches knurled with age
And thrust with youthful heat
In passionate embrace

We shagged as Larkin said
For us it was our prime
The year was sixty three
'fore Eva called her time.

And left me failing.

I cried, I wept
I couldn't rid the cancer from her soul
I tried, inept
I couldn't free the evil of her self
I couldn't purge the poison in her head
I cried, I wept.

Eva recovered from that first attempt at suicide, but only in a physical sense, for the scar of trying was a constant reminder. It was etched so deep that no amount of therapy could find the hurt to erase. No watchful eye could see when the torment was about to be unleashed. No gentle tone could soothe that waking beast when its roar is unheard. Its quiet work was done in her loneliness and concealment, manifesting itself in a playful dolefulness.

That aura surrounded her when we met up again at Hornsey College of Art, where I was helping a friend. Tony had been at school with me, but we had not been particularly friendly and he had not been one of the "coffee club" crowd. I had got in touch with him after my India trip as I needed someone to help me with the photographs. In return, I offered to help him with a light show he was devising for a band that was performing at the nearby Alexandra Palace. Tony was excited by the psychedelic music scene and was in the forefront of the linked art movement. I hardly recognised this new incarnation from his faceless schooldays – thin faced, with a goatee beard, clothed in the uniform of the moment – jeans, T-shirt and embroidered denim jacket.

A feature of the light shows that Tony put together was the projection of images relating to the song being played, onto a giant screen behind the band. That was to be my job and, in particular, to be in control of the projector's heat shield. At crucial moments, I was to remove the shield, the projected transparency would emulsify, bubble and illuminate the band with a scorched writhing image in a triumph of psychedelia. We were rehearsing for the gig in one of the college studios when she walked in.

"Oh, hello." Eva looked at me and spoke with a nonchalance that negated three contactless years. "What brings you here?"

"You two know each other, then." Tony only seemed slightly surprised, vaguely remembering the school connection.

"I'm helping Tony with the show tonight," I replied, trying to keep up an air of normality.

"Be careful with my slides, they're part of my final year project." Eva gave me the sly grin that I remembered from when she told her mother that "Peter and I are just off on a country walk, we'll be back late afternoon". I looked at Tony with a puzzled expression.

"It's all right, she knows that they're going to be destroyed. She's teasing you," he said.

"Thanks, Tony." It seemed like I would need to get to know Eva all over again. If that was what she wanted.

She did.

Our first years together again were a blur as we launched ourselves into the back end of the sixties. I made my films, wrote, travelled and continued to develop my outer shell that blocked off any show of emotion.

Eva, perceptive Eva, could see through this façade, and manage to make the most of an opening if it arose. Those moments were best. I surrendered to her empathy and dwelt long in the softness of her embrace. We read each other's body-Braille with searching fingertips. A tension felt was a tension shared. A clutch revealed a racing pulse, an insight to the heart. Who needs words, we said with our eyes. Perhaps we should have talked more.

Too often we were not together. Eva had her own trips that distanced us. That light show at Alexandra Palace had caught the attention of a rising band that was seminal in the burgeoning psychedelic era. Not that I knew them, but they soon became a reflected part of me. Eva and Tony became part of the Pink Floyd entourage. I clung to her through the music, drifting into drug-induced hallucinatory moments that conjured up Eva's concert backdrops.

Her fame grew. Her lighting designs and images were sought after by the alternative rock movement. America beckoned and soon the Velvet Underground performed laconically in front of her sombre patterns. Later I would learn of a curious link with this band.

Success brought confidence. It seemed to change her physically. The gawky adolescent I first knew had metamorphosed into a strutting luminescent female. Her blonde hair had been chemically transformed into a vibrant, glowing red. She used it as a motif, self-portraits featuring in the stage shows. These were recognisable as Eva only through the eyes, heavy with mascara, that pierced a gaze through the hair-tail drawn across her face by outstretched fingers. One of the bands used it as an album cover.

Twenty silk-screen prints of that face, each in a different set of fluorescent colour, adorned the wall of our flat. They were spectators to our lovemaking. This was conventional in terms of practice, but often bizarre as regards environment. Eva needed to experiment, to use our personal ecstasy as a model for the relationships in a concert, the use of light and sound to bring an audience to orgasm. There was always music when we made love. Loud, rhythmical, insistent. Rolls of tin foil on the walls and ceiling, formed into concave and convex shapes, folded and scrunched, reflected coloured lights on us. Colour wheels, projected slides filled with soap bubbles, all shaped the passion.

A transparent tent was erected over our bed and lights and images shone on the exterior. Our senses succumbed to the vibrant patterns that surrounded us. We writhed to the movement that enveloped us. We tossed, we turned to each colour change, each transformed motif, each strident chord.

And then there were the quiet times, lying there, often stoned, listening to Dylan. No movement, communicating through the clasped hands at our sides.

And then the bubble burst. Psychedelia gave way to glam-rock. Bolan, Bowie, Ferry. They didn't want their persona to be subverted, to be inferior to their surroundings. They strutted, they pranced, they had no need of craven images. They were incarnate.

Eva could not adapt. Work was patchy, infrequent, unsatisfactory. Her confidence waned. She became sullen, withdrawn, listless, the stupor concealing her inner turmoil. She felt the shrivelling, shrinking, scorching destruction of her slides. It was her pain. Tears of dripping emotion. She projected her iconic face on the white wall of our living room, removed the heat shield from the projector and stood facing the beam. Her features dissolved and she absorbed the self-destruction.

When the light was pure and blinding, she slid to the floor and sat with her arms clutching her shins, her chin on her knees, gazing at emptiness. I would find her like this. Often. I would huddle alongside and squat. Reach out. Stroke that red hair. Run my thumb down her cheek and across quivering lips. I led her to bed and lay her down.

In the dark she spoke. With anguish. With effort.

"I'm afraid. What's happening to me? I feel so worthless." She cried. Tears born of despair. Tears that would only dampen the depression, nurture it and further its growth.

What could I do? My words were platitudes, born of desperation.

"Work will pick up. You're really talented. There's loads of stuff you could do outside the music world."

"That's not the point. I felt alive doing the concerts. The music touched me. It became my core. It became my being." Eva shook as she spoke. I couldn't tell if it was anger, frustration or pain that moved her. She glared at me in the half-light, then gazed through me. I was transparent to her. She felt that. I felt that. I had nothing to give her.

I tried.

"I'd really like it if you illustrated the credits to that documentary I'm doing on the Navajo Indians. There's a whole mix of art and spirituality that would stimulate you. Bring you out of yourself."

"Maybe I don't want to be brought out of myself. Maybe whatever has captured my spirit doesn't want to let it go."

"What?"

"I mean I feel possessed." She said it almost rationally, in a state of calm. For a moment, for the first time, I sensed her turmoil. Her possession seemed tangible to me. I wanted it to be that. It meant that Eva was retrievable as long as she could be purged of her inner demon.

I was on my knees by the side of the bed. I clutched her hand and drew it to my chest.

"Eva, feel this. It's my heart. Sense its beat, its rhythm. Take its life force. Let it enter you." Strange words came from me. Something intuitive, something deep was guiding me towards a potential cure.

"My pulse is strong," I continued. "It will drive out whatever has taken you over." My heart was racing, trying to generate the energy for the healing process. Eva lay back in a stupor. She writhed and pulled her hand away.

"Don't, don't," Eva sobbed, "I don't understand what you're doing. It won't help." She turned over and buried her head in the pillow. A stifled scream urged me to go. I was at a loss. Whatever was animating me had gone. My brief moment of attacking Eva's despair was at an end. I felt rebuffed in my attempt. Annoyed, angry that she hadn't responded, that I hadn't affected some miraculous healing.

It was the last time that there was any sense of communication between us.

My New York face continued its stare as I relived my past, those irredeemable moments.

My work took me away. I left Eva to her suffering. It was what her parents had done. Were doing. They didn't have much respect for me and blamed me for the lifestyle that Eva led. It was not what they had wanted for her and they had taken no delight in her fame. Her world was alien to them. They didn't understand its rebellious nature; it didn't conform to the structure of their life, so it made it easier to reject her and avoid any responsibility for her unease and anguish. It was all too difficult and would have smeared their cultured existence.

So Eva joined the Valium generation. The small yellow tablet with the big V smiling at you. She would hold it between her index finger and thumb and examine the pill's features, gaze into its chemical essence, challenge it to right her wrong. Then it was swallowed. A morning ritual that smoothed her day. I abdicated control to it and travelled. Got on with my life.

We spoke on the phone. Always at a distance, conversation limited to the practicalities. How was the filming going? When would I be back? That sort of thing. She told me of her daily routine, which amounted to body maintenance and not much else. When we were together I was aware of the drowsiness the drug was causing. Anxiety had given way to listlessness. She compounded it with alcohol. Her enthusiasm for sex disappeared. It was difficult to tell if it was a side effect of the Valium or endemic to her feelings.

Another assignment took me away. More phone calls. A brighter voice at the end of the line surprised me. There was an animation I hadn't encountered since the Pink Floyd days.

"I'm working, Peter," she said, "illustrating some children's books."

"Great. How did that happen?"

"Oh, through an old college friend. You don't know her." Eva's voice faltered slightly.

"What are the books about?"

"The usual stuff. Anthropomorphic animals living life in the woods."

"Bit like Winnie the Pooh, then."

"Yup."

"Look forward to seeing it in a couple of weeks when I'm back."

"See you then."

"Bye."

I never saw the drawings. I'm not sure if Eva's commission ever existed. I was sure that the Valium had pushed her into a fantasy dream-world. I hope it gave her comfort in her last days. I returned to Eva's body lying in the re-erected tent of our previous passion. Both bottles that lay on the floor were empty, the pills and the vodka. The flesh was cold as my fingers softly closed her eyes and touched her lips.

It was an act not intended to be discovered; undertaken while I was on my way home and incommunicado. Poor Eva. Her note to me lay close by, on the floor, as if it had just slipped from her hand as she succumbed to the drugs. It was written in her personal hand, not the psychedelic scrawl of past work. It was addressed to Paul, the name she used when she wanted to touch another part of me, get beneath my surface, be endearing.

Dear Paul

By the time you read this I will have left you. Left you with my sadness you wanted to share, but I was unable to give. Now I am to be released, it is yours to take on. You have the strength to tackle it and take it to your core. To enhance your being. I was not able to do that and ultimately it destroyed me. You may feel that the tone of this letter is strange as it has an inner strength that is at odds with what I am about to do. It is the reverse. It is an acceptance that calms me to the task. Dear Paul, survive and take me with you. I loved you once. I love you still, but it was not enough.

Yours ever, Eva

Those words are seared to my soul and have been shared with no one, concealed from the inquest. I wanted to retain this Eva for me, the pain, the love, the guilt.

My image in the window reached out to me, clutching the letter as if saying "Yes, I was the catalyst, the bringer of your dream. I put you in that state of inherited sadness, that loss of passion, that gnawing of emotion, that emptiness, hollowness, a void waiting to be filled. And put you into a state of reception."

The window could bring no more of the past and I sat down, still clutching the cup with its remnants of cold coffee and becoming morose in that hotel room. The street sounds of Manhattan punctuated my brooding on past traumas and anxieties. I seemed to have no control over my inner demons. They materialised and plagued me, crowded me into the emotional state that I suffered in Safed. I felt the enormity of my experience. I felt insignificant.

I felt possessed.

5

London 1978

What did he look like, this Hayyim Vital? This man of my dream? I could picture how he was dressed as in the visions from that night, his robes swirling around his calf. As were all the crowd, all of Israel gathered, waiting and weeping in impending gloom. But what of his face? His features. His eyes – mostly his eyes. How could they see through time, to an innocent, and view me as a receptacle for a drama that lay within him? To possess me.

And I was possessed. The past months had been a glazed existence. A surreality. A division between my physical needs and the fevered searching of my mind that came to a halt with the discovery in New York.

Back in London, the curtains in my Camden flat hung heavy. They absorbed the light and what little energy I had, forming an enclosure as I lay on a threadbare couch, self-contained, languishing. The ceiling did not divulge my mystery. No image there. No face to be seen in the texture of emulsion on wood-chip paper. No reflection in the sheen of that white-painted surface.

The light melting through the curtains faded. In the gloom I lit a joint, inhaled and watched the glowing red embers at its tip. Incandescent, a flash of illumination, then subsiding into a passive wait for the next breath. A hit. The brain lifted and allowed subconscious activity to take over. To direct the flow. I lay with my eyes closed, seeing. Watching the mists in front of me. Watching faces emerge from the clouds. Watching them morph into others. Other faces, other beings. Then they came. All Israel. Faces of wisdom. Eyes set deep in features framed by different textures of hair. Rounded locks that covered the head and ears, vertical strands descending from the chin and cheeks, furry moustaches that concealed the mouth. Except for the motion of speech. An opening appears. A cavern to the interior that exhales a calling. Each figure drifts towards me, dissolves, changes. Until one remains. Stationary. Eyes fixed. Slightly moist. The rest of the body emerges from the cloud. An outstretched arm. Then two. A desire to embrace. I reject the intensity and come down from my high. I sleep to provide the next day with a sense of purpose.

Soon I had no need to use drugs. I developed a meditative technique that enabled me to conjure the faces at will. It provided a degree of comfort to have them available, but I felt myself sliding, descending, removing myself from my twentieth-century existence. I hadn't spoken to anyone since my return from New York three weeks ago and needed contact, to move on, get back to work, continue my researches and accept a parallel life.

"George, it's me, Peter."

"How are you? Where's all that dream stuff taking you?"

"Can we meet? I'd like to talk. It'd be easier than over the phone."

"OK. When?"

"Are you free this evening?" Now that I had broken the spell, I needed the quick reaction.

"I'll have to rearrange something. Nothing that's a problem. You sound a bit desperate."

"Thanks, George. Eight at the Queen's Head suit you?" It was the pub where we had our first meeting, which made it an appropriate venue.

"See you there."

"How can it be the same dream? That's incredible." I hadn't wasted time with George. I told him straight away. It came out as a frantic rush. A release. The relief to share it with someone was great.

"I need to get hold of the book now. To check my memory. Really make sure I wasn't imagining it. I couldn't possess it at the time. I was just too freaked."

"So what makes you so certain?"

"Vital's dream starts differently. There's some stuff about him walking through Safed and meeting up with deceased rabbis. He meets up with a crowd of Jews and the similarities start. They're too much of a coincidence."

"Tell me."

I visualised the text in the book.

"Well, there are steps in both dreams and a crowd of people gathered. The people in my dream were dressed in a style of clothing that could be typical of Safed in Vital's time. I'll have to check."

"What else?"

"Both dreams have the sun high in the sky, about midday, when it disappears and there is darkness. There is chanting from the crowd – Vital describes it as weeping."

"Freaky!"

"I appear in my dream and ask someone why the crowd is chanting. Vital talks about meeting a stranger. At the end of both dreams the light returns. I'm sure there are more points of contact, though."

George sat in silence when I finished speaking. What was he thinking? He had experienced my manic state in Safed. Did he think I'd finally flipped and invented a strange scenario?

"What do you make of it? Any explanations?" George's practical and analytical mind needed something tangible to grasp, to provide an answer.

"I've no idea. I just know I've got to follow it up. Find out as much as I can."

"So who's this guy Hayyim Vital?"

"From what I've read about him, it seems he's quite a character. His main claim to fame was that he was the main disciple of a guy called Isaac Luria."

"When was that?"

"Second half of the sixteenth century. Safed was a bit of a hotbed then of Kabbalistic thought and development."

"Kabbalah? Isn't that all about Tarot Cards and magic numbers?"

"That's more of an offshoot, like the occult. The basis of Kabbalah proper, if you like, is a mystical interpretation of the Bible. Luria put together a whole systematic view of creation and the meaning of life."

"Sounds heavy."

"Luria couldn't write it down himself and it was Vital who documented it all. Most Kabbalists now use the Lurianic system. They seemed to have had quite an extraordinary relationship."

"I'm intrigued."

"Well, for a start, Luria originated his thoughts in Egypt and had a vision that he should got to Safed to impart his knowledge to Vital. At the same time, Vital was told by a soothsayer that a sage would come from Egypt and teach him his wisdom."

"No shit! And a soothsayer ... thought you said it had nothing to do with the occult."

"I did say Vital was a bit of a character. Seems like he abandoned his Jewish studies for a while and went into alchemy and astrology and all that stuff. Even after going back to his religious studies, he still sought advice from female diviners."

"This whole thing gets crazier and crazier. So what else have you found out?"

"Mostly background stuff. Like the relationship between Luria and Vital was pretty intense and only lasted a couple of years as he died quite young."

"Who?"

"Luria. Of cholera, I think. I've got pretty interested in Kabbalah myself."

"So, are you going all religious then?" George said it with a hint of concern. The question shook me. Is that how it appeared to an outsider? That I had surrendered to a fanaticism?

Judaism had been a cultural rather than religious phenomenon for me. Even the cultural side was latent, not overt. It was reactive. I appreciated the Jewish joke, understood its wryness intuitively. The suspended blue note of Hebrew melody conveyed an instant empathy. Without being aware,

I was drawn to Jewish authors. Their material may not have been explicit in its conveyance of Jewish ideas, identity, religious themes, but somehow the essence came through the books to touch me. If I looked in the mirror I recognised features sculpted from Semitic ancestry. I had a rabbinical look. A face of puzzled containment that revealed a questioning of knowledge held within.

Now George was witnessing an explosion. A release. Somehow my researches, my exploration had opened a path within me. He had equated it to religious experience. I had not perceived it that way, or even thought about it in those terms. My last visit to a synagogue had been an enforced barmitzvah, the rite of passage for a thirteen-year-old boy.

"I'm not sure, George," I replied after a long pause for thought. "Dabbling with religious concepts has had some effect. I don't have enough understanding of what being religious means to answer your question."

"So what interests you about Kabbalah?"

"I suppose the philosophical side of it. How its structure can relate to ideas of the cosmos and also to an individual. There's this academic called Gershon Scholem who's written some of the definitive books. He says that for some Kabbalists the intellect itself is a mystical phenomenon. Sort of disappearing into your own intuition."

"I'll take your word for it, but do you think you've had a mystical experience?"

"I'm frightened to reply to that. An admission becomes a commitment to something that I have no knowledge of or perhaps don't want to be part of."

George's probing had me on a metaphysical back foot. I couldn't bring myself to tell him to stop his mild interrogation. I wanted to know the answers myself.

"Perhaps I'm being too direct. I'm asking questions that are outside of my own comfort zone. What is mysticism anyway? Sorry for all this shooting from the hip stuff, but I'm struggling to piece it all together. You know me, Peter, I like rational answers to rational things."

George sat back in his chair, caressed the pint glass in front of him and took a deep swig. It gave him time. A liquid pause for thought. His next words were unexpected.

"I'd like to help you," he said. "I'm really fascinated by all this. Would you mind me being involved? Doing some research, having discussions. That sort of thing." I was swept back to that drive away from Safed. To that tear, that emotion I felt for him. I struggled for words of acceptance. George grinned.

"Sleep on it," he said. "I must have surprised you. Call me when you've made a real decision."

We left the pub together, saying goodbye at the door, George to make his way to his flat in Maida Vale. Camden was three miles away, six tube stops with the change, thirty minutes of bustling public transport. So I walked, the night air stimulating my mind to consider the events of our meeting,

Why had George offered to help me? That was uppermost, as to be honest it wasn't like him. He was caring and considerate at the human level, but it was more to do with practicalities of living – helping me to move, that sort of thing. This was something different, something that would have to rub off on him, affect his own sense of being as it had affected mine. Perhaps it was his own search for a deeper spirituality, a sense of existence and awareness. He was no different to many people I knew who were in "questioning mode". George never discussed politics, but his red beard was a personal banner for a socialism that seemed in decline with the Callaghan government. A mystical quest was diversionary and alluded to higher things than the immediate problems of living and coping in a crumbling left-wing environment.

I suppose the main question was what was it I was trying to uncover, to reveal. George had an organised mind and a systematic way of looking at things. Maybe he could help on the contextual side, the factual stuff and leave me to ponder on the meaning of the dream for *me*.

I phoned George the next day to take up his offer and we met that evening to discuss a plan. There was strangeness in this whole concept for me, floating as I was in some magical realm with the possibility of being buffeted by George's research. It had to be that way, to drift on the wind of fatalism.

In the pub, George continued with his directness.

"You've obviously done a lot of research yourself from what you've told me last night. Anything written down?"

"Not a lot, it's all in my head."

"Never mind, just let me know your sources."

"Well, it's mainly Gershon Scholem's stuff. That has the history, players and theory. I can't really lend you his books as I refer to them a lot."

"I'll get my own. What about the book that had your dream?"

"I need to see it again now. Sort of a confirmation that I didn't *dream* that episode."

"I can believe that. Anything else I should know?"

"There is a local museum in Safed. I was thinking of getting in touch with them to find out more about the house and sixteenth-century life there."

"That's the sort of thing I can do. Leave it to me."

"Thanks." I said it with a real sense of gratitude, feeling the antithesis of the loneliness and despair I encountered in New York.

"OK. Give me a few weeks to think about things and do some digging and then let's meet again. But keep the contact going." George had seen into my anguish.

The next weeks were unsettling and I felt in limbo, waiting for whatever George had discovered and resisting the urge to call him.

Finally the phone rang. It was his voice.

"Let's meet," he said, "there's quite a bit to talk about. Could I come round to your flat? It'll be more private."

"You'll have to ignore my squalor. I've been too preoccupied to worry about the state of my flat."

"Don't worry, as long as we can sit comfortably."

"You've done a lot of research, but it's not terribly coherent," said George, commenting on the limited notes I had given him.

Most of the material was within me. I had my own comprehension, a ragged book of knowledge, piecemeal and holistic.

"I know, I know. I have this obsession, a determination to find out, uncover, reveal things. But I don't know to what purpose. I'm not sure where it's taking me." I had trapped myself. The reality was that each step, each new piece of information was a challenge to my psyche. A confrontation.

"I think we should step back a bit," George proposed, "it'll give you a chance to absorb it all properly and help you to move forward with it."

"What do you suggest?" I was willing for George to lead me through the mire.

"It may sound a bit too analytical, but it would be interesting to break it down into a number of different areas to investigate. It'll give us a focus."

"OK. You obviously have some ideas. Tell me."

"Well, firstly we can look at 'externals', anything that may have been an influence in having a mutual dream."

"Mutual dream?"

"I've been doing a bit of reading myself. A mutual dream is one that is shared by two or more people, normally at the same point in time. Yours is separated by 400 years. Sort of puts it in a different league."

"So what are the influences?" George had me intrigued.

"Well, the house itself and its location are probably the main ones. The fact that the dream had been documented could also have been a factor."

"But I had no knowledge of Vital, let alone read anything of his."

"I know that, but other people had. There may have been some energy, some vibe that you picked up."

"George, you're freaking me out. I didn't think you believed in psychic experiences"

"I don't, but I'm not ruling anything out."

"So we have externals. What else?"

"Then there's the dream itself. There are some specific symbols within it that would be good to analyse."

"Such as?"

"The steps and the people on them. The sun and its disappearance. The chanting. The light reappearing. The flashing and the symbol you saw. I managed to get a copy of the book you mentioned with Vital's dream. Reading it there's a whole bit about the stranger who no-one understood except for him. That we should look into."

"George, you amaze me! I'll need my own copy of the book, though."

"I got two!" George smiled. We needed something to break the intensity.

"Thanks!" I grabbed the copy from him as he brought it out of his briefcase.

George waited as I read Vital's dream again. And again. He remained silent as I closed my eyes and thought about the dream, imagined myself in Safed. I recaptured the feelings and sensations from my experience. I trembled and felt panic and anxiety as the dream took me to an unknown realm. Vital's dream took over within me. I strode the steps with him and acknowledged his peers. I was transparent to them. The dreams commingled, but who was the doppelganger, me or the hermit?

George diffused the moment. He was concerned that my descent did not become too deep. That the immersion only cleansed and clarified my thought processes. That the blackness did not become permanent.

"Tea?" A necessary reality punctuated my stupor.

"Thanks, George." For the suggestion and for breaking my mindset, I mused.

Over the steaming mugs we discussed the other aspects of George's plan. He was keen to know more about Kabbalah. Like me, he found its systematic view of purpose to be intellectually intriguing. We both felt that being exposed to this wisdom, this knowledge, might provide an insight into my mystery.

"I got this letter back from the archivist in Safed. It's pretty interesting." George handed it to me to read.

It stated that the house where I had the dream was "known". It had survived the major earthquakes in 1759 and 1837 and now stood in isolation in what once was a terrace of houses overlooking the old cemetery. Its survival and the connection with the witch had given it a reputation of being possessed. It was possible, thought the archivist, that witches had owned the house for a number of generations as practitioners of the black and white arts tended to run in families. The archivist was more of the opinion that the witches were likely to be soothsayers that locals sought out to be told a prophesy. Adera, when she bought the house from the white witch, had given to the museum some decorated bowls that she had found in the cellar. They had been identified as fifteenth or sixteenth century and were typical of the bowls used for oil divination.

The location of the house was also intriguing. According to the archivist it was less than 100 metres from the Ari synagogue. Ari was the popular name for Isaac Luria. It was the Hebrew word for lion and was also an acronym of the Hebrew words for "the Divine Rabbi Isaac". The disciples of

Luria were known as his "lion cubs". The most prominent "cub" was Hayyim Vital. Luria had a house built where he could study with his select group. This was no longer standing, but our friendly archivist informed us that the site was less than 20 metres from the house. A footstep echoed across 400 years.

"Wow!" I said, almost unbelievingly.

"I know, I felt shivers up my spine as I read it."

"And what state do you think I'm in? I feel like someone has walked over my grave."

"Your grave! Come on, Peter, you're not dead yet." As ever George tried to lighten things, sensing my melancholia and not wanting it to deepen.

"And neither is Hayyim Vital, it seems. He's haunting me with his dream. Or his soul is still floating around."

And where did my soul reside? Those investigations into Kabbalah were definitely unsettling me, causing me to question my sense of self, my own feelings of identity. Many years of sublimation since teenage questions had buried my spiritual being, my soul. And now, little by little, it was being exposed and gradually unpicked until … until what? What would be revealed?

My lack of fulfilment? The emptiness, the void within needing to be filled? It was as if I was replaying the Lurianic creation myth at a personal level. I had suggested to George that my interest in the Kabbalah was intellectual, academic and observed objectively. What was in fact happening was a somewhat subliminal impact on my psyche. It didn't need the detailed understanding that would come from years of study to feel the impact of the concepts, and to succumb to this idea of creation as a metaphor for my self-renewal. And tremble at the thought of the infinite.

Ein Sof was a Kabbalist term for God. It encompassed the perception of God as an unbounded presence that was beyond human understanding. The metaphor for *Ein Sof* was a continuous, ever-present source of light. This Infinite light filled all existence and left no space for finite worlds and beings to exist. The first step in the Chain of Creation was for God to contract and conceal the Infinite light, creating a void in which finite existence could endure. This process was termed by Isaac Luria as *tzimtzum*. The first created being, Primordial Man (Adam Kadmon), was formed from a thin ray of divine light which penetrated the void. Adam Kadmon was then responsible for the next stages of creation, the emanations of God's attributes through the ten *sefirot*. These divine emanations served as a channel for a life force and a mechanism for the revealing of God to man. The Tree of Life was the popular construct of the *sefirot*. It was an instant symbol of transcendent power.

My intuitive awareness of these complexities reminded me of some words of Einstein I had read as a teenager. These gave me as much a personal philosophy as I allowed myself. I could repeat this passage as a mantra:

> *"The most beautiful thing we can experience is the mysterious. It is the source of all true art and science. He to whom this emotion is a stranger, who can no longer pause to wonder and stand rapt in awe is as good as dead, his eyes are closed. The insight into the mystery of life, coupled though it be with fear, has also given rise to religion. To know that what is impenetrable to*

us really exists, manifesting itself as the highest wisdom and the most radiant beauty which our dull faculties can comprehend only in their most primitive forms – this knowledge, this feeling, is at the centre of true religiousness. In this sense, and this sense only, I belong to the ranks of devoutly religious men."

Our researches progressed. The combination of my brooding, contemplative exertions and George's drive, enthusiasm, focus and analytical ability was synergistic. We came to an opinion that there were a number of viewpoints on the dream. It had been a catalyst for enquiry into Judaism and Kabbalah; it was forcing me to confront my identity and acknowledgement of "Jewishness"; it was an entity that had its own existence and relevance.

"Where are we with the specific symbols you mentioned a while ago?" I had my own thoughts on these, but was curious to see what George had come up with.

"Where do I start!" A spark lit George's face. He was uplifted, a semblance of the old George seeped through. "I'm moving towards Jungian notions of interpretation as well as the obvious Kabbalistic link."

"So you think I've drawn on the well of the collective unconscious?" Jung's concept of a second psychic system of impersonal and universal consciousness that an individual inherits had an intrinsic appeal for me. It was something I could relate to.

"Well, yes. I'm thinking specifically of the light symbols in the dream. The sun and light are fundamental to life and for many cultures the absence of light is frightening and despairing."

"I've read a bit about that. Do you remember the stuff we got on eclipses?"

Our researches had taken us to the Royal Astronomical Society. The sun disappearing at midday could have been an eclipse. Again an oddity emerged. During Hayyim Vital's lifetime there were three total solar eclipses that were visible in Northern Israel. This frequency was unusual, as any local region on the earth's surface would normally experience that event once every few hundred years.

"Yes. It's possible that an eclipse planted itself in Vital's psyche."

"The chanting and wailing has a collective unconscious feel to it as well. Some North American Indian tribes would sit in a circle and sing during an eclipse until the light returned. It was a way of overcoming their fear."

This perspective started to drag me from my melancholy. A liberation from the pull of Judaica. I felt an animation, a pulse of excitement.

"Anything else, George, along these lines?"

"The steps have a symbolism, a Jacob's ladder linking two worlds, linking you to your forefathers. The dominant figure at the top with the outstretched arms could have been an ancestor calling to you."

My ancestors! How far back? What is their calling? There was an immediate impact from George's point. The self-questioning that I had been undergoing prompted a need to understand my roots, the filtering of the collective unconscious through tribal and familial traits. I knew little of my background. History stopped with my grandparents in the murk of middle and Eastern Europe. My father told me that I had been named after a cousin of my grandfather, Paul Levi. Paul had been a lawyer and prominent member of the German Communist Party and was reputed to be a lover of Rosa Luxemburg. He took over the leadership of the Party after she was murdered in 1919 and died in 1930 after an attempt at suicide.

I connected to the socialist background, but was wary of his method of death. In my own gloom, I didn't wish to consider genetic predisposition to self-destruction. I was burdened with death.

It was beyond the recent history that intrigued me. This '"ancestor" in my dream was in ancient dress, so were there familial ties in sixteenth-century Safed?

"George, I feel a need to go back to Safed, just to see the place again." There were too many unanswered questions. I might not be able to find all the answers in a return visit, but the compulsion was great.

What was it that now compelled me to revisit the place that I had fled in panic and anxiety? Fled in a rush that had left no time to dwell on the causes of that frantic state.

Being drawn into the world of the original dreamer, Hayyim Vital, that mystical figure of the past, created a need for me to trace his footsteps. Those of his life and his dream, and to reflect on the conjunction of our dreams. For in mine, one man emerges from the crowd of all Israel to speak to me, whereas Vital confronts a stranger, a dervish.

But it was more a desire to see the physical manifestation of Safed where these events took place – its lanes, houses, synagogues. These were tangible. I could run my fingers across the bricks and observe the coating of dust on my skin. Engrained within those particles of time was the story of a place that needed to be revealed and, once uncovered, would allow me to breathe anew.

All this is what drew me back.

"Funny you should say that. I was thinking it myself. It was prompted when I bumped into Robin the other day."

"Robin?"

"You remember, the sponsor of our aborted project."

"Oh yes. Has he forgiven me?"

"More than that. I told him why we were unable to complete the film. He's fascinated and thinks there's a programme in it."

"A programme! What did he mean?"

"It's sort of around the topic of the impact of dreams on the dreamer. Your story triggered something he'd been thinking about for a while. He'd be willing to fund a speculative shoot in Safed to give him substance for a treatment for selling it to a broadcaster."

"You've obviously had more than a five-minute chat in the corridor. Why have you kept it from me till now?" I was angry. I had allowed George to take over too much.

"Hold on, Peter. I didn't commit to anything. I just thought it would be best to get as much from him as I could before I discussed it with you. The next step is really up to you. You should talk to him directly."

"What are his ideas?"

"I think he'd like you to go back to the house and get your impressions. Maybe relive the dream there. He'd also like to film you talking to the modern-day Kabbalists who live and study in Safed, to get their impressions of your experience."

It was an attractive proposition, but did I want to be drawn deeper into the Kabbalah and have contact with unknown scholars? How would they view me? How would I react to them? Reading about Judaism enabled me to keep an objective distance from its reality. Direct contact with exponents was a different matter. What would it open up in me?

I succumbed to my fates. It was an opportunity that I had not conceived. I would let it determine its own course of events. George and I would leave for Safed.

I had never spoken much to George about Eva and the strangled relationship I had with her. It was all too personal and difficult to explain, so I withdrew from it.

But now George and I were returning to Safed, I felt compelled to tell him all. Offload. Somehow free myself from this burden I carried. I used the captivity of our flight to begin my exorcism. George, as he always did, listened with a thoughtful intensity.

"Perhaps you should stop now," George said as he watched the welling of emotion in me. "We can talk more in the hotel."

"There is more, so much more," I inwardly sobbed. "I never realised how much I miss her."

"I know. I always sensed your emptiness. It reminds me of what Eliot says in the Hollow Men."

"I never knew you ready poetry!"

"Not a lot, but I was struck by the title. Anyway, the verse I remember is where he talks of a shadow falling between emotion and response."

A DREAM UNTOLD

I was taken aback with George's insight. Was my burden that apparent? Eva's legacy had reinforced the barrier to my inner self. My feelings were lit with the gloom of her existence. My hollowness was the vacuum of the dark space between, well, my emotion and the response. My relationships were tinged with uncertainty. My reality was superficial and defined by externalities. I could not be other than my work.

And now I was to be the other side of the camera. Revealing myself to enable the next stage of the journey that the dream had inspired. The anticipation began to sublimate my melancholy. Put it in another place.

Safed beckoned and with it an arousal of the senses. As we drove near, the sky said it all. Grey and brooding with atmospheric presence, it embraced the hills of Galilee, adding weight to the climb to Safed, increasing the burden of expectation. A return to the house and an opportunity not conceived, of meeting with men of insight, a glimpse of wisdom, and enlightenment.

A citadel with no walls or gated entrance. Encrusted energy guarded this place, drawn from two millennia of throbbing minds. A shaft of light broke through the clouds, but the source was unclear. It connected a humming throng with ethereal diffusion. It pointed the way to the house with its own portents and connections. Safed, the mystical city; Safed the city of dreams; I felt that everyone had their own story in this place. Some would say that no story is personal, that they all belong to Safed and are lent to an individual for a purpose to become each person's defining moment. A moment that is simultaneously of no time and of infinite time. It is this transcendence that enables the connectivity.

As we approached the house, that house, we looked deep into the valley below to the ancient walkways of the cemetery, where a millennia of dead are buried. The air seemed thick with their souls; air that permeated the brick of dwellings ravaged by earthquakes and time. It penetrated the peeling plaster of the terraced cottages. The plaster flakes mingling on the stone floors with the shedding skin of their intense occupants, forming a physical union that replicates the spiritual. Safed, the city of souls.

I had returned.

THEN

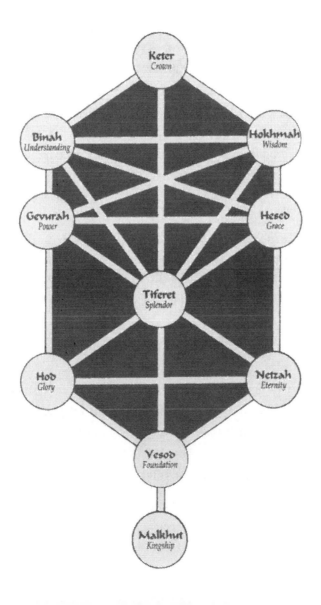

6

Safed 1570

In the sky above the hilltop town the three stars announcing the start of Sabbath had been joined by many more. With dawn some hours away, their glow added to the brightness of the crescent moon, illuminating the flat roofs of terraced houses. A shadow was cast upon one and inside Hannah Vital stirred. The whispers emanating from her husband Hayyim's lips had woken her as they had done many times before.

Lying there entranced, Hannah wondered what Hayyim would tell her in the morning as the murmurings signified he was participating in a dream. She was privileged to be the first to hear of his visions as he told of them on his wakening.

They were profound, elevating, prophetic. But most of all they positioned Hayyim in the highest ranks of rabbis. Above many of his contemporaries in Safed, Sagis, Halevi, but mostly above that upstart Ibn Tabul. Hannah was proud and could hold her head high among the women of Safed. Was her soul not the reincarnation of Kalba Savua, whose son-in-law was the illustrious Rabbi Akiva? Had she not been impregnated with the soul of the wife of Tinneus Rufus, the governor of Judea? Through her good deeds the souls of the sodomite Savua and the evil Rufus would be purified. Had not Hayyim told her that the cleansing of his soul would be hastened by her acts? He was a *tzaddik*, a righteous one. Soon the righteous ones of Safed would create the conditions for the coming of the Messiah.

But this night seemed different. As Hayyim's whispers grew louder, Hannah could make out a word, one word repeated with increasing intensity. YHVH, the divine name. Sweat came from Hayyim's brow and he jerked upright without the aid of his arms. His eyes blazed open. He screamed.

"Another one, Hannah, another one."

"You were saying the name, Hayyim. In your sleep. I heard it. What is it?"

"I was dreaming, Hannah, of being in synagogue and meditating on the four letters of the Divine Name. And as is the custom, the *Tetragrammaton* formed the shape of Adam Kadmon."

"And was the flame lit?" asked Hannah, aware that this mythical figure representing the limbs and body of primordial man could blaze with fury.

"With a fierce red, so bright and glaring it pierced me and I rose to the heavens on its sparks." Hayyim faltered in his description as the intensity of recalling these images filled him with dread. Hannah clutched his hand and looked softly into Hayyim's tormented eyes. Her expression of love allowed him to regain his composure and he continued.

"The shape was before me as I ascended to the heights. From my loftiness, I turned to look down and the letters floated towards the cemetery below, to the graves of the holy ones."

Hannah held fast to Hayyim, her grasp becoming tighter as she shared his terror.

"And the *Tetragrammaton* settled on a tomb and became … became…," Hayyim sobbed. The final words lay in his mouth, waiting for the reality of their deliverance.

"… a body, the body of a boy."

Hayyim dressed slowly in the emerging glow of an early dawn. The rituals and observances to be performed on rising became secondary as he pondered on the deaths that had all Safed in turmoil. There had been three in the past two months. All young boys, and the Council of Rabbis wailed in their hopelessness to find reason for these deaths. Their goodness clouded the possibility of seeing into the mind of the murderer. And what of motive? What possessed this evildoer to drag the life from these innocent souls and force a still-warm corpse into a sacred shape to be left on the graves of those they revered? Such a desecration was an insult to the piety of the community.

And now a fourth? The image from his dream overpowered Hayyim's thoughts. He forced himself to concentrate as he uttered the blessings while putting on his Sabbath cloak, a velvet robe of crimson hue. The material oozed through his fingers, conjuring a semblance of blood. Blood that was not of the body. It was not flowing or a pool or a congealed mass.

As Hayyim examined his appearance in the mirror, the thin vessels in his eye projected a rich redness that matched his robe. And as he gazed the eyes became those of another – wilder, fiery, burgeoning with evil.

"It is the murderer," shuddered Hayyim, "he dares me to reveal him."

But the face remained obdurate, hidden in its own darkness, unlike the images of rabbis that Hayyim could conjure in his meditations. Those who bore his past soul in transmigration and would speak to him with their wisdom.

"I have lost the ability to see into the diabolic mind," Hayyim reasoned as he reflected on the time he was 21 and turned his back on his *Torah* studies and immersed himself in alchemy, astrology and the rituals of witchery.

"One must dabble with evil to recognise evil," were the words of his teacher Joseph Karo, when he was welcomed back to his study circle three years later. But the stain was still there. It cast a shadow on his attempts to cleanse himself, move forward, become the revered and rightful successor to Joseph that he felt was his destiny. What penitence was appropriate? His teachers could not advise him. It was beyond them.

Hayyim could sustain his stance no longer and continued with his preparation for attendance at the Abuhav Synagogue for the Sabbath morning service.

"Hannah, I must leave now. Today, of all days, I should be among the *minyan* and tell Rabbi Joseph of my dream."

"Fly, Hayyim, fly," his distraught wife wailed, still overcome with the drama of the night. "The murderer must be found."

"And it is for the community to uncover him. Our Ottoman rulers have little interest in helping us. The Council of Rabbis must decide what to do. But it should not delay our Sabbath lunch!"

Hannah's face lifted at Hayyim's remark. A little levity, even in the most harrowing of times, is always welcome, he would say. All things need their counterbalance.

She gazed lovingly at him, attired in his finest clothes. Like all marriages, theirs had been arranged and as a tender girl of 16 she had initially been dismayed at the thought of sharing her life with a man who had grown portly after his return to the fold. His dumpiness was in contrast to her litheness, the black of his hair illuminated the redness of hers in its distinction, and her height was sufficiently above his to make her bow in seeming obsequiousness when they embraced.

But their minds met more easily as Hayyim, unlike many men, enjoyed discussing spiritual affairs with her. And valued her opinion. But these deaths, these terrors afflicting Safed, they were beyond her experience; they were from some other realm that only Hayyim, perhaps, could comprehend.

As he bustled through the streets and entered the narrow lane leading to the synagogue, Hayyim's mind was pulsing as it searched for some explanation for these events. Getting closer to the house of worship, a foreboding intruded on his thoughts. A sense that the actuality of his vision was about to be realised.

In spite of his earliness, a buzzing crowd was already assembled in the courtyard. Approaching them, the hubbub became words that could be discerned. Body. Boy. Cemetery. Grave.

The body had been seen from the path above the burial ground. It had not been identified as it was forbidden to enter the graveyard on the Sabbath. The talk was of the strange posture of the corpse. The legs had been pulled apart to form a right-angled arch with a narrow gap between the trunk and arms that lay straight down. Hayyim recognised this as the shape from his dream.

Eyes turned towards Hayyim as he drew nearer, filled with an expectancy of revelation.

"Whose child is missing?" he asked, halting in front of the throng.

"The Halevis' son did not return last night. Menahim is out searching for him now," came a voice that Hayyim recognised as that of Abraham Galante, a leading disciple of the great sage Moses Cordevero.

"Halevi the weaver?"

"Yes, and it is retribution for his sins." Abraham's words seared through the crowd and bore the portent of the authority he drew from the devising of rules to obtain piety.

"Abraham, it is wrong to criticise a man facing tragedy," responded Hayyim.

"When a man places wealth above piousness, when he blasphemes and makes false commitments to his workers, when he misses prayer to meet with merchants, then he must expect censure at any time."

"That may be so. But why now? You are harsh, Abraham."

"Because of the severity of the sign."

"The sign? What meaning is this?"

"May I remind you of the 26th rule of my list of practices."

"Recite it for us, Abraham, so that we may all understand your reasoning."

"Rule 26 states that an individual ought to be careful with respect to taking false vows and oaths, for through the sin associated with doing so a man's children are stricken, as it says in Jeremiah *'In vain have I smitten your children'*...."

The crowd shifted in fear; Rule 26 was unique in that non-adherence could lead to that dire punishment. An eerie silence descended, which was only broken by a blazoned voice.

"I saw that the body of the child lay awkwardly. It appeared of the shape of the *Tetragrammaton*."

Abraham Galante spoke. "Then it is as I have said. For the letters of YHVH add to 26."

"Then it must be, then it must be," rose the crowd, lamenting as in congregation.

"Menahim's sins will ruin us all," came an anonymous cry from the midst of the masses.

"All of our sons will be lost," was the response from the herd.

Taken aback at the display of panic, Hayyim stood back, distancing himself from the ranks of the distraught, and addressed them: "Friends, do not be alarmed. We are a pious community and our foundation is secure. But we must pray with more fervour to seek the repentance demanded to overturn the evil that is among us."

As Hayyim concluded, the imposing figure of Joseph Karo strode into the courtyard. Even he was affected by the state of turmoil and so put aside his rationality to succumb to the hysteria.

"This is a sign for us all to revert to an ascetic and austere life. Our mortal souls are to be punished, And I ..., I must die at the stake to repair for my sins." Joseph drooped as he expressed what many knew to be an innermost desire, but one of aspiration rather than fulfilment. Stating it stunned the crowd, who loved and revered him as their master

But Hayyim Vital spoke for them all. "Oh wise one, I beg you not to think of this fiery end. Your wisdom is needed on Earth. You must guide us on the path of contemplation."

Joseph regained his composure and assumed his mantle of leadership. "Then we must burn these unworldly thoughts in the fire of meditation. Come, recite the *Shema* with me."

A DREAM UNTOLD

Shema Yisroel, Adonoy Elohenu, Adonoy Echad.
Hear O Israel: The Lord is our God, the Lord is One.

And the crowd calmed as their devotions brought them closer to the Divine essence.

Sabbath afternoon, the period between lunch and the evening service; this was the time that Hayyim reserved for peaceful contemplation. A period for renewal and refreshment of his whole being in preparation for the week to come. So he reflected on that which was uppermost in his mind and on the words of his father Joseph, may his soul rest in peace.

"Safed has changed much since you were born," he had told his 20-year-old son, "the people, the atmosphere. There is a new energy that excites the mind and increases our wisdom. But with it, I feel, there is a sense of foreboding."

"I am aware of it too," responded Hayyim, "but tell me why you think this is."

"Our cousins have brought the pain of the Inquisition, I fear. It still clings to their being, even after three generations."

"It seems we have paid a price for the knowledge of Kabbalah they brought with them!" commented Hayyim, suppressing a cynical smirk.

"That does not become you, Hayyim; they have suffered much and we must continue to welcome them. Especially as their persecution and expulsion help bring the coming of the Messiah. The healing of their wounds has great power," admonished his father, who was aware of the challenges to orthodoxy that his son was starting to make.

"A date is proposed, within this age, is it not?"

"Many believe it will occur in 1575, when our community will be pure of soul."

Pure of soul. Those words brought Hayyim back to the present. The community strove to achieve this perfection in many ways, but it was the negation of the body that struck Hayyim, unable to distract his mind from the murders.

Rabbi Karo had spoke of ascetic practices outside the synagogue this morning. The rituals mostly related to food and drink and on enforced lack of enjoyment when partaking, such that fasting brought gratification. In fact Joseph had said that it would be perfect if it were possible to exist without food and drink altogether.

Even more extreme were the Fellowship of Penitents. Hayyim observed this group of *conversos* at prayer, weeping and tearful. He watched them on the street as they practised flagellation, wearing sackcloth and ashes. He noticed their fasting, some for three days each week.

As a teenager Hayyim was disturbed by the sight of them, unable to understand their motivation. He studied their expressions as they whipped their own backs into bleeding sores. Gaunt and emotionless, of another world, the curtain of their eyes preventing Hayyim from seeing into their soul.

"I must comprehend their darkness," thought Hayyim, and he began to look beyond the *Torah* and his Talmudic studies. After the death of his father, he immersed himself in the dark arts, striving for a meaning that was not forthcoming.

A DREAM UNTOLD

But he had retained one practice from this period of experimentation. One that complemented his visions and directed his insight. One that calmed a raging mind. And one that enabled him to retain contact with the white witches of Safed.

So that night, after the evening service, with his breath-warm prayers still striving for the firmament, Hayyim made his way to the house of Soniadora, the soothsayer.

An inclined lane led to her abode overlooking the cemetery. The slope quickened his pace and an archway soon came into view. Through this was the field above the witch's home. Hayyim paused and allowed the dark air to enfold him as his gaze rested on the roof at the foot of the bank. Beyond and below was the cemetery, the drab flatness of the roof seeming to provide a step into the chasm of graves. Shadows flitted among the tombs and then stilled to retrieve the body of Judah Halevi.

Hayyim made his way down a gravel path and entered the terraced garden, wild of weed and herb used for Soniadora's potions. Walls of pale blue bounded the property, the hue revealed by the purity of the moon's reflected light.

"The colour wards off the evil eye," Soniadora had told him.

As Hayyim stepped into the courtyard, she opened the arched door leading to the main room of the house and greeted him.

"Welcome, Rabbi Vital," came as words of warmth from a woman of indeterminate age. Some said 20, others 60. But none could remember her birth. She was dressed in a shapeless robe that concealed her slimness, long blond hair cascading over her shoulders, framing a heavy brown and black beaded necklace.

"It is not too late, I hope," replied Hayyim.

"Your need is now; these murders trouble you. Please come in," was her response of lightness and understanding.

Hayyim followed her into a room that had the arched ceiling, thick stone walls and alcoves typical of the design favoured by their Ottoman rulers. It was in sharp contrast to the simple, square layout of his own home.

Thick carpets adorned the floor and the stone window seat. Candlelight was unable to penetrate the gloom of the recesses on two sides of the chamber. Soniadora invited him to sit on a stool in front of a low copper table in the centre of the room.

"What is it you desire, rabbi?" she asked, looking down on him.

"I seek a prophecy, wise woman, which will help cleanse our town of its horrors."

Silently Soniadora retrieved from the blackness of an alcove an engraved metal bowl, a pitcher of water and a small narrow-necked bottle containing olive oil. These she placed on the copper table. She sat on a stool opposite Hayyim and filled the bowl with water.

"I must know what you see in the oil, Soniadora." Hayyim was impatient as he watched her drip olive oil into the vessel.

"I must cast a spell first, as is customary." The incantation echoed in the chamber as her hands concealed her face in a motion similar to that performed by Hannah when lighting the Sabbath candles.

The drops sank and then rose to form a thin film on the water's surface.

"I see a crescent shape, which is good, Rabbi Vital, something fortunate is denoted. I will divine again for the details." Soniadora went outside to empty the bowl, filled it again with water and slowly dribbled in the oil.

"I see a message. The letters are clear. They say you have a desire and thirst to know a discipline called Kabbalah. You will comprehend that which no others have understood. A great sage will come this year from Egypt and he will teach you his wisdom."

Hayyim was pleased with this prophecy. Gaining insight into the mysteries of this ancient knowledge would bolster his desire for greatness and confirm the elevated nature of his soul.

"But what of the murders?" he cried, remembering the purpose of his visit.

"For this, the sage will bring deliverance. I can tell you no more."

"Goodbye, wise one, and thank you."

At this Hayyim took his leave and began a thoughtful climb of the steps that took him to his home near the *khan*. He entered, silently acknowledged Hannah, sat down on the wooden chair in his study, and waited.

Many in Safed viewed the murder as the work of a *dybbuk*, the tainted soul of a sinner. But who of them had been possessed and driven to perform these dark deeds? And would the revered Joseph Karo be able to exorcise him, or her, as he had done so remarkably in past cases? His first public exorcism was burnt into the memory of the populace.

A young boy had been in torment and spoke of strange and wondrous things, driven by the spirit that had entered him. The spirit did not respond until Karo threatened it with the punishment of excommunication, and then it spoke of the history of its soul. It had passed through various Gentiles before becoming lodged in a dog that the boy's father had killed. The soul sought vengeance by entering the man's son with the intention of killing him. Karo expelled the soul by reciting the *Aleinu Leshubeah*, the prayer that concludes the daily service. He declaimed it seven times, forward and backward, and decreed that the intruder be banished to the wilderness. And so the boy was healed.

And so the people of Safed witnessed the eternal battle between good and evil.

Caleb Pinto woke and automatically said the prayer before rising that reflected the belief that one's soul departed to the higher realms during sleep.

> *"God I thank you. You have returned my soul. Great is your faith."*

Something stirred within him. There was uncertainty in the truth of the words he had just uttered. In his somnolent state there was no recall of the dark events of the night before. He rose and looked out from his home in the street that nestled beneath the Citadel of Safed. It was here that most of the *conversos* lived. Not that they wished to be known as *conversos* now. Their tribulations in Spain and Portugal were of the past and they no longer had to hide their Judaism or let it drown in baptismal waters. Fleeing from persecution, they left their homes and property and struggled in their journey to Israel, valuing its sanctity over material wealth.

Joseph Karo was one of those who had made the journey east, aged only nine when his family fled from Portugal in 1497. It took nearly 40 years before Joseph finally arrived in his spiritual home and became the great scholar and codifier of Jewish law.

During his time as Chief Rabbi, Karo defended the *conversos* by pronouncing forgiveness and proclaiming that they should not be humiliated but be able to integrate into the community.

The Pinto family had prospered in this climate and Caleb's father Abraham had helped establish the Portuguese synagogue.

"And you, Caleb, will maintain our standing," were words of gentle encouragement that emanated from Abraham when his son took office in the synagogue.

The Sabbath sun was soon to rise. In the half-light Caleb could make out the cemetery below as he peered across the rooftops of the Jewish Quarter. He was wakening from his trance, the fixated state of his possession. The memory of his tragic deed returned and he raised his hands to his face. They were disembodied. Not his hands. How could they be? He was not a murderer. They were the instruments of death. It was not he who encircled them round the throat of Menahim

Halevi's youngest son Judah. The boy had looked up to him, had given him a reverence that few in Safed offered the *conversos*. In spite of the efforts of Karo, they were still regarded with contempt for their baptism. But this was no justification for the slaughter of innocents. We have come to Israel to greet the Messiah, his father had told him. There was a fervour in the land that the Messiah would soon reveal himself in the hills of Galilee. It would bring redemption and an end to the exile of the Children of Israel.

This much Caleb knew. But what was it that had compelled him, that had taken over his soul, his essence, his purity. And then left him. Left him with an image that brought him to the brink of madness. An insanity of desperation. Judah was his fourth victim. No, not his. Not him. Guilt was elsewhere. He had not the courage to reveal that he was the mechanism for the outrage. He drew back, professed horror with the others in the community. Expressed wonderment at the reasons for the deaths. Offered no help in the search for the perpetrator.

He was respected in the community and was prominent in the "Baaley Teshuvah Society". How could he, a leader of the Society that sought to achieve forgiveness for the sin of conversion by sincere repentance, disobey the Sixth Commandment?

The glow of the ascendant sun illuminated his face. He felt its warmth, its acceptance that should allow him to start a new day. But these cosmic powers were insufficient to overcome the stirring from within. Caleb quivered with its embodiment. His body contorted and shook. A silent scream echoed in the hollow of his mind. The voice raged in its desperation and inability to be heard.

His father, Abraham, entered his room. For Caleb was unmarried and lived with his parents. It was a source of concern that a match could not be made for him. Many whispered in private that he was a sodomite and had no desire to procreate.

"Good day to you, my son. Are you at prayer? I will not interrupt your devotions." Abraham observed Caleb's movements at the window and mistook them for the ritual motions required for entering a state of meditation.

Caleb turned. Away from the window. Away from the sun's rays. But the radiance was within him. His face shone. It distorted. Caleb uttered words in a voice not his own.

"*I am the lover of Lilith, the wife of Satan.*" Caleb twitched. He convulsed. Abraham felt the heat of his breath and cowered beneath the torrent that followed.

"*The Messiah must not come. My soul is in torment for abusing the Holy Name and I could not be redeemed. I possess you to prevent the redemption I sought.*"

Abraham looked up. His son appeared to him through tragic eyes. They implored him for a release from this bewitchment.

"What evil spirit possesses you, my son? Who are you? What are you?" Abraham addressed the mortal and incorporeal elements of Caleb. No answer came. Abraham, in his fear, recalled the public exorcism that he had seen performed by the sage Joseph Karo. He would seek his help.

The spirit within Caleb was obdurate. It remained silent. The sage Karo could not provide the balm. Abraham implored in muted tones. His arms outstretched, one caressing the cheek of his cowering son, the other pleading with Rabbi

Joseph. The threat of excommunication passed through Caleb and did not touch the *dybbuk*. Negation of its evil power was beyond the known exorcism abilities of all in Safed. The community wailed in their hopelessness. How many more of their children would die before the visitant was satisfied? Captivity for Caleb was not feasible when confronted by a creature of supernal strength. And death for Caleb? That would release the evil soul until it found a new being to impregnate. And who would this be? Any of those among us, they thought. Thus the fear of execution was great.

And so Caleb was left to be alone. And be watched. And when the spirit raged, all doors were shuttered and barred. And none ventured out.

Isaac arrived unobtrusively into this brooding atmosphere, exchanging glances with the inhabitants of the hilltop town whose name was derived from the Hebrew word *sufim*, to observe, such were its commanding views of the surrounding countryside.

And it was to the distance those residents looked as Isaac passed by with his wife and teenage daughter, strangers in their midst who they could not welcome, such was the fear in their hearts.

Tired after their journey from Cairo, Isaac had not allowed his family to enjoy their travel and take in the sights of Alexandria, Jaffa, Jerusalem and Tiberias, through which they had passed.

"We must proceed with haste," Isaac had told them. "The community is in urgent need." They did not question his want for speed; the intensity of his desire was overwhelming.

For the first few nights they stayed at the *khan*, built by the Ottomans at the behest of Joseph Karo. It was much like Mordechai's home in Cairo, the rooms of the inn looking out onto a central courtyard. Familiar surroundings allowed the women to settle, while Isaac, with the generous amount of money that Mordechai had settled on him, sought out a home for them.

"I must gain the trust of the community and let their awareness of my wisdom grow as I plant the seeds of my knowledge. We shall live close to the school of Rabbi Moses Cordevero and I shall attend his study group."

And so he joined Hayyim Vital in Cordevero's classes on Kabbalah. He kept silent as Vital declaimed his knowledge and grasp of the highest wisdom. He observed the demeanour of this man whose face he had seen in the Nile and noted his impatience and arrogance, an internal conflict in Hayyim's aspiration to greatness and the humility it required.

Isaac remained wordless on the relationship that was soon to be revealed. A reputation grew and spoke for him as his insights spread among the people. This stranger has great learning, they uttered. His *Torah* knowledge is exceptional, his commentary full of sagacity, his interpretation a wonder.

And Isaac learnt of Caleb, the possessed one, and of the inability of Joseph Karo to exorcise him. "This torment," thought Isaac, "this agitation has stirred the air and this is the disturbance I felt on the banks of the Nile. It is for me to heal, to succeed where Rabbi Karo failed."

Isaac retreated. He wandered the hills around the city and breathed the potent air and watched the luminescent clouds engulf the green ridges of the valley. He sat on ancient rocks and communed with those who had gone before. And the means of exorcism came to him. Rabbi Karo could only expel a soul, but the *dybbuk* in Caleb was also in need of redemption. "I must reach into the possessed one and release him from the hold of Satan," he thought.

The rocks grew cold as night descended and still Isaac sat, his eyes shut, enclosing the images in his mind. Pictures of evil, of the devil that held Caleb. And as this vision grew clearer, the curses of Psalm 109 came to him.

> "Appoint over him a wicked man and may a Satan stand at his right."

Isaac repeated these words to himself, felt the power of them as a mantra and an invocation. Swaying as he stood, heady with the exertion of his excogitation, he made his way back to the city and vowed: "It is time; tomorrow I will make myself known to Rabbi Vital."

As was customary, after a long day of study and concentration, the students of Moses Cordevero engaged in informal discussion. It was an opportunity that Hayyim took to tell of his visions and establish his position within the group.

"Upon a wall I saw a serpent's egg about to hatch," he began, "and I threw it to the ground."

There was a murmuring around the long table at which they all sat. Isaac lifted his eyes and gazed intently at Hayyim as he continued.

"The egg broke open and two serpents emerged, one male and one female. They entwined and clung to another as if in sexual intercourse." Heads began to nod as understanding of the symbolism grew.

"I took a pure white stone and threw it at their writhing, decapitating one. The freed head escaped and as I searched for it I came upon a white tent which I entered." His curious colleagues were now gripped by this description of Hayyim's battle with evil.

"Inside the tent was an inscription. It read *'whoever desists from and destroys evil and whoever chases away evil sinners and impurity from himself, and throws off the evil inclination, I will make my highest servant'*."

Isaac watched Hayyim as the allusion from the dream inflated his being. "There are many sides to this man," he thought. "The potential of greatness must battle with his lack of humility."

Hayyim completed the account by positioning himself in the place of greatness. "Upon reading this inscription, I surmised that the reward is so great that I must kill the other serpent, which I did. And then I awoke."

No discussion ensued, as there was no desire among his peers to discuss Hayyim's assumed eminence once again, and all save Isaac left him alone with his dream.

"You must endure the presence of evil strongly, Rabbi Hayyim," spoke Isaac now that they were alone, "as I feel the chill of the wind in Safed."

"And its rawness afflicts all our hearts. It is the gush of that lost spirit, Rabbi Isaac, it settles not."

"There is a way, I believe, to rid the poor soul of his scourge. I have studied much and the *Zohar* gives guidance in the use of prayer for exorcism." Hayyim was stirred, for Isaac was zealous in his assertion.

"What can you bring that our master Karo could not?"

"I can see into the heart of man. I perceive with all my being the source of his troubled state. And then I am at one with the sufferer and his cause. The power of this unification will expel and redeem the *dybbuk* and release Satan, who stands over this evil soul." Isaac looked into his companion's eyes as he spoke. A stillness of conviction penetrated Hayyim that assured him of Isaac's ability to succeed where Karo had failed. But there was more to this revelation.

"Rabbi Isaac, I am convinced you must try to exorcise Caleb. I will take you to him. But there is something more. You are from Egypt, are you not?"

Isaac softened his expression into a loose smile.

"Yes, Rabbi Hayyim, I am from Egypt. You have been expecting me. We are to be close. It is part of my destiny to teach you my system of Kabbalah. We are to be pure of soul and lead the way to redemption."

And so began the mortal story of Hayyim Vital and Isaac Luria.

It is a story of opposites. Of master and student. Of humility and arrogance. Of actual and potential. Of patience and frustration. Of intuition and perception.

And how Isaac guided Hayyim to the wisdom he so desired. And sensed when the antithetic forces were subdued and Hayyim was ready to receive each particle of knowledge. And allowed him to grasp the system he envisaged. So that all could benefit from his insights.

Although they saw each other every day, much to Hayyim's dismay, Isaac held back from engaging him until he sensed a calmness within his pupil. "And first," Isaac determined, "I must allay the differences between us and we should bond through our transmigrations." And so it was, on a day after Sabbath, Isaac invoked their first discussion.

"We should talk of our soul history, Rabbi Hayyim," he began.

"Yes, I am most curious of mine. I feel it should substantiate my pre-eminence," an eager Hayyim responded with his need to put himself at the centre.

"But first you should hear of my soul ancestry. And then you will see how we are linked."

"It is from Adam we both start, as all do," responded an anticipatory Hayyim.

"Yes. I will enlighten you with a few of those most dominant. I have traced my transmigration from Adam to his son Abel to Moses and to Shimon bar Yohai, the originator of the *Zohar*."

At the sound of these illustrious names, Hayyim grew expectant. But a growing awareness caused him to hold his tongue and allow Isaac to proceed without interruption.

"And yours, Rabbi Hayyim; as I am from Abel, you are from Cain. And our linkage continues through history."

Isaac did not reveal all the details. As with much of Isaac's knowledge, Hayyim would need to have evolved into the fit attitude for acceptance.

"And the nature of this link, Rabbi Isaac?"

"You are to be my spokesman, Hayyim. As Aaron was for his brother Moses and Rabbi Abba was for Shimon bar Yohai. It is for you to take my wisdom forward."

"But why me, teacher? Why have you chosen me in advance of the others? There are many outstanding scholars in Safed." Hayyim would remain vexed and unable to progress until he knew the answer and be able to face the community.

"You were disclosed to me by Elijah. That you were chosen in heaven makes it clear to me that the greatness of your potential surpasses the others."

Isaac went on.

"The greatness of a man is not measured by how he is esteemed by his peers. It is the purity of the soul that is the determinant. I have looked into them all and not one is as unblemished and suitable to receive my teachings as you." Isaac drew back and allowed Hayyim to absorb his words.

Hayyim was humbled by Isaac's view of his essence. This stab wound at his hubris invoked a feeling of anxiety. "An unblemished soul," that is what Hayyim heard. And it should remain unblemished, untainted by deeds of omission.

"Oh Hayyim," he thought, "you are chastened by this man. His expectation belittles your conceit. Your piety should be unquestioned and elevated at all times. Stand in awe at this demand."

All this Isaac saw in his disciple's mind and was content with this invocation of self-awareness. Both remained silent in reflection until Hayyim felt ready to speak.

"Rabbi Isaac, I accept my role with deference to your great insights. I look forward to our discussions and receiving the fruit of your wisdom."

"That is good, Rabbi Hayyim, already you have learnt much. And now we must turn our minds to the unfortunate Caleb. You must tell his father of my plan to exorcise him."

"Abraham is desperate. I will tell him of the measures you wish to take and I am sure he will agree."

It was a short walk from Isaac's house to the *converso* quarter. In Hayyim's mind, as he walked silently alongside his mentor, the distance was not physical. Another world was to be opened to him, as an observer and pupil, one of transcendental power put to the most mysterious of uses, to redeem a lost soul from evil intent. If this pious young man, so esteemed not only in his community but by all of Safed, could be afflicted, then what might happen to any one of them? An awareness of his own vulnerability chilled Hayyim as he directed Isaac to Caleb's home.

Abraham Pinto was waiting outside the house as Isaac and Hayyim approached. Caleb was alone inside as his mother had gone to stay with her sister in a neighbouring street. She was much disturbed by the involuntary behaviour of her son and could not endure the pain of another attempt at exorcism.

"Welcome, rabbis. Caleb is in his room. He is willing for you to free him from his anguish." Abraham greeted them with a tremulous voice. His anxiety was apparent for he was placing trust and the healing of his son in the hands of an unknown.

"That is good," Isaac said, "the expulsion of the *dybbuk* must take place in the sanctity of this home. The spirit should not be humbled in front of a crowd."

Isaac and Hayyim followed Abraham into the house. The plastered walls were cracked and stuccoed flakes crumbled under their feet as they climbed the stairs. "See, Hayyim, how this place sheds its skin," mused Isaac, "it is a good sign for the expulsion."

Abraham opened the door to Caleb's room to the sound of scurrying feet. His son had been anticipating their arrival with ear and body flattened against the door. As they entered Caleb shuffled quickly to the opposite corner, slid to the floor and sat with his knees against his chest, releasing a ponderous sigh. He hugged his shins and gazed at Isaac with a pleading supplication. Hayyim stood back to observe his master.

"Caleb, I can see that you are troubled and wary. Your eyes have pity in them for the wrongs you have done. Approach me as a friend." This Isaac said in a gentle, but commanding voice. The sound seemed to permeate the wall behind Caleb, at first to bring comfort and then to exert some hidden force that persuaded him to rise. Isaac reached out as Caleb's halting steps brought him close.

Isaac continued. "Now, Caleb, I must stand behind you and look over your shoulder. I will see what you see."

Hayyim and Abraham remained motionless and watched as Caleb approached the window, Isaac turning as he passed, their movements so calm as to not disturb the air in the room.

"I must now feel the anguish of your soul," Isaac intoned as he gently grasped Caleb's wrists, lifting his arms in supplication to the distant hills.

"You must understand what I am doing," explained Isaac, for the benefit of Hayyim. "As a physician can recognise ailments of the body in the pulse, I can feel the vitality of the soul through the coursing of the arteries. The greater the transgression and sin committed, the lighter the pulse."

Hayyim was transfixed. This was the meaning, he thought, behind the *Zohar* passage that tells of the ten varieties of pulse, recalling that each variety was named after a Hebrew vowel with which it had a rhythmic affinity.

For an eternity the pair stood motionless as Isaac attuned himself to the evil that was submerged in Caleb's life forces. Eventually Isaac relinquished his hold, suppressed a shudder, and spoke.

"You are indeed possessed, Caleb. It is for me to rid this evil from you and I should begin the exorcism. Please remain as you are while I stay behind you."

Caleb looked around hurriedly, searching the room for his father in a sign of desperation. Abraham absorbed a penetrating gaze, replying with a supporting nod that seemed to disturb a flock of sparrows resting on the rooftops opposite. Other noises permeated the room – sounds of children's laughter, the rumble of a cart, doors closing as neighbours went on their daily business.

"Abraham, can you please close the shutters?" requested Isaac. "We must shut off the outside world before I begin."

Warily Abraham circled the bonded pair, not wishing to touch them in case he broke the spell that Isaac seemed to have over Caleb, and reached out to the wooden slats. As he drew them back a shadow descended on them all before the room was calmed in the diffusion of light.

"Where should I stand, rabbi?" asked Abraham nervously.

"By Rabbi Vital's side at the back wall," replied Isaac, "and then I can commence the exorcism."

Isaac began by inhaling with such deepness that all air in the room seemed to have been sucked into his lungs. As he did so his head arched backwards, directing his being to the heavens. Again he clasped Caleb's wrists, this time more firmly and in a resilient bond. On his exhalation he intoned the verse from Psalm 109 into Caleb's ear.

> *"Appoint over him a wicked man, and may Satan stand at his right."*

With alternate breaths he said the verse both forward and backward to reinforce its magical power. As Isaac chanted, the room grew cold. Nothing stirred. The repetition grew manifold and Isaac contemplated on the power of the prayer whose intent was to force the spirit to speak, to reveal its name and to answer questions.

"This *dybbuk* is stubborn," Isaac whispered, breaking off from the recitation. "Bring me a *shofar*. A blast from the ram's horn will be necessary to assist me in the task."

Abraham exchanged a puzzled look with Hayyim as they left the room to get the instrument.

"The trumpet has great power in putting demons to flight," explained Hayyim. "It is as in the New Year, when we blow the *shofar* over a well to subdue the evil spirits before drawing water. It is the same with Caleb, this must be done before we restore his life force."

And what of Caleb during this healing? The Psalm entered him. The image of Satan on his right overwhelmed his being.

A tortured silence pronounced judgment on the battle for his soul. The pain of his ancestors rose within him. This was his Inquisition. Soundless screams shuddered from quivering lips. But his body remained calm and still as Isaac's passiveness flowed into him. At Isaac's command, Hayyim blew the ram's horn and its wail resounded in Caleb's ear. And Isaac's recitation became sharper and more insistent. He added the words "Depart, depart quickly" after each verse. He invoked the *Tetragrammaton* and decreed that the spirit leave from the space between the nail of the big toe and the flesh such that the body is not damaged. He commanded with the power of the names he had used that the spirit should not harm, nor enter any Jew's body again.

Caleb writhed and wrestled with Isaac, releasing himself from his clutch. He turned and faced all in the room with contorted face and the fiery eyes of the murderer. Saliva moistened his lips, his breathing became quick and unsteady, his mouth opened to grasp the void between him and the other mortals in the chamber.

And the spirit spoke.

"I am the soul of Joseph Della Reina."

Isaac was unmoved at the sound of this infamous name, continuing to watch over Caleb as Abraham gasped in recognition of the fallen Kabbalist, then whispered to Hayyim, "My grandfather told me of this man from friends who lived in the same village in Spain. It is said he sold his soul to the devil."

"We must remain quiet," responded Hayyim, "and hear the voice of the spirit."

The spirit of Joseph continued.

"*I am the lover of Lilith, the Messiah must not come. I possess you to prevent the redemption I sought.*"

"And what of you now?" Isaac adjured.

And Joseph said, "*I have been punished and driven away by the Supernal Court for having conjoined with the soul of demons.*"

And Isaac asked, "What are the sins for which you have been punished?"

And Joseph said, "*I bowed to Satan and made offerings. I used the Holy Names for my own benefit and for the good of my mortal body, rather than for the sake of the holiness of heaven.*"

And Isaac asked, "Why have you entered Caleb? What is his transgression that allowed you to possess him?"

And Joseph said, "*He has no sin. It was for his strength that he was chosen.*"

And Isaac asked, "Why did you invoke Caleb to murder the children?"

And Joseph said, "*It was Lilith's doing. She seduced me and turned my thoughts of redemption into evil deeds.*"

And Isaac asked, "What was Lilith's purpose?"

And Joseph said, "*To thwart the process of cosmic salvation by tainting the pure soul of the victim with the sin of murder.*"

And Isaac asked, "Do you now wish to be free of Lilith's embrace?"

And Joseph said, "*For ever more.*"

And Isaac prayed and lifted his arms over Caleb. And Caleb felt the divine power emanating through Isaac and engulfing his inner demon. Drained and exhausted, Isaac had a last measure to perform before the *dybbuk* could depart. The soul of Joseph Della Reina was to be redeemed.

He asked, "How did you die?"

And Joseph said, *"By my own hand."*

And Isaac said, "All these sins prevent you from entering Gehinnon. Do you repent?"

And Joseph said, *"For all my sins."*

And Isaac said, "Then I expel you from the body of Caleb and relieve you of your limbo state. You will enter Gehinnon for your soul to be purged before joining all others in the World to Come."

And the soul of Joseph Della Reina departed the body of Caleb.

News of the exorcism quickly spread among the community. What power, they thought, was in this man from Egypt that could dislodge the *dybbuk* that had resisted the attempts of Rabbi Karo. And not only dislodge the spirit, but bring peace to Caleb such that he was able to regain his place in the community, the power of their belief in possession absolving the *converso* from his crimes.

And his learning continued to amaze his fellow students in the academy of Moses Cordevero. All were in awe and would speak of him thus.

"He overflows with the *Torah* and he speaks with the voice of an angel."

"And he understands all, even the language of the natural world."

"Like that of the trees and the birds."

"And before a thought comes to us, he knows it already."

"He is aware of everything, even our future."

"He sees into our very souls."

And Hayyim remained silent as his peers queried the destiny of the man from Egypt. But Isaac was not imperious and was respectful of Cordevero for the few months of their time together. Death came early for Moses and all of Safed were in mourning as they gathered in the burial hall to pray for the departed soul of the 48-year-old sage. The black draped coffin rested on the handcart that had borne the mortal remains of all the past *tzaddiks* of the mystical city and the congregation were silent as the 80-year-old Joseph Karo stepped forward to perform the funeral oration. His head was bowed with age and reverence. Tears flowed as Karo spoke, his mind full of memories and the witnessing of an 18-year-old prodigy who had become the pre-eminent master of Kabbalah.

> "He was the pearl that gleamed in the hearts of all. He had time for the most simple and the most learned. His students flocked to him as a gazelle races from a flowing brook. They would toil day and night under his inspiration. Today the Holy Ark of the Torah is to be hidden away in the grave. Who can replace this most illustrious of men?"

As the bier made its way through the narrow cobbled streets of the city, buildings brought their own sadness, shielding the procession from the sky, casting a gloom on the mourners. The cortege entered the open space between the last terrace of cottages and the boundary wall of the cemetery. The rumble of the iron wheel on stone changed to a dragging scuff as the wheels encountered the dry earth of the path to the gate.

One by one the funereal procession made their way down the steep hill of the graveyard to the departed rabbi's last earthly home. Clouds formed above them, the mourning of heaven reflected in the weight of their greyness. In this closing gloom two pillars of fire suddenly illuminated the burial cart and accompanied it on its slow journey.

"We have a sign of Rabbi Moses' greatness," proclaimed Isaac, "the divine flame is a compliment shown only twice a generation."

The throng murmured, for no other of the grief-struck crowd had witnessed this accolade from paradise. And then all spoke at once, save Hayyim who stepped outside the group to stand between them and Isaac.

"The new rabbi is a chosen one."

"He alone among us saw the pillar of fire."

"We must look to him as Rabbi Moses' successor."

"A new era has started."

And Hayyim took his turn. "But he must choose among us who are to be his disciples."

The murmuring stopped. It was not fitting to have such thoughts before the esteemed Cordevero was cast into his grave. And Hayyim's interjection reinforced the silence. What did he mean by this? It was not customary to have an elite group in Safed.

"The soul of Rabbi Moses must be dispatched before his successor can be allowed to emerge," interjected Joseph Karo, "and we must surrender his mortal remains to the earth."

And so the coffin was laid in the grave. The congregation sprinkled the dust of the burial ground onto the casket as manna from heaven to nourish the deceased one on his journey. The dust became clods as each of them shovelled from the waiting mound of soil until the grave was full and satisfied. And they stood back and recited the prayer for the dead to ensure that the departed soul of Cordevero would find its rightful place in the cosmos.

Silence reigned as their minds joined the spirit of Moses in a concord of farewell. Eyes lifted as one, the elemental forces within them bearing Cordevero's chariot to the heavens.

But the mystery of Moses' sudden death confused them all. "Why was he taken so early, when lesser sages can live to a great age?" was uppermost in their mind.

Sensing the dismay, Isaac delivered an oration to pacify the collective distress.

So, it was time for Isaac to speak again, to make the final oration full of cryptic words that mystified the throng until his allusions became clear.

"The verse states," began Isaac, "that *'if a man committed a sin punishable by death, and he is put to death, you shall hang him on a tree.'* A sin implies a deficiency in the totality of a person, but there was no deficiency in Rabbi Moses to warrant his early death. So, how then can we explain his passing?"

These cryptic words mystified the throng, but Isaac held them in his thrall and continued with the explanation. "The words, *'you shall hang him on a tree'* may also be read to imply that we 'hang' the reason for his death on the primordial serpent who caused Adam to eat from the 'tree' of good and evil."

Nodding of assent greeted the erudition. Glances were exchanged and hidden thoughts shared. Had Rabbi Moses relinquished his mortal existence to make way for this man who could bring *tikkun olam*, the healing of the world?

So Isaac led the pious of Safed up the steep path from the tombs of the ancients to the gate of the cemetery. As one they looked down to the burial place and pondered, the past behind them and an unknown future.

"There is no doubt," said Jonathan Sagis. "Rabbi Isaac is the rightful heir to the mantle of our beloved Moses."

At this the throng dispersed, each contemplating Hayyim Vital's assertion and speculating if they were to be part of the circle. And curiosity about Hayyim's special relationship was in their minds.

That person, that Isaac, that ascetic from the Nile, stopped on the path and waited for his solitude. He viewed his domain and chose the sites of his ministry. There was to be the *mikvah*, the ritual bath, for cleansing the body. Here should be his study house for elevating the mind. And not 50 paces along should be the synagogue as the place to unite the spirits of his disciples with God.

Isaac felt the embrace of the air, its touch an acceptance from the sages interred below. Acceptance of his plan, acceptance of him as the emergent leader, acceptance of his divine authority.

He stood and looked upwards. He opened his arms and breathed deep the atmosphere of this place. He grew large and encircled the space between heaven and earth. The surge of destiny coursed through his anchored body.

He quivered with awe and drew his arms across his face to shield his eyes from the horizon of dreams. An inner voice proclaimed his readiness to commence the task of universal redemption and he conjoined with the heavens to seek guidance for his task.

Those who looked down on him from the town felt the radiance emanating from him, and then turned away to give privacy to the conjunction. In the setting sun, Isaac returned to his body and made for home with the prescience of work to be done. Now he was to choose those who would help fulfil his task. They will come and be revealed, he thought, they will come.

Hayyim looked up to the fields surrounding the Citadel. They were full of poppies, which formed a red-patterned path inviting him to ascend to the heights. He resisted their pull and mused on the day's events as he walked through narrow streets. Cobblestones reflected a hazy sun that was curtained by an expanse of soft clouds. They seemed to form a roof over the city, creating a barrier to the heaven above. A light rain settled the dust on the paths snaking through the Jewish Quarter. Tiny rivulets trickled through the miniature gulleys formed between the cobbles, the water being absorbed at intervals in patches of earth, where time had eroded the path. The dampness of the soil gave the impression that it was the source of the stream, contradicting what he knew to be true. Hayyim smiled inwardly as he reflected that he could not trust appearances. He had been told that earlier today, admonished by his teacher.

Hayyim and Isaac had just completed their daily walk in the slopes and fields surrounding the Jewish Quarter. The Ari favoured the open air for discourse; the freedom allowed him to expand the thoughts and ideas that came to him in meditative sessions. The discussions that day had reached a critical point.

Hayyim's mind was reeling with the profundity of Isaac's utterances. His body trembled with an unease and an expectation that it was to be the vessel of containment. At times the silence between them spake loud. It magnified the disciple's thoughts, his interpretation. It was that, which had been his downfall.

"Do not interpret. You must absorb, must feel, must become the knowledge," his teacher said as he expressed puzzlement.

"But teacher, I must understand first and understanding comes from interpretation." Hayyim spoke with exasperation.

"You must clear your mind and be prepared to accept that which wishes to be revealed," replied Isaac patiently.

"I must know what you wish to reveal to me." A frustration was building up in him. He felt that his role as the Ari's preferred disciple was being undermined. If future generations were to benefit from his wisdom, he would need to grasp the principles of Isaac's system and how to apply them.

"As the *Zohar* states, Hayyim, *'permission to see is granted only with eyes concealed'*. You must first learn to see with your eyes closed."

"But how am I to attain this ability, master? Are there rituals I should undertake?"

"It is too soon to lift the lid," Isaac continued. "You must be patient. I will determine the time."

"And when will that time be? How will I know?" Hayyim replied, concealing his vexation.

There was a lengthy pause before Isaac spoke. They both knew the significance of this moment.

"You asked the question because you are not ready. Your soul is capable of comprehending the wisdom revealed by my system, but you are not aware of it yet, it is hidden to you. You must prepare yourself by purifying your mind."

"And how do I accomplish that, teacher?" responded a subdued Hayyim.

"You should never get angry, depressed, haughty or impatient. You should not discuss commonplace matters. You should maintain a modest image of yourself and be filled with inner joy and fear of sin." The Ari announced a strict regime to the bemused Hayyim.

"You must study in the prescribed manner," he continued, "you must obey the rituals I have set. This will give you the ability to ascend the spiritual ladder. And then we will both be ready."

For the remainder of the walk back to Isaac's home silence prevailed. Although he had visited Isaac many times this was the first awareness that Hayyim had of its closeness to Soniadora's. The denseness of trees separated the two abodes, shielding one from the other, keeping the antithetic influences on Hayyim apart. A fig tree, however, its spreading branches reaching like tentacles to the respective houses, made a tentative connection.

Isaac plucked a ripe fig as he passed the tree, broke it in two, giving one half to Hayyim.

"Let us share this fruit as we are to share my wisdom," a now smiling Isaac uttered. "Imagine its fleshiness and sweet taste before taking it to your lips and its succulence is revealed. Learn this about all things."

"Thank you, Rabbi Isaac. You have left me with much to contemplate."

"Until tomorrow, then." Isaac accompanied the now ritual farewell greeting with a wry grin as Hayyim headed back through the streets in a curious state of being. Again he was honoured, yet humbled.

"Hannah, I am perplexed," Hayyim confessed to his wife, "Rabbi Luria has chosen me to be his agent on earth. Yet he will not reveal his secrets. He tells me that my soul is the least unblemished of all in Safed, yet he keeps me apart from his other students. He even has Hiyya Rofe, one of my pupils, within his inner circle!"

"You must be patient, Hayyim. Is that not one of the practices that Rabbi Luria wishes you to follow?" Hannah reminded him of the set of rules that Hayyim was commanded to obey to ensure the purity of his soul.

"It is indeed. I can only admit to you the difficulty of keeping to these precepts. I have to avoid killing the slightest thing, even the gnat that bites and bleeds me."

"That is indeed difficult," consoled Hannah, "but it must be God's will as uttered by Rabbi Luria."

"Indeed, Hannah, indeed." Hayyim paused and retreated to a pensive questioning of his role. Isaac had recognised in him all the weaknesses of his youth. He had known of his study of alchemy and magic and other forbidden rituals. Hayyim had told Isaac of his visit to Soniadora and her prophesy that he was to teach him his wisdom. Isaac respected this power. Did he not have it in himself? That it was in a woman did not trouble him, unlike many of the sages in Safed who felt that the domain of a woman was in the private realm of hearth and home.

Women have potentiality, Isaac would say. The *sefirot* have a feminine side of understanding and judgment. And all the upper *sefirot* feed *Shekhinah*, the female divine presence. This represents the eternal balance that must be sought between man and woman to achieve harmony in the Tree of Life. We cannot attain redemption, believed Isaac, if chaos exists through an imbalance.

Hayyim had gleaned these insights during his discussions with Isaac. But the detailed systematic view that underpinned everything was withheld. Again he thought of his earlier discourse. You must see with your eyes closed. You must see with your eyes closed.

"I see with my eyes closed," whispered Soniadora to the nocturnal air.

It reached the ears of Hayyim as he walked out into the night after his talk with Hannah. I must overcome this barrier, he thought. I must progress. A half-moon illuminated the way from his house near the Abuhav synagogue. It was not the light he needed. He knew the narrow streets well and the path to Soniadora's house was ingrained. His feet needed no instruction. A small flight of steps led past the weaver's house, the cries of his children rebuffed by Hayyim as his senses were focused on this one action. He needed guidance from the witch.

A candle glowed in her window. She is home, it is good, she will advise me. Hayyim reflected before entering. Is this right? Perhaps it should come as an enlightenment from within.

"Enter, Rabbi Vital," welcomed Soniadora. "I have been expecting you."

Hayyim could not ignore this sign and crossed the courtyard to the half-open door where she stood. He went into her now-familiar home. One day he would ask what lay within the alcoves on the two sides of the room without windows. They had an infinite darkness that contained the secrets of divination.

"I am troubled, Soniadora," a hesitant Hayyim responded, "and need your help to seek the source of what is ailing my soul."

"Your soul is not unwell, Rabbi Vital, it is to other things we should look. Do you wish me to perform a divination?" Soniadora asked the question to ease Hayyim into a receptive state. His agitation was not conducive to a good reading and she needed to calm him first.

"My master says I must see with my eyes closed. That is my difficulty. I cannot grasp his wisdom without this faculty. His insight is great and I must develop an awareness that approaches it." There was a pause as Hayyim sat down on a low stool beside the ornamental brass table where Soniadora performed her soothsaying. She was startled by Hayyim's admission. He must indeed be distressed, she thought, to divulge these feelings.

"Then I will divine with my eyes closed," she at last said. "I will use the stones."

Soniadora disappeared into the concealment and returned with a box containing three smooth stones, each of a different size. They were marked with mystical symbols. Hayyim recognised the intersecting lines and circles that represented the *sefirot* Tree of Life formation. The others were inscribed with patterns made up of Ashurite letters.

"We must use a different bowl for this method," spoke Soniadora, as she replaced the dish on the table with one that was larger and adorned with more letters. She filled the bowl with water and carefully poured a thin layer of warm chicken fat onto the surface.

"Are you ready, Rabbi Vital?" she asked. "Please tell me your concern."

Hayyim drew a deep breath and told of his troubles. Soniadora picked up the stones and closed her eyes. She gently dropped the smallest, fingertip-sized pebble into the water and listened to the faint whistle it made as it fell through the air and penetrated the covering of fat. A pause as Soniadora absorbed the meaning of the sound. This was repeated with the other two stones, the largest being the size of an eyeball.

Soniadora laid her hands on the table, either side of the bowl, palms upward. Her eyes were still closed as she saw into Hayyim.

"You will be able, Rabbi Vital, you will be able." The words floated from Soniadora's mouth. Hayyim felt relief that the capacity was within him.

"Does it say how?" Hayyim still needed direction.

"I must see the pattern made in the oil." Soniadora opened her eyes and gazed at the bowl. The surface appeared unbroken. The chicken fat had closed around the openings made by the stones.

"This is a sign, Rabbi Vital. You must close your mind before seeing within."

"And how am I to close my mind?"

"That is for you to determine. But remember you have three parts to your being. The body, mind and soul. Think how your physical nature affects your mind. You will come to it."

"Thank you, Soniadora. You have been of great assistance. Now I must go home to pray and sleep with these thoughts. I am confident the answer will come."

And that night Hayyim dreamt of these things. He saw himself purifying his body in the *mikvah*. He donned clean clothes of untainted white and entered a room where no sound could be heard and saw that he had closed his eyes. He felt his mind divesting itself of all thoughts and becoming devoid of sensation.

He woke in this dream state and meditated on the supernal universe. It seemed as if his soul had left his body and ascended on high. He imagined himself standing in the celestial cosmos, where he sensed that the Spirit had rested on him and that secrets were to be revealed.

"I saw with my eyes closed, master." Hayyim told Isaac of his dream and the preparation for meditation that it contained.

"That is good, Hayyim," Isaac acknowledged, "but the truth can be mixed with falsehood. You must discern what is revealed and reject those idle concepts and ideas which do not conform to the teachings of the *Torah*."

Hayyim nodded, accepting his teacher's advice.

Before he could ask for enlightenment, Isaac continued. "There is a journey we must take that will flame your ability to interpret the teachings. And then you will be ready to comprehend my wisdom."

Morning came quickly as Hayyim, in eager anticipation, joined Isaac on the descent to Tiberias on the shore of Lake Kinneret. A bright sun illuminated the still water as Isaac studied the shoreline.

"We must rent a boat and row to this point," Isaac told Hayyim. "It is clear from the markings on the surface that this is the place."

Hayyim was puzzled, but had learnt by now not to question his master. All would be revealed, he mused, for that is my destiny.

From the fishing dock they rowed south towards a place that Hayyim recognised as the tomb of Rabbi Meir Daal HaNess.

"Stop and dip your oars," commanded Isaac when they were about halfway there. As they drifted, Isaac waited till they were aligned with the pillars of an ancient synagogue on the distant shore.

"This is the place where the water will flood you with the insights of the Patriarchs. Here, drink this." Isaac took the pitcher that Hayyim had been looking at curiously during their journey and filled it from the lake.

Hayyim took the flask from him and swallowed the brackish water without questioning.

"Here," Isaac explained, "is the final resting place of the Well of Miriam that nourished our forefathers in the wilderness. And in honour of the sister of Moses, the water is now imbued with the power to aid understanding of the *Torah* and give the ability to remember all."

Hayyim lowered the pitcher and looked into the face of his master with a new assurance. No longer would he strive for illumination, for he was ready to be taught.

No more words were spoken between them on the return to Safed. Each had much to contemplate and the next steps were pivotal in the belief of both men. In their silence the same theme was considered by both, but from their differing perspectives. Hayyim was still concerned that he was not included in Isaac's study group, but he could not demand to be included as that would not comply with the practice of humility that Isaac stipulated for him. It would also display arrogance, which was also forbidden to him.

"'Now that Hayyim is prepared," mused Isaac in his silence, "I must enlist his help in forming a select group of the most pious individuals, as many of my students are not equipped for the task that lays ahead."

Tired after their long day, the gates of Safed were a welcome sight as they climbed towards the city. Each of them felt a need to emerge from the cocoon of the journey and establish contact before taking their separate paths for the night.

"We must sleep on our thoughts," Isaac said, "and meet after the morning service. We have much to discuss."

Hayyim's concern welled inside him. "*Speak now, tell of your unease,*" came from a voice resounding in his mind. Overcoming his deference, Hayyim uttered his perturbation. "My tiredness will overcome the spark you fed me today and I will no doubt sleep well," Hayyim replied, "but there is a matter troubling me …"

Isaac interjected before Hayyim could articulate his concerns. "I know, Rabbi Vital, but do not despair. It will be resolved tomorrow."

The words came as a gentle pouring that bathed Hayyim in calm. His wonderment for his teacher was intensifying with each day. Were there no limits to the capability of this man, he thought? And as they walked, before departing, a sparrow flew in front of them, chirping as it burrowed into a hedge.

"Our colleagues await our return with great curiosity," Isaac remarked as he observed the bird nestling into the branches.

"His song tells you this?" asked Hayyim, knowing that the answer lay in the verse from Ecclesiastes that they chanted in unspoken harmony and unison:

> "Don't revile a king even among your intimates.
> Don't revile a rich man even in your bedchamber;
> For a bird of the air may carry the utterance,
> And a winged creature may report the word."

"Yes, Rabbi Vital, the language of birds discloses the actions of men," Isaac declared when the verse came to its end.

Hayyim was overcome by Isaac's intuition. He knew all that was around him and there was reason in all his actions. Hayyim resolved to remain silent on his concerns and let Isaac guide him on the day to come.

The morning service was over and Hayyim made his way to Isaac's house. He walked past the Bannai Synagogue, the oldest *shul* in Safed. It had been built at the burial site of Rabbi Yossi Bannnai, a Talmudic sage in the Roman era. To the amusement of some and the consternation of others, the grave was located in the women's gallery on the ground floor. The symbolism was pertinent to Hayyim, as he had reverence for the role of women in spiritual life. Isaac's home was in view as he descended the steps from the synagogue, as also was Soniadora's house, the pale blue walls that enclosed the terraced garden forming a backdrop to his destination. The proximity of the two homes filled him with a curious mixture of disquiet and ease. Both were places of enlightenment for him, but the connotation of witchcraft and magic attached to Soniadora left him vulnerable to condemnation.

Isaac's study house was newly built. His Uncle Mordechai had financed its construction by raising money from friends and business acquaintances in Egypt. They considered it a "good deed" to perform this task, which allowed Isaac to concentrate on his life's work. The house was in a chosen location in Safed. Through the window in the study room Isaac could see the cemetery. No houses blocked the view. That was important. He could look down into the tombs of the deceased *tzaddiks* and meditate on their souls. And this was how he prepared himself for the morning he was to spend with Hayyim.

Visions entered his mind as he pictured the wafting heavenwards of the departed spirits. And how the levels of the soul dictated their ability to conjoin with the Source of all things.

It was this concept he would discuss with Hayyim today, for it was crucial to his mission. Only those who could attain the highest level of *neshamah* would be acceptable for the task.

"Welcome, Hayyim," greeted Isaac as his disciple entered the courtyard of his master's home. "Today is auspicious as last evening was the night of the new moon. It symbolises our beginning and the endeavour we have this day. You are to help me in the choice of learned men who are to comprise a fellowship of disciples."

Hayyim was benumbed. To be Isaac's primary student was one thing; to have power over the learned men of Safed was another.

"This is an honour," responded Hayyim as Isaac stood waiting for a reply.

"The honour is to serve God, Rabbi Vital, it is not for you to inflate yourself. Remember your humility as we proceed and you will have clarity in your thinking."

"My admonishment is just, master. The task is unexpected and I have much to learn. Please tell me the purpose of the fellowship and how we are to judge our colleagues."

Isaac stood quietly and let the silence speak to Hayyim. The two men faced each other and each saw a different wisdom. Hayyim knew not to expect an answer. It was for him to reason out an explanation.

"Come Hayyim, let us have some refreshment. I smell the coffee brewing." Isaac broke the quietude and took his student's arm. A steaming jug awaited them on a table in Isaac's study. They sat, recited the blessing before drinking and took a small bowl each. Cradling the vessel and watching the vapour rise, Isaac began to talk.

"Contemplate your coffee, Hayyim, and liken it to the three aspects of the soul."

"How so, master?"

"The *nefesh*, or lowest soul, is as the bean before it is roasted and ground. It contains the potential of the drink we are about to imbibe. We are all born with a *nefesh*; it is how we proceed that will determine if it can ascend to the higher levels."

"As good or bad coffee can be made from the same bean."
"Indeed."
"And the next level, the *ruah*, master."
"As the *Zohar* instructs us, the *nefesh* is close to the body that nourishes us. With the right preparation it becomes a throne on which the *ruah* may rest. The *ruah* betakes itself into the earthly Garden of Eden to enjoy its pleasures. As we enjoy the taste and stimulus of the drink."

Hayyim clasped his hand around the bowl and took it to his lips. The vapour from the hot liquid drifted across his face as he mused on what Isaac had been saying. He took a draught and spoke.

"Our word for breath, *neshamah*, also refers to the highest soul, does it not?"

"Yes, Hayyim." Isaac waited.

"And it is *neshamah* that ascends to the highest place so that the purity of our essence can join all those above."

"That is so."

"As the steam from the coffee contains its aroma and merges with the air."

"That is the analogy, Hayyim. But what of the breath?"

"We can equate the steam to breath. And it was the Divine breath that Genesis tells us was blown into the nostrils of Adam to give him life."

"Continue."

"And when we wake each morning we give thanks by reciting 'My God, the *neshamah* you placed in me is pure.' We say this as the *neshamah* of a human being leaves him every single night and returns in the morning."

"I hope you will appreciate your coffee in a different way now," joked Isaac, "but as I told you earlier, the purpose of today is to enlighten you in the choosing of disciples for our hermetic circle."

"So it is those with the purest of souls we must select?"

"Correct, Hayyim, but how are we to identify them?"

"As those whose souls can reach the highest level of *neshamah*?"

"Yes, Hayyim, and it is here that you must learn from me again, as you did at the exorcism of Caleb Pinto."

Hayyim paused and reflected on what he had heard. Now he was to be instructed in something that would give him supremacy over his fellows. At the same time, he would need to sublimate this power to retain the esteem of his teacher. Was this inner turmoil purposefully created by Isaac, so that he, Hayyim, would enhance his self-control? Even this awareness, in Hayyim's mind, was a sign of his development.

"Now, Hayyim," Isaac continued, "I must tell you of how I propose to use the ancient art of metoposcopy to identify those who can attain the highest level."

"Metoposcopy! I learnt of that during my studies of alchemy and astrology. Is that not the art of predicting a person's future by divining what is in their mind?"

"That is so. But what is in a person's mind or in their soul manifests itself on the forehead in the form of lines."

Hayyim suddenly felt defensive. What symbols were displayed on his brow and what could they reveal?

"Do not worry, Hayyim, I know you well enough by now for you not to worry about my sorcery!"

"Master, you should not joke about your powers."

Isaac smiled, for he recognised the totality of the world and that humour had its place. "Just so, Hayyim," he responded, "but those of limited understanding may view me as one with magical powers. But to continue. These lines that I see form letters which tell me much about the person. And the message is most significant during their devotions or when interpreting sacred passages."

"So you are to observe our colleagues during the study group and identify them this way!"

"Correct, Hayyim. I do not expect you to learn this technique immediately. It takes many years of concentration and awareness of our fellows. It is that you should be conscious of what I am doing during the class and from my manner try to determine those who I have judged suitable."

"I will try, Rabbi Luria, I will try," a humble Hayyim responded. "You have left me with much to contemplate. And when is this process to start?"

"I have no need to tell you, it will be apparent to you. Now finish your coffee, it must be cold by now."

The two men merged into noiseless solemnity for the remainder of their meeting, each ruminating on what lay ahead.

"Until tomorrow," said Hayyim at last, choosing a propitious moment in his meditation to stand. Isaac did not respond. Still deep in concentration, his aura transmitted a farewell.

And who were the members of the hermetic circle, these pious men of virtue? Chosen in unknowingness, the criteria for selection could not be discerned. It was not by age or community, for all were represented. The local Musta'arabs, the Sephardim from Spain, the Maghrebin from North Africa, Ashkenazim from the Germanic lands, Italians and French.

In all, 38 men of the many who had been drawn to the charismatic Isaac formed the clique of Safed, the Kabbalistic fellowship.

Addressing Hayyim after the day's study, when all had left bar these two luminaries, Isaac pondered further.

"We have our names," he said. "Now tell me what you have learnt about them."

"All are pious, there is no doubt," replied Hayyim, "and you have seen deep into their souls for their worthiness …"

"And, Hayyim, you wish to tell me more."

"I feel that not all are equal in their importance."

The words did not come as a surprise to Isaac, but it was his desire that Hayyim came to this himself. If he was to maintain his primary status then it was for him to judge his fellows.

"Tell me of your thoughts, Hayyim."

"There are some who were born into the darkness of the night, and it these who have the strongest cravings to seek the light."

"And these are…"

Hayyim grew with excitement as he declaimed his knowledge and enlightened his teacher. "Some 21 of us. And even these can be divided."

"How?"

"Into those born into the first half of the night, when it is darkest, and those in the few hours before dawn."

"Tell me their names," enquired an intrigued Isaac.

"I have drawn a list, master, and provided notes on each person so that you will know whence they came."

"Thank you, Hayyim. Let me read it now."

Hayyim handed over the parchment containing all 38 names, divided into a hierarchy of four groups.

THE DISCIPLES OF RABBI ISAAC LURIA

These names I divulge to my teacher, the Rabbi Isaac Luria, as those whose souls can reach the highest levels. Of all communities do they come. And of these the following are the most devout.

- Hayyim Vital, Musta'arab
- Jonathan Sagis, Sephardi
- Joseph Arzin, Musta'arab
- Isaac Kohen, Ashkenazi
- Gedaliah ha-Levi, Maghreb
- Samuel Uceda, Musta'arab
- Judah Mishan, Musta'arab
- Abraham Gavriel, Ashkenazi
- Shabbatai Menashe, Ashkenazi
- Joseph ibn Tabul, Maghreb
- Elijah Falco, Sephardi

And the next in order of their piousness are

- Moses Alsheikh, Sephardi
- Moses Najara, Sephardi
- Isaac Orcha, Musta'arab
- Solomon Sabon, Musta'arab
- Mordechai Gallico, Maghreb

> Jacob Masad, Musta'arab
> Joseph Altun, Ashkenazi
> Moses Mintz, Ashkenazi
> Moses Yonah, Sephardi
> Abraham Galkil, Ashkenazi
>
> And the following, whom my teacher has recognised, but I cannot ascribe to the higher groups are
>
> Yom Tov Tsahalon, Joseph Kohen, Jacob Altarats, David Kohen, Isaac Kerispi, Shimon Uri, Israel Uri, Abraham Arubas, Israel Levi, Joseph Canpilias, Judah Ashkenazi and Elijah Almiridi
>
> The fourth group is of three names only
>
> Abraham ha-Levi, Moses Meshamesh and Judah Romano

Isaac unrolled the document and as each name appeared before his eyes the letters dissolved into an image of who they represented. As the last name faded before him, Isaac rolled the full list on his tongue, absorbing this sign of them so that he would know them at all times and who he should look to as his primary acolytes.

"Thank you, Hayyim," he said at last. "Our fellowship is now ready to lead the community in *tikkun olam*. Tomorrow we will refresh their minds in the fields beyond and let them breathe the pure air."

"And this renewal will transcend the rivalries and tensions among the communities."

"Yes, Hayyim. You are indeed becoming my true disciple."

"Behold these rocks," Isaac would tell them. "It is here that Rabbis Eleazar and Abba sat when Rashbi revealed the mysteries of creation."

And he would sit on the same rock as Rashbi, the Rabbi Shimon bar Yohai, the originator of the *Zohar* a millennium and a half earlier.

"In the beginning," Isaac quoted from the *Zohar* commentary on the first verse of Genesis, "when the will of the King began to take effect, he engraved signs into the heavenly sphere that surrounded him."

The disciples remained silent as the enigmatic phrases of the radiant book wafted heavenwards. Isaac gave time for contemplation before he continued.

"In the beginning was when God began the process of Creation. That is before the emanations were emanated and the creatures were created." Isaac paused again. His pupils had varying degrees of knowledge, but he would direct his words to the novice. Even the most erudite would learn anew and be refreshed from the hidden depths contained in the words.

"And his supernal light filled entire existence. There was no space whatsoever, for everything was perfused with that simple, boundless light." An image of the unimaginable was being created for his rapt audience. The metaphor was indistinguishable from the actuality.

"When the will of the King began to take effect." Isaac moved on to the next phrase in the opening sentence. "By this we mean His desire to create the world and to emanate the emanations." Another pause before Isaac invoked the unspoken declaration of His will.

"He ached to bring to light the perfection of His deeds and His names and His appellations. This was the cause of creation of the world."

Isaac did not invite questions or discussion. It was for each to absorb, contemplate, and come to his meaning in their own time and way. They could debate among themselves, without the constraint of their master present. An air of expectancy loomed as Isaac continued with the last phrase of that overwhelming beginning. This was the link to the world they knew.

"His desire was to become manifest," began Isaac's commentary, "and His engraved signs are the gestation of the *sefirot*. It is in the *sefirot* that his attributes are revealed."

A ripple of recognition spread through the students. The *sefirot* were fundamental to Kabbalistic understanding and provided a framework for spiritual and practical living. A common image confronted them: the ten emanations that formed the Tree of Life.

Isaac paused and by his own will directed their gaze to a high rock above his left shoulder. He watched as they contemplated the markings on the sandstone and as all the lines and circles engraved by time coalesced into linked emanations they formed the image that was forever burnished on their soul.

Isaac saw that the reflection of the Tree of Life was in all their eyes and so continued. "But the highest *sefirah*, *Keter*, the crown, the God-Head, transcends them all. It is the first impression in the heavenly sphere and remains in the world above and the world below."

A light breeze ruffled the grass that separated the master from his pupils. The blades first bowed to Isaac and then rippled towards the disciples, as if carrying the hidden message.

Calm descended.

Isaac left.

Moments passed.

Elongated time to meditate on the profundity of the Ari's thinking. As the light dimmed and brought a coolness to the air, discussion was needed to warm their collective souls.

"He leaves us too soon," questioned Jonathan Sagis, "his spirit feeds our thinking. My mind is poorer when he is not present."

Joseph noted the edge in Jonathan's voice. It was the vexation that preceded anger. He spoke.

"Calm yourself, Jonathan. Our master rues the state of ill temper. It is corrupting to the soul and keeps the spirit of purity at a distance."

The others nodded. The North African Ibn Tabul had written of the Ari's pious custom of avoiding anger. You understand it well, Isaac had told him, your commentary adds much to the precept. Hayyim suffered an air of aggrievement when he learnt of this exchange, for he was zealous in the protection of his favoured position with Isaac. He remained silent as Jonathan breathed deeply and took Joseph's words to his heart. To still his body, to contemplate on the anger remedies prescribed by Isaac. These were too drastic for the tinged emotion he felt, but the depth of awareness was sufficient to soothe his rising tide. As it was with all teachings.

Touch the surface and be aware of all that lies beneath. Let it infuse your being and direct your existence. All wisdom is within you; find yourself and it will be revealed. The way of Isaac. To be attained by them all.

Shabbatai Menashe was next to speak.

"He is humble among us. See how he follows us on our walks, so that we may feel honoured."

"Happy is the man who belittles himself in this world. How great and exalted he will be in the next. Our master lives the wisdom of the *Zohar* to the limit." Solomon Sabon, who was a teacher himself, quoted the aphorism as he stood and exclaimed to his colleagues. "We should aspire to his trait of modesty. Only then will our devotions be pure and untainted by personal ambition."

"And also to his lack of vanity," added Hayyim. "He is not concerned with the wearing of fine clothes. But he honours his wife by dressing her well to the limit of his means."

"He always has money for charity," observed Judah Mishan, perhaps the wealthiest of them all. "It is his regular gift of gold florins that provides the wine for our Sabbath ceremonies."

The disciples settled themselves on the rocks in the meadow. Isaac's vision hovered over them, drawing out the multitude of stories regarding his righteousness. Each of them had been touched by an experience, some action of the Ari, which elevated him in their thinking.

Samuel Uceda, who was to write much about his master, captured the mood of that afternoon. "Our master is a man of great piety." Samuel's trembling and reverent voice broke into the reverie of the group. "He is unlike any other."

These words were a signal to leave. The sun was beginning its rapid descent behind the distant hills, warning them that there would be just time to return to Safed for the evening service.

As they walked in silent contemplation, none would utter the thought that consumed them all. The image was beginning to form of Isaac. A role that is God-given to one in each generation. Each of them believed that God, in His compassion, would send them a redeemer. And in unspoken unity, it was to their master their minds turned. To the dawning of a messianic age and to the Ari as Messiah.

NOW

7

Safed 1978

Robin and Adera were drinking in the bar as George and I arrived at the hotel. Both were in their fifties. Their mothers were sisters, but there the similarity ended. A closeness was apparent, for they had grown up together and had stayed with the same family when they were evacuated during the war.

Post-university their lives had taken different paths. George had filled me in on their background during the flight. That hairiness of his contained the lives of all the people he had contact with, a receptacle for the results of his natural curiosity and desire to understand the bigger picture.

Sports-jacketed Robin still retained the schoolboy ebullience of his early days as a trainee producer with the BBC, following the traditional post-Oxford route into the organisation. The informality of being in Israel had passed him by as he was wearing his usual shirt and tie, knife-edge creased slacks and well-buffed shoes. Clean shaven, his whole image was one of wanting to present the power of his position as founder and head of Myriad Productions. That he was tolerant of my mercurial and moody temperament was because I was the renegade film-maker latent in his being but never expressed.

Adera had been the rebellious one in the family. Dropping out from university, she had evolved from fifties beatnik, through sixties hippy (the image she still retained) to eclectic entrepreneur. She had settled in Israel after the '67 war, when she had joined the ranks of impassioned individuals who had gone to support their homeland.

Money almost came to her by default as she helped other immigrants find homes and profited from the dealing in property. Purchasing the house in Safed had been an act of love, though, and not just a business transaction. The whole context of the town and the exotic ownership of the place had inherent appeal. It had remained unchanged since she had bought it, for to alter anything, she surmised, would offend its history and destroy its ambience. Staying there, she said, was to be at peace with the world, which was why she was fascinated by my story and how this seemingly tranquil environment had so disturbed me.

Robin waved at us and we went over to them. Adera was the first to speak, brushing aside her long mousy hair as she turned from the bar.

"Hello. young man. I've heard a lot about you …"

"Don't overwhelm him," interrupted Robin, "he's got a busy time ahead."

"Ever the conciliator," joked Adera. "Well, at some point I'd like to hear all about it."

"And I'd like to know more about the house," I replied.

"If you both don't mind, I'd like to avoid any talk about the house or Peter's dream. I don't want anything to impact the filming."

George looked at Robin in puzzlement, "That's an odd statement. How can the filming be impacted?"

"Not the physical process, George," Robin replied. "It's to do with Peter. The less he knows, the more he'll be able to reproduce the feelings he felt at the time when he tells the dream on camera."

"So where are you filming me for this?" I asked, knowing the answer.

"We'd like you to tell the dream in the room where it occurred. Perhaps your first contact with the house since the dream and your telling it in situ will bring some freshness to the story. Give it a greater sense of reality."

"Why wait until tomorrow?" I was already uneasy and sensing a drama unfolding in me.

"Gilad, the sound engineer, is not arriving from Tel Aviv till then. The idea is that we will all be set up in the room, you come through the door from the patio and start talking without a pause." Robin coolly articulated his plan that left me with a sense of foreboding.

Robin wanted to capture my dream. He had read my notes, heard me tell the story and could visualise the context. A straight narrative with imagery could not convey for him the enormity of what had transpired within me. I had to tell the dream from within. Let it emanate as involuntarily as it had entered.

"So what shall we do for the rest of today?" I asked.

Adera responded, taking charge after Robin's put-down: "I know a lot of people in the community. I could take you to see someone who could tell you a bit more about Luria and Vital if you like … and if Robin doesn't mind!"

Robin smiled at this hint of sarcasm. It was obviously something he had been used to over the years. "OK," he said, "but we want to start the filming tomorrow morning – so don't whisk Peter away anywhere."

With a flurry of her long skirt, Adera took my hand and pulled me towards the door as I exclaimed, "But I haven't checked in yet."

"Oh, Robin can do that. It's what he's good at," teased Adera. "I want you to meet Jacob."

Adera did not draw breath during the ten-minute walk to Jacob Kretzmer's home, filling the air with a continual stream of chatter to fulfil her promise to Robin.

On the fringes of Safed, looking west, the houses seemed derelict or half-built. Bricks littered the grey, dusty road bordered with weeds. Children, with their *peots* and *tzizits* flying in the wind, played football on the rubble. Adera pointed out three of them. "Those are Jacob's sons. We're close to his house."

The boys waved, evidently recognising Adera, and gave me a quizzical stare appropriate for greeting a stranger.

Sitting at his desk in a small study, Jacob filled the room with his size and presence. Welcoming us, with nicotine-stained teeth smiling through a dense black beard, he opened the conversation with the wisdom of a storyteller.

"There are many stories and legends of the Ari. Some, perhaps, are from the imagination. But for a Kabbalist, imagination is part of his reality, so all can be considered true."

"What is known of Luria the person? And his relationship with Hayyim Vital?" I asked Jacob these questions because I wanted to get beyond their Kabbalistic system and delve into their core being. Vital had got inside me with his dream. I needed to perceive the man and through him his master, the Ari.

"You are familiar with Rabbi Vital's *Book of Visions?*" Jacob prompted.

"Yes, that is how I discovered the similarity between my dream and that of Vital. I have only read the extracts that are in the Louis Jacobs book, *Jewish Mystical Testimonies*."

"The *Book of Visions* has much autobiographical detail and also records many discussions that Rabbi Vital had with the Ari. Do you read Hebrew?"

"No."

"That is unfortunate, as there is no English translation of the book, other than the extracts you have read. You will have to rely on oral transmission to glean what you want."

"In keeping with the long history of Jewish oral tradition!"

"Exactly! There is something that will provide background. Rabbi Vital transcribed much of the Ari's system into a book known as *Etz Chaim* – The Tree of Life. He wrote an introduction that gives a strong sense as to the nature of the Ari. I have an English translation which you may like."

Jacob went over to his bookcase and took down a box file with a stack of photocopied sheets.

"There is much interest now in the Ari, so I keep these to hand." Jacob passed me one of the pages. It felt as if I was about to handle something sacred. I focused on the words and became transported. This was a personal statement. It was written to reach into the future, to tell others of the transcendence of this man.

The Ari overflowed with Torah. He was expert in the language of trees, the language of birds, and the speech of angels. He could read faces in the manner outlined in the Zohar. He could discern all that any individual had done, and could see what they would do in the future. He could read people's thoughts, often before the thought even entered their mind. He knew future events, was aware of everything happening here on earth, and what was decreed in heaven.

He knew the mysteries of gilgul [reincarnation], who had been born previously, and who was here for the first time. He could look at a person and tell him how he was connected to higher spiritual levels, and his original root in Adam. The Ari could read wondrous things [about people] in the light of a candle or in the flame of a fire. With his eyes he gazed and was able to see the souls of the righteous, both those who had died recently and those who had lived in ancient times. With these departed souls, he studied the true mysteries.

It was as if the answers to all these mysteries lay dormant within him, waiting to be activated whenever he desired. He did not have to seclude himself to seek them out. All this we saw with our own eyes. These are not things that we heard from others.

Jacob remained silent as I read. He observed my reaction to the words, took note of my body language and the sense of awe that overcame me.

"It would be wonderful to meet a man like that," I finally uttered, "one who could understand so much by being at one with the whole of existence. He was a special person."

"And this is a special place," added Jacob, "and now is a special time."

Adera and I looked at him and waited for an explanation.

"Many of us have come to Safed in the last year or two. There is a magical atmosphere here which emanates an irresistible attraction. We all feel that there is 'something in the air' which causes us to remain, even if we intended, like I did, to have a short visit."

Adera gave me a knowing glance, unstated words of "you must have felt it too". She was right.

I had succumbed to Safed's vibe before the dream expelled me with its agitative force. I harnessed the energy to fuel my researches and gain some basic knowledge of its significance. And to determine that which now linked me to this place. I was in a state of heightened awareness, receptive to any input.

But for now I could not absorb any more and bade farewell to Jacob.

Returning to the café where we had arranged to meet Robin and George, my mind was in turmoil, struggling to cope with an enormity. It was as if I had been given an instant injection of 2000 years of Jewish intellectual thought and wisdom.

George sensed my anxiety. He had been there before; witnessed my exposure to the then unknown force. He did not want me to take flight again. I succumbed to his knowingness that the approach Robin was adopting was critical filmically, but more importantly, a step in my continuing quest. I had to confront it.

I glanced at the pictures of Israel adorning the walls of the café. One, of the Mediterranean coastline just south of Haifa, brought memories of my escape from Safed after the dream. Of the emotion and despair. Of the mystery and power of that subconscious implant.

"How was your meeting with Jacob?" asked Robin.

Adera looked at me, waiting for my response.

"He's not what I expected, I suppose. I had this image of Kabbalists as being withdrawn and totally focused on an inner world. He was, well, normal and full of life."

"Was it useful? Did you learn anything?" Robin probed with purpose.

"He was very knowledgeable about Luria and Vital and had a lot of anecdotes about them. It was the sense of place, though, that came through for me as well."

George dived in at this point, knowing the effect that Safed had on me first time around.

"How did he describe it?" he asked.

"It wasn't so much a description, more about feeling the aura and absorbing the lingering presence."

"Do you think he's worth filming?" Practical Robin brought me back to reality.

"There are some others I can introduce you to who are equally charismatic. Depends on what you want."

"Thanks, Adera. Let's see what emerges after we film Peter tomorrow. Someone who could provide some interpretation of what all this means to him would be useful."

A DREAM UNTOLD

After that, George and I left Adera to join Robin in Turkish coffee and contemplation.

The café was in Jerusalem Street, the main thoroughfare of Safed. It symbolised the city's mystical nature with no start and no end. It formed a circular route around Citadel Park, the mound that was the site of the ancient fortress destroyed by the Romans.

It was a clear day and I began to appreciate the layout of the city. Below me were the narrow terraced streets of the old Jewish and Arab Quarters. Each roof seemed to form a coruscating tile of a larger structure that concealed the occupants and purpose of the town. It drew the eye to the cemetery in the valley below. At this distance, the tombs were indistinguishable from rocks nestling in the vegetation. Looking deep into that place gave a feeling of infinite presence, the dead occupants bonding with stone that had witnessed Creation.

We walked along Jerusalem Street, past the police station and the Davidka Mortar, a monument to the 1948 War of Independence. The long stone stairway of Ma'alos Olei HaGardom came into view. This bisected the town, with the Old City and Jewish Quarter to one side and the Artists' Colony, founded in the abandoned Arab Quarter in 1949, to the other. The steps stretched down to the road that bounded the cemetery.

I looked down the staircase. I gasped. I imagined myself at the bottom looking up, my eyes directed to the heavens. These were the steps of my dream.

I began walking down the steps with George in a trance-like state, my mind full of Vital's account of our shared dream.

A DREAM UNTOLD

I was going down from the khan of Safed by way of the stone steps leading to the market-place ....

The fact that these steps were of a different era was immaterial. Physicality was not the issue. It was the linkage. Their symbolic power of connection was great: to the past; from heaven to earth; of the spirit in mind to its manifestation in the art of the adjoining colony. I felt all this as I descended.

Many of those who had departed this life came down to the road from heaven and they all came to greet me.

Men in Hasidic garb, unchanged from its eighteenth-century origins, drifted upwards and seemed to pass through me, talking, not noticing. Their discussions dissolved into the atmosphere to join those of the past. No words are lost in Safed. They remain in the air waiting for a receptive ear.

Then we all came to the Jewish Quarter where I saw all Israel gathered.

We reached the bottom of the steps that opened out onto a dirt- and rubble-filled square. A crowd of men were assembled, seemingly for no purpose other than to be there. I felt like a stranger in their midst, not wanting to stay and not wanting to go. The air chilled as the sun disappeared behind a dark cloud.

The sun had set at noontime and behold there was a thick darkness over all the world and all Israel wept bitterly.

The assembly turned to the same direction and began to pray. Was it time for the Minhah, the Afternoon Service, or was there another purpose? In my daze I took it for the wailing of the dream. My subdued primary senses took the half-light for darkness. We walked around the gathering unnoticed. They swayed and shifted in ritual motion, generating a pious energy directed at the heavens.

.... the sun shone once again as before.

The gloom lightened as the dark shroud of vapour continued its journey across the sky, revealing a newborn glow. As at the end of my dream, I was uncertain of my conscious state and felt rooted to the ground, unable to move.

"Our hotel is this way." George's words shook me from my trance. "We could go into some galleries en route."

It took me some time to respond. Time to traverse 400 years. Time to adjust to the current reality of my physical being. Time to form words, not thoughts.

"Sorry George, what was that you said?" came a triggered response.

"I thought we could visit a gallery or two on the way back to the hotel," he repeated patiently.

"I think I'd just like to meander through the Old City. I didn't take in too much of it on the first visit. I want this link that I have with it now to guide me. I want to walk the streets of Luria and Vital."

"OK," agreed George, "but remember we have to keep away from the house."

As we walked, an overwhelming awareness of unfulfilment was generated. Buildings spoke of destruction and reconstruction. The causes were indeterminate. An earthquake? The War of Independence? Deterioration from neglect? New developments sprouted on terraced mounds, projecting unplastered faces to the mountains beyond. Everywhere was the feeling of unfinished business. A town in waiting.

We ambled in silence. I ran my fingers along the walls of narrow alleyways. They crumbled slightly, leaving a dusty residue on my fingertips. I did not remove this tangible evidence. Did not wipe away this remnant of the past, this bond with previous residents, this marker from history.

Luria came to Safed to explain his system to Hayyim Vital. He did it as they walked together. In the streets of the Jewish Quarter, in the open spaces and fields beyond. Perhaps even in this alleyway. Vital gained his understanding as he listened and questioned. Their words echoed off the walls until they were finally absorbed in the cracks and crevices. Settling in the brick. I looked at my fingers and the fine dust told me of this. But there was another story. I knew that. There was a significance in the transitory nature of the buildings. A symbol of something that was unknown to me. Beyond intuition. It lay deeper, more fundamental. It was clear that I had just touched the surface.

George and I had separated after our post-lunch stroll. He recognised my need for solitude and went back to the hotel. Safed felt different to me. Welcoming, rather than the rejection of my first visit. I felt a vibrancy that counteracted my foreboding of the next day's filming.

An afternoon of ethereal activity transformed me. A precious time when the outsider looking in became an insider looking out. It started when I ascended to Citadel Park, the green mound that laid a protective presence over the city and its inhabitants. Rose bushes were in bloom, a profusion of yellow and white. The sun and the moon. I paused at a bench that was set back in some green shrubbery. An arbour of calm, inviting the passer-by to grasp its prescience. I sat. My gaze was drawn to a single budding flower on the other side of the path, its tight petals restricting the desire to blossom. Perhaps by tomorrow, with another day of light, it would unfurl and reveal its latent beauty. Each bud was different, would require a different amount of illumination before its flowering.

Involuntarily I drifted into a meditative state; my eyes were closed. The rose floated in the black void in front of me. It twirled, bobbed and metamorphosed into a face. As in my Camden room. Now in another home.

The features distilled through the initial fog of contemplation. No beard, no wizened visage. The hair was red, just above the shoulder. And red lips, enticing. Eyes that were unmistakeable. It was Eva. As the dead of Israel came to me in London, so my English soulmate appeared in Safed.

She spoke as if in a dream in the reflective mode of meditation, and I listened in acceptance. The pursed mouth softened; voiceless words emerged in soundless timorousness and echoed inaudibly in the dark chamber of my mind.

"I have been with you, Peter," came her passion. "I have watched you suffer the agony of my angst. I have seen your self emerge in your journey. And grow with the acquired knowledge of your being. This next step is yours alone. Farewell Paul."

Eva's face suffused into the boundless backdrop of my brooding vision. I drifted in my sentient void until the chill of time unlocked my reverie.

The rose bush was still there. I was still in Safed, sitting on this bench, feeling the call of fateful happenings.

I stood and shuddered. The shock of Eva's suicide and the intensity of emotion that followed had been supplanted by the fervour of activity relating to the dream. Her subliminal message denoted a salvation from the destructive power of that last note, our final corporeal contact.

She had always guided my thoughts, been a balm to my conscience. In death more so. Her legacy. Our veiled dialogues following her death were often suppressed, but the awareness of them sustained me. Now, she had fulfilled her objective. I had drawn strength from the sadness she had left me. It was time to move on.

"Her red hair was unmistakable. I remember her well." Words of mordant expectation uttered by a man whose life now had relevance beyond a chance meeting. A moment of diluted epiphany and connectivity that reinforced the emerging bond between us. In each other we revealed ourselves in mirror acquaintance.

A DREAM UNTOLD

Irwin Steinberg, the artist I had stumbled upon in my post-meditative stupor, had his studio in the Jewish Quarter. He did not want to be divided from his roots, he told me, so he kept this side of the steps. Examples of his work were propped up on the walls outside the crumbling cottage that served as his workplace and home. One picture struck me and had a resonance. A man with outstretched arms standing at the top of some steps. The figure was dressed in robes with a round hat. It was not the exact image from my dream, but close enough to enquire of the artist its provenance.

"It is a common stance for Kabbalists," he explained, "the man is a Hasid extolling the greatness of Shimon bar Yohai at his tomb in Meron."

"The reverence seems to fill his body. Who was Shimon bar Yohai?"

"He is reputed to be the originator of the *Zohar* nearly 2000 years ago. Each year on the anniversary of his death many people make a pilgrimage from Safed across the valley to Meron."

I had read about this. It coincided with the archaic festival of Lag Ba-Omer. Bonfires were lit in the sage's honour, accompanied by much singing and dancing. Crowds came from all over Israel, gradually turning the event into a "Jewish Woodstock".

I turned from the painting and the transparency of his first appearance became visible. His slim build was accentuated by the Hasidic uniform of the close-fitting, shiny gabardine coat tied with rope. *Peots* caressed his shoulders, the black curls resonating with his speech. They appeared to sprout from his skull cap, which enveloped the top of his head to give an appearance of baldness that emphasised the vertical lines of a straggly beard. A white shirt, without the ornamentation of a tie, and light gaiters completed his monochrome look. He must have been around 40 and had the gaunt look of an ascetic.

Now aware of his dress, an American accent became discernible and I grew curious of his background. "How long have you lived in Safed?" I asked.

"I finally settled here a couple of years ago. It's odd how this place affects you. My first visit was for a few days. I came back for a week and stayed a month, then two. And now I'm still here!" Irwin smiled as he said it and reflected on his comments. He continued. "Many of us were drawn here in the late seventies. Seems like there was something in the air."

"I've heard others say that and I've felt it too." That was as much as I wanted to reveal. My dream-like state precluded talking about the dream. I was in receptive mood and wanted to find out more.

"Do you mind me asking about your background?" I added. There were so many gaps I had to fill. So many stories abounded. All part of a universal picture. All connected.

"Not at all. It is what Safed is about. The sharing of history. By the way, my name is Irwin Steinberg. Very Jewish-American."

"Peter-Paul Levi. Very Jewish-mongrel! Pleased to meet you."

"I have not always been this orthodox," he remarked, noticing that I had discerned the nature of his appearance. "I came to it when I realised that the decadence and drugs of the sixties could not bring spiritual peace. Psychedelic enlightenment proved to be momentary. The roots I thought I had severed were still intact, though somewhat bruised. A little nourishing turned me round."

"What were you doing back then?" Something was beginning to stir in me. An anticipation of a link between us. I was in a flurry of listening activity. A mix of elongated and encapsulated storytelling. I wanted to hear it instantly. And to get to the synchronistic moment.

"Let's just say my lecturer at Harvard was Timothy Leary. My hobby drew me into his circle and I became his court photographer. You know, at that big house of his in New York."

"You mean Millbrook, the one Tom Wolfe describes in his 'Electric Kool' book?"

"Yes. That was a crazy time when Kesey and his Merry Pranksters visited us. I tried to give the Prankster activity a philosophical context. A nihilism. That was probably the turning point for me."

"Music was pretty fundamental at that time. All part of the movement. Were you involved with any of the groups?" The leading question had an inner rationale. I already knew the answer.

"Very much. I took concert photos and portraits of most of the leading players. My main involvement, through Leary and Andy Warhol, was with Lou Reed and the Velvet Underground. I was a bit of a groupie."

My heart began to palpitate as I asked Irwin the next inevitable question.

"Did you ever come across an English girl, Eva, who did some work on the light shows for the Underground?" Irwin paused, then replied.

"Her red hair was unmistakable. I remember her well. She had the same haunted look as their singer Nico. Why do you ask?"

"She was my girlfriend." Irwin noticed the tremor in my voice that triggered a need to enquire.

"Was?"

"She died nearly three years ago." I was willing to say more but needed the prompt. Irwin was visibly shocked.

"I'm sorry. A young life of talent. There was an energy that was compelling to those who came across her." Irwin broke off for a moment. I knew he wanted to ask about her death. I pre-empted the question. Eva's re-emergence in meditation gave me a desire for openness.

"Before you ask, it was suicide. She was a manic-depressive. I travelled a lot. It happened while I was away." Strangulated and rapid words emerged from my mouth.

"That must have been very distressing for you. Would you like to talk about it?"

I nodded in acquiescence. There was something about this stranger that invited me to be candid. I had never really spoken about Eva's death in any deep way. With George it was still superficial. I had sensed that he did not have enough ingrained understanding to provide me with the level of solace that I required. Not that I was aware of that. Intuitively I felt it was a cultural thing. Irwin, Eva and I shared something collective that needed to feed any discussion I had about her death.

"Let's have some tea. I've adopted the Middle Eastern custom of keeping a samovar boiling. Come."

Irwin led me to a back room that was lined with books. The ornate urn was bubbling gently on a carved wooden table in his sparsely furnished living quarters. We sat on low stools around a copper table as he handed me a glass of mint tea.

"It's very refreshing. Try it with some honey if you want to sweeten it."

"Thank you." I took a sip and opened the conversation.

"What hurt me at the time was the attitude of Eva's parents at her funeral. It was as if she had never existed for them. They recited the mourners' prayer, but that was about all. She had had a brilliant career and in her best moments was kind and considerate. That was all ignored." The image of her black draped coffin in the burial hall returned, along with the feeling of the suppressed tears of the time.

"Suicide is regarded as a sin by Orthodox Jewry," Irwin explained. "It is perceived as a denial that human life is a divine gift and constitutes a defiance of God's will for an individual to live the life span allotted to them."

"That point was made strongly by the rabbi at Eva's parents' synagogue. They didn't have the strength or willingness to resist his views. They just wanted the funeral to take place."

I fought back the desire to shout and declaim and express my inner feelings. As I had stifled them before, being a persona non grata in the eyes of Eva's parents. Irwin noticed this sublimation from the trembling in my voice. He continued with his matter-of-fact explanation, probably thinking that this was the best way to deal with me.

"The ruling on the burial service actually stems from Safed. Joseph Karo states in his Codes of Law that there are to be no rites of mourning over a suicide. Eulogies are specifically excluded."

Eva's life negated, reflecting her ultimate despair. And my despair. My emptiness.

"'*Suicide kills two people, that's what it's for.*' I heard that line in an Arthur Miller play a few months after her death. How I related to that."

What was I saying to this man? He sat looking at me passively, his body in soft relaxation, his eyes drawing me out, his pause inviting me to go on.

"Eva bequeathed her death to me." The words of her note raged in my mind. "She broke free from the obsessions in her distraught life. Left them behind. I couldn't help her. I couldn't help her." My distressed voice reverberated in the room. Its echo shook my body, compelling it into supplication. Eventually Irwin spoke.

"You feel guilt for her death?" Guilt, the word that had been shrouded within me, confronting me.

"I'm not sure I could have prevented it. Many people said that to me. She had gone beyond the cry for help and intended discovery. A finality had set in. That much I knew in retrospect. Yes I do feel guilty, in defiance of that logic."

"Don't forget it, I knew her too." Irwin said it in a direct, almost angry manner. His demeanour changed. He leant forward accusingly.

"Knew? In the biblical sense? Did you?" I responded with this semi-comic phrase. My accusation somehow settled him. He drew breath in the realisation of what he had said, hoping to suck the words back out of the air.

"You don't have to answer me," came my pre-emptive reply. "I knew what she was like on her trips. And the environment she was in. It must have been inevitable."

This common bond brought a calming between us. Irwin felt he could now talk openly about Eva, tell me things about her I wanted to know.

"It was one-off at a party after one of the Underground's concerts. We were all heady from the atmosphere and, well, other things. Eva had taken some of my portraits of Lou Reed and Jon Cale and turned them into a rampant collage of sensuality. She projected it onto the wall of Lou's flat and danced it front of it. It was an extraordinary moment. She seemed to take their vitality from the image and let it possess her. It gave her a power that she wanted to exercise. I succumbed. It was more of a transduction than a seduction. I'm sorry."

"Don't be. I know, knew, that side of her. Her domination that stemmed from insight."

Irwin sensed that I no longer wanted to talk of Eva and asked, "Tell me, what brings you to Safed?"

As I told him of my dream , the effect it had on me and my subsequent researches, Irwin remained quiet and thoughtful. Even when I divulged the commonality with Vital's dream there was no reaction, no interference with my telling, a waiting for me to finish recounting this phase of my journey.

"So now I am here for this filming. There is a compulsion for me to undergo this, an unstoppable momentum in a journey to … I just don't know," I concluded.

With her obviously still on his mind, Irwin's response seemed to harp back to Eva. "Hayyim Vital had relationships with powerful and insightful women also." It seemed as if he was glad of the opportunity to discuss something in his background that had remained concealed. Now, as a Kabbalist and Orthodox Jew, it was something that required penance.

A reference back to one of the eminent mystics was perhaps the start of a cathartic process. We would share it together.

"I have read that he would consult soothsayers. Is there more?"

"He wrote extensively in his *Book of Visions* about a number of women who he consulted at various times in his life. One, called Soniadora, he sought out when he needed a prophesy or some advice on future events. Although the Bible forbids the use of divination, it was tolerated in Vital's time."

"Was it she who spoke of the Ari coming from Egypt to teach him his wisdom?"

"Yes. Vital was also quite a vain man and had a high opinion of his importance and rank within the community." Irwin became animated. This was obviously a topic he knew well.

"He was quite a complex character, then?"

"Well, yes. As you probably know, he was the Ari's principal disciple, which did cause some problems with his peers. The rivalry is well documented."

"Tell me more of his female relationships." I was curious. This was something I had not been aware of.

"He had a particularly strong association with a woman called Rachel Aberlin. Her husband Judah was very wealthy and helped support Luria's activities. Vital and his family lived with the Aberlins for a time."

"What was the nature of their relationship?"

"There is nothing written of any improper behaviour between them, if that is behind your question." Irwin smiled, hinting that he had thought the same as I.

"No," he continued, "Rachel seemed to be a medium for promoting his pretensions."

Irwin stopped talking and went to a pile of prints that were stacked against the wall. He shuffled through them and produced a picture of an old woman standing in front of a window that looked out on the night sky. Two ethereal figures could be seen floating among the stars. The woman was engaged in some laundry activity. The room in which she was standing reminded me of the house of my dream.

"I came across this in one of the local galleries. I bought it because it reminded me of a dream in Vital's book. The dream is reflective of the high opinion he has of himself." Irwin now went to his books and pulled out a battered text.

"This is a Hebrew translation of the *Book of Visions*. In it Vital recounts not only his own dreams but those of others who dreamt of him." Irwin went to a page that was bookmarked.

"I won't read it all. But basically it describes a dream that Rachel had about him. It tells of how he ascended to Heaven and told her of the greatness of his status there. He interacts with a great angel who advises him not to open a treasure that has been closed since the creation of the world. By opening it he would be detained in Heaven and not be able to fulfil his mission in the mundane world. A great sage guards the treasure for him, for only Vital has permission to open it. Vital then descends to earth."

"So you think the two figures are Vital and the angel?"

"That's how I wish to interpret it. I said it was reflective."

"And the old woman. Not Rachel, surely?"

"Perhaps not. It was the juxtaposition that attracted me."

I looked at the picture. I closed my eyes. I drifted back to what I knew of the house and its provenance.

A DREAM UNTOLD

"I was told that the house where I had my dream was previously owned by a white witch. She was reputed to be a hundred years old and was employed in the ritual washing of the dead before burial. Maybe the image is of her. It certainly forges a link with Vital through the house and my dream!" Irwin laughed.

"In Safed all things are possible. If you believe it, then it is true."

"You have given me a lot to think about," I replied. "I am not sure I could absorb much more. I would like to continue our discussion another day, if that's OK."

With the thoughts of the deceased in my mind, I emerged from Irwin's studio into the breaking twilight and trod funereal steps towards their burial ground.

8

Peter Paul from the house of Levi made his way to the deep valley between Safed and Meron. The cemetery loomed in front of him. A movement in the air disturbed the stillness of dusk. The sound of voices carried in the gentle wind. The murmuring disciples returned for the evening service to join their master, the Ari. Inviolately and with the transparency of the past, they brushed through this man of their future to the synagogue beyond.
Peter stopped until the air was once more calm and descended to the ancient hollow.

I saw the dusk, the unseen sun dropping from its curtained clouds into the nestling hills. In the descending gloom a loneliness overcame me and with it the need to take a solitary walk through the cemetery, skirting the grave of Luria and into the valley beyond.

I wanted to feel the chill, sit on rocks burnished by the robes of sages, take a primal energy from the granite as an unmoved body, transfixed, isolated, watching the darkening sky. Waiting for the first star. I exchanged glances with passing strangers, alien in their Hasidic dress, with fur hats signifying the East European origins of the garb. But it was I who was the outsider.

One looked at me longer than the others. Our eyes engaged as he probed deep into my psyche. He sensed within me a link into his mystical world. Unable to stay and question the source of his puzzlement, he signalled a hidden invitation to seek him out and pursue the connection.

"But you are not ready for that." An inner voice came to me as the doleful Hasid strode purposely away after our transitory encounter. Not ready. I had articulated this to George on the evening before the dream. It was an involuntary outburst that signified an inability to understand the nature of Safed. And this time? The stranger represented a world that was an anathema to me. I had no desire to be drawn into it. But Irwin had opened the door and now, somehow, I was – uncontrollably and with a timing that seemed predetermined.

I did not feel the cold in my darkened room. My walls were the hills and my window had no frame. I could see all about as I drew warmth from the rock that was my chair.

The lamps of Safed joined the stars as a backdrop to the focus of my gaze. A gaze fixed on the burial ground through which my Hasidic mind-reader had passed. With eyes wide open, I saw a distant flare briefly illuminate the graves. A silhouetted figure lit the lantern above Luria's tomb, the glow revealing a moment of prayer followed by a circling of the corporeal remains that lay enclosed beneath. A flickering shadow was cast on the grave that gave the appearance of searching for cracks in the stone to conjoin with the body within. His incantations echoed across the valley and floated high away to the heavens. And then the shadow disappeared as the human form no longer concealed the light. It was as if the pneuma of this person had joined Luria's soul in its nightly ascent.

I sat mesmerised by these visions and four hundred years passed as I spent the night on that rock.

The sun rose on the city. An awareness of the day dawned and a need to make contact with the reality of the present stirred my body. In solitude I walked up the hill; each grave observed my measured steps and I dared not look round, fearful of their presence. Luria's tomb stood out in its blueness, the same hue as the walls of the house, the colour proclaiming his stature. As I closed the gate of the cemetery and stepped on to the gravel that would return me to the hotel, I felt the touch of all the hands that had been through this portal.

George was frantic as I arrived. He was consumed with anger born of concern, but his irate words did not disrupt my somnolent state.

"Go freshen up," he yelled. "We have to be at the house in an hour."

I stood alone on the patio facing the knurled wooden door. Inside the room was Robin, with George and Gilad the sound engineer. Waiting for me. A reverse of the black-robed presence that had manifested itself before.

Four flagstones separated me from the source of my panic and anxiety. One for each century that connected me with Vital. Each step would bring me closer. Each step would increase the palpitations I was feeling. Imbalance was the best way to describe my state – an adrenalin surge fuelled by my physical presence and countered by the continuum of my overnight trance.

A DREAM UNTOLD

I was about to re-inhabit the dream. Not to describe, not to tell the story, but to step back into a subconscious realm that would provide its own articulation. Crouched figures were before me as I entered. A floodlight glared and a muzzled microphone hung in the air. I turned away, took an initial look at the window seat where I had lain and began to speak.

The voice was not recognisable as mine. It quavered in time with my body's tremor. Cadence and pitch were uncontrolled. The now familiar tale stuttered in the place of its being.

I raised my arms in softened remonstration against the vision I was creating. Staggered movement punctuated the telling as I searched for a place of comfort and respite from this ordeal. Words in my mind prompted my speech, strangled phrases to be elaborated.

> *Steps steeped in the light of day.*
> *Outstretched arms.*
> *An ancient horde.*
> *A vanished sun.*
> *Darkness prevails.*
> *The chanting crowd*
> *The chanting crowd ripples in my mind's eye.*
> *I cry out*
> *I cry out "what are they doing?"*
> *Two strangers meet.*

I pause and enter the vision.

> *Two strangers meet.*
> *The light dims the room*

A DREAM UNTOLD

Two strangers meet.
I am suspended.

Two strangers meet.
I am alone in the room.

Two strangers meet.
I hear the chanting of the crowd.

Two strangers meet.
I see the darkness of the day.

Two strangers meet.
I sense a man approach.

Two strangers meet.
I discern his presence.

Two strangers meet.
I make out a voice.

Two strangers meet.
I hear his name.
Two strangers meet.
I know this name.

I am with Vital.
I am the dervish of his dream.
I am in his dream.
He is in my dream.
There is turmoil.
Our lives are intertwined. Enmeshed. There is a linkage I cannot perceive.

The light returns to me. I see George behind the camera. Robin in a state of anxiety, Gilad uncertain of the sounds he has captured.

The tumult of the dream is made physical as I sink to the floor and sob uncontrollably. The film crew silently leave me to my lonely catharsis. The weeping subsides and I am released from this abstracted state of being.

I dare not leave the room. I am enthralled. What century lies outside? My cocoon channels me to past and present.

I gaze at the room, taking in each of its boundaries. Two alcoves with their infinite blackness; a window through which only the heavens can be seen from my lowly perch; the door, knurled with age and imagery that transfixed me on the fateful night.

Now it was a gateway. A gate, that metaphor for a transition of state. And time. As I stared open-eyed, the voice came. From behind me. From the void. Gentle, feminine, soft, pleading, in a language not of me. The current me. An incantation in an ancient tongue.

At first the words had no meaning. But soon there was a common tongue as they penetrated my being. I heard with my soul.

The voice became insistent, commanding, directing.

Who are you? I shout from within. A name emerges from a recess in my subconscious.

It is I, Soniadora.

Then you have bewitched me, I cry, grasping my sanity.

No, Peter, I am here to guide you.

You know my name, I stutter, how do you know my name?

It has always been with me, she murmurs, *I have waited for you.*

And now we are together, then what? I ask.

Stay in Safed, she says, *live in this house, live as Hayyim lived.*

I calm down. She brings me succour. She will be with me. I must tell them of these plans. George, Gilad. Robin must arrange for me to stay here. I must get my things from the hotel.

The door opens. I have risen and unlatched it to greet the sun burning its will on those of us below. Voices break through its beams.

The eyes of Peter Paul glowed red from the sun that burnished the inside of his skull. It was an outward manifestation of the internal world that blazed within him. He saw hills and mountains clinging to the earth's crust that was his cranium, reaching out to the blue hollowness of his brain. The driftwood of heaven floated in this primordial space.

And angels rode these chariots and spoke with the voice of Soniadora.

"Come Peter the Levite," they would say, "now you are without time. All are assembled before you. Receive their wisdom and tell those of your mundane world of this knowledge."

And Peter Paul was to go forth amongst the populace of Safed.

A DREAM UNTOLD

And stride the dusty streets.
And proclaim the divine truths of his revelation.
And all would make way for this figure amongst them.
And watch with awe as he returned each night to the house of the witch.

"Peter." A sound recognised as one made by George. It came from the direction of his face. He knows me. I know him. I must ask him to do what I require. I mouth the commands and he looks past me. To Soniadora.

"I will be OK, George. I must do this." I see two more. They were with me also, inside the house. They will understand.

I see them dance and move their arms. Their wild motion engulfs me with a fervour that strives to entangle me. Capture me.

I sense their craving to prevent my need to stay. All understanding is gone. I am conscious of their dematerialisation. I am subject to an ethereal bondage.

And led away to a distant place. To sleep.

I wake in a room I recognise as the hotel. My eyes meet the picture on the wall. Long grass ripples in a breeze swept down by the mountains behind. There are faces in the room. They sway with the grass as I look through them. Hollow words echo towards me from another dimension. My back arches away from the sheets and raises my contact with their world. A container for my senses – sight, speech, hearing, smell. I smell their fear, their nervousness as they speak. I touch the sounds that emanate from them, grasp their floating meaning, take them to my mouth and swallow their intent.

"Breakdown …"

"Peter, you've had a breakdown."

"We're worried about you."

"Concerned …"

"Home …"

"We need to get you home."

"Someone …"

"Doctor …"

"You need to see someone. A doctor."

"Home …"

"Get you home."

"This is my home. That house. I have to stay. It is predetermined. You have no control over me." I fired my response at them. A salvo of short, sharp sentences, hoping it would make them flurry, disappear, leave me. And the room disgorged them, flowing with my vituperation. But one was left.

"Peter, it's me, George. The others have gone. We are alone. Let's talk." The face that was George exuded calm and gentleness. So I rise in the warmth of his empathy and look down on our discussion and watch the rhythm between us.

I swayed as George implored. He reached out as I effused in statement of my intent. The pattern of our movements became a struggle. Neither would relinquish their position.

I stood before him in my nakedness. Vulnerable. I felt his vulnerability from the projection of this bareness. Only skin concealed my soul, the seat of my resolve. A frozen moment in our dance.

The body that was George sat. Immobile save for arms that rose and swung to conceal his face. With hands of despair. I drank in the sounds he uttered. It was what I wanted to hear.

"Peter, it is obvious you are in a troubled state. We can't force you back to England. But if you stay, we must arrange for someone to keep an eye on you."

A resolution. A chink. An opportunity. An overwhelming moment. But no sense of outward joy to match my inner rapture. How my feelings were sublimated. There was no way to release my tension, so I suffered an acceptance.

"And I will stay in the house. Irwin. I met Irwin. He's an artist. We talked. He'll be with me." A confusion of words that wrapped themselves into some sort of meaning. George nodded in acquiescence.

"How do I find Irwin?" George asked.

"In his gallery of the lost souls. Let their breeze direct your feet as they return to their creator."

George smiled. With Adera's help and those cryptic clues, my ministering angel would be found.

"Adera has told me of Peter's breakdown, but I am not sure I can help." These words came from a bemused Irwin as he welcomed George to his studio. "Could you explain what Peter wants of me?" he continued.

"Well, basically he wants to remain in Safed and live in some sort of deluded state. I just don't know how it's going to develop, but for the time being it would be to watch over him and make sure he comes to no harm," answered George as best he could.

"I'm willing to try. We did get on quite well the other day. He's had quite an experience and I must say it does interest me."

"That's great. I'll obviously be in regular contact with you. There may be a point where professional help is needed."

"You're right. I don't know if Peter mentioned it, but I spent time with Timothy Leary in the States. I witnessed a lot of people on LSD and dealt with many who had bad trips. It's possible that experience would be useful."

"Well, good luck. If there is anything you need or Peter asks for, just let me know."

George left and Irwin contemplated the situation he was facing. Eva as a link between him and Peter was something he didn't want to reveal. Discussing it would expose his own weakness and also his intimate knowledge of Peter. After their lovemaking Eva had confided in him. Told him of her life in London with a man she loved but could not commit to. Of a relationship that had a buffer of unknowingness which kept them apart. Separated them from passionate reality and left much unsaid. Not that Peter was devoid of emotion, she had said, it was just that he put up a barrier to your understanding what he was really feeling, and it forced her to do the same.

Irwin had absorbed this flurry from Eva without asking why she had chosen him to unburden herself. Maybe there was something of Peter in him, some hint of what a freer, more open Peter could become.

Now his own immersion in Kabbalah had taught him the need to redeem souls, which was reinforced by his natural compassion.

All this had been unstated in his meeting with George, but this inner knowledge made it easy for him to say "yes" to this request for help.

Irwin came to see me in the house. My eyes were transfixed on the dust that lay on his arm as he placed a bowl of salad on the table. Which wall had he brushed against? Whose home? What past was contained in those particles? My mystic friends had scurried through the dry streets, sending the clouds of fine gravel to settle on brick. To coat the passer-by. To transform Irwin into a messenger. Or was the dust borne by the wind to settle on him? Soul flakes left in the air on the nightly journey heavenward? Whose spirit had come to rest on Irwin? All I could see was this patina denoting previous existence. I took Irwin's hand and brushed these remains into a bowl. Soniadora would tell me of their provenance.

Our eyes met during this gesture, which Irwin did not question.

"How are you, Peter?" An innocent question, but how to respond. Each word meant something different to me. The physical state inferred by *how*. *Are* expressed uncertainty over my existence. *You, Peter*. Was I?

I was hungry. Yes, I was hungry.

"The food, that looks good."

"We should eat, then. When did you last have a meal?"

I touched my face, felt my dry lips, brushed my parched cheek, fingered the new growth on my chin, ran my forefinger and thumb down my neck and gently squeezed my throat, slid the palm of my hand down my chest and felt the hollowness within. A voice said "long ago".

"Where are the plates and cutlery?" Irwin continued in practical mode. A pause. "Don't worry, I'll find them."

We ate in silence, communicating with eye contact. Fleeting glimpses of revelation. My saviour. Redeemer of my soul.

He will guide you, said Soniadora. *The manifold paths leading to the way. In his eyes is the reflection of your embodiment. Go with him and take his instruction.*

Irwin was concealed from the voice. His intuition drove us towards our mutual destiny.

"We must communicate, Peter. You must tell me of your feelings. What is troubling you. Driving you into this state. Then I can help."

I nodded as Soniadora had instructed. My querulous look belied the desire to embark on this course. Another me observed the turmoil in my mind. I struggled to connect my feelings to my actions. I wanted to embrace Irwin, let him know that I needed his help. But couldn't. An anger built up. Confused frustration erupted. Shouting, pushing emanated.

"How, how, how?"

A startled Irwin backed away from the rigidity of my purpose. He saw deeply into my fixed gaze and rejected the animosity. Thought suffused him and I saw the tension flow out from his body. I implored expectation, ready for his message.

My neck strained as my head arched back and my eyes followed as Irwin rose. His head arched back and his eyes looked upwards as he sought the means to enable a dialogue untinged by madness.

And he searched through his wisdom and learning in this devotional stance. I too was static, absorbed in the slowness of my breath as I waited for his word. It came.

"There is a mystical way of writing," a voice proclaimed, "that may help you reveal the source of your unease. The ancient sage Abraham Abulafia used it as a meditative technique. I know that Hayyim Vital thought highly of him."

Irwin paused to judge my reaction. Mentioning Vital was the right stimulus. For a fleeting moment, as he said his name, my fragmented self became whole.

"Be at peace, Peter. I will return soon with the relevant text. It is important that I quote Abulafia correctly. Then you can borrow from his technique."

"Come back, come back!" I shrieked in acceptance.

"Many people think that some of the *Zohar* was produced through automatic writing." Irwin had returned quickly with the texts he required.

I looked blankly.

"About the time of the Ari," Irwin continued, "there were Kabbalists in Morocco who contended that mysteries were revealed by this method."

I remained confused. Did Irwin want me to add to these religious tracts? He saw my desperation.

"I'm trying to give you the context, Peter. My idea is that you can write down thoughts that you cannot speak by this technique. OK?"

I silently agreed with a pondering look that asked *How?*

"The basis is to get yourself into a state of readiness. Abulafia describes it like this." Irwin opened the book he had brought with him and read.

"Take the pen in your hand, like a spear in the hand of a warrior. When you think of something, uttering it in your heart with specific letters also express it with your mouth. Listen carefully and 'watch what emanates from your lips' as it says in Deuteronomy. Let your ears hear what your lips speak, and with your heart, understanding the meaning of all the expressions."

Watch what emanates from your lips. That seemed to summarise the sensation when Soniadora spoke. A soft pallor of excitement tinged my body. I was in a hurry to start, to see my voices manifest.

"Do not rush the process," observed Irwin as he perceived the aura of my eagerness. "Abulafia meditated on permutations of the letters in the name of God that he had written. That is not what you must do. You should first enter into a meditative state, which you have told me is something you can do. Let your arms hang limply by your side and when you feel a presence, take the pen as Abulafia describes and commit whatever has imbued you to paper."

I nodded. What would emerge? Would I be able, as Abulafia said, to understand with my heart the meaning?

"I have brought you paper and a fountain pen. The flow of ink is much more conducive to this type of activity."

Irwin handed me a large envelope. Inside, waiting to be etched with my enigma, were the instruments of an intended salvation. A bridge between two realities.

9

I look back on what I have written. This story of mine. A report on a life. A significant event that changed the state of my existence and flung me into a transcendent mode of discovery. Until the breakdown and an attempt to describe my psychotic state. If that is what it was. A confusion of truth and time that is my current makeup. Dissociation viewed with a mirror reflecting a self-realisation. Images within, shrinking to infinity as they bounce between the hardened external ray and my burnished incubus. All temporal sense vanished during this episode. How long was it before Irwin's intervention? Perhaps 400 years.

Day the beginning

I am sitting at the table on the patio. The freedom of space and light appeals. No intervening construction between the heavens and my pen. As Irwin instructed, I calm myself. First the breathing exercise. Four breaths inward. Hold them for a count of four. Exhale in the same rhythm. Repeat and feel the body slow and begin its detachment. Ground my feet and have the sensation of the cold stone imbue its solidarity. Let the earth rise and overcome the ownership of my limbs. Continue the inhalation and exhalation. Slower and deeper now. Arms hang limply. The focus on externality diminishes and the breathing rhythm becomes automatic. The blackness of closed eye sight retreats inward and drives out directed thought. Emptiness prevails and creates its own energy. The potency stirs and the voice that is not a voice emerges from its unknown conception. A hand rises to take up its spear ready to wound the paper, release its pulp and sketch a mindscape on its blankness.

Lightness, lightness. Encrusting all. Deliberating and taking its path to destiny. Taking all that its rays land on. To all that respond. Take warmth and its actuality into their being. Transforming them. Helping them to walk and take steps towards an infectious oblivion. When dusk descends the leader loses its appeal and cannot be followed. Emotionless and lost in their own vacuity, the bleakened souls reach out in the darkness. And touch each others' stony heart. I see all this. I float down and observe the maelstrom. The whirl of pneuma taking the dance floor of ether. Past and present emerge and call a tune of disparate rhythm and harmony. Confusing the essence of the floating partners as they grasp the antennae of nearby prancers. Where next, as the music of deathly persuasion reaches an evensong crescendo. Black shadowed lines of hooded participants crowd in subdued march towards a distant valley. Gloom. Vanishing point. Endless streams of organising thought take them to an oblivious end. The observer has a proud stance across the divide and bridges their ascendancy, in control of the pace and direction. Listlessness and somnolence as the light has unimpeachable success to drive out the primeval inclination. End of sightlessness and vision emerges. All is peace.

The paper remains at rest. I look at the words with blurred sight. My focus is beyond the page. The heat of my gaze dries the ink and makes the text sacrosanct, unable to be changed. That is the way it must be. I put the writing away in an envelope to shield it from the light and prepare it for the judgment of Irwin.

Bare feet caress the stone beneath. Slide across the smoothness, ground by centuries of footsteps. A toe turns inward in sensuous motion and exerts a pressured touch in an attempt to excite the inertness. In seamless motion, the body that is I rises and shuffles to the door. Movement and the friction of the journey vibrate through my limbs. A warmth enters me as the room beckons. I cross the threshold and turn to face the light. I disrobe so that it can embrace my nakedness.

Soniadora approaches from within. Her outstretched arms grasp the cloak that is her identity. The billowing folds enclose me from behind as those arms caress my chest. Firm fingers find a partner in my aroused member as her hands slide down my body. She whispers in my ear *"Do not resist"* as an encircled palm clutches gently at the expectant organ. Soft enduring pulses bring the uncontrollable response. My ejaculate spurts upward and then descends as wasted seed to be scattered on an unassuming floor.

THEN

10

Safed 1570

Hayyim shuddered in the night. Forbidden feelings thrust through his sleeping body, an image provoking the sensation. It was cloaked and billowing, with long blond hair framing eyes the blue of her house. It was Soniadora who aroused him in his somnolence. He writhed to deny his sin, prevent that which was impure. Her face loomed large and concealed the vision of his night. The warmth of her breath subdued his struggle, its light breeze caressing his face. The sigh from his open lips mingled with this presence and formed their union. Quavering in peaceful submission, the involuntary ejaculate materialised from his loins. And still he slept.

Its warmth was revealed on wakening.

"Hannah," wailed Hayyim in despair, "I have sinned. I have wasted my seed in the night. The *Talmud* likens it to being a murderer."

Hannah was troubled and knew of the consequences.

"You must tell your master," she said, as she sat upright in their marital bed that was now defiled. "He will tell you of your penance."

Hayyim reflected on her comment. A nocturnal emission ranked high in the list of transgressions and its expiation would be onerous.

Isaac's study was bare of books; its austere walls imposed a naked presence on his thinking. When a need for reference arose, the library that adorned the classroom next door provided the counterpoint to his contemplations. It was in his study that he received the distraught Hayyim.

Isaac gazed thoughtfully at him. He could discern the troubled state of his disciple and the unintentional nature of his wrongdoing. The reparation for his misdeed must not deter him from our divine mission, mused Isaac, and the penance should repair the damage to his soul and increase his understanding of the infinite wisdom.

"You must fast for one month," pronounced Isaac. "That is the prescribed *tikkun* for this sin. However, your intention during the fast is determined by how your seed was wasted. Our colleague Moses Yonah has enumerated the ways in which this can be done."

Hayyim was aware of this list. Discussion on the sexual transgressions was rife among the disciples as they formed one third of all the sinful acts that required some rite of purification. Sexual relations were only permitted between a wife and a husband, for the union was a metaphor for divine love and the act contributed to *tikkun olam*, which was the ultimate objective of them all.

"You tell me that your orgasm came from a fantasy and that at no time did you touch your member. That is the least offensive manner." Isaac paused to reflect on the objective he must set for Hayyim during the fast.

"The fasting will subdue your physical aspects and elevate your inner self. This will enable you to remember your mission in the world." Isaac briefly stopped again. All fasts had this intention. What could he get Hayyim to draw from this misdeed?

"I liken this incident to a bad dream. In this case you must draw joy to yourself by means of the fast. That is the *tikkun* for the dream. And that will be the *tikkun* for your delusion."

"I will start my fast at sunrise tomorrow, master, and spend the rest of today in preparation for the attainment of your order. But first I must understand the meaning of joy, for am I not one who exudes his rejoicing?"

"Reflect on the words of Psalm 16, Hayyim,

> 'You make me know the path of life;
> in Your presence is a fullness of joy,
> in Your right hand everlasting bliss.'

And also remember how you applied yourself the last time I instructed you to fast."

Hayyim bowed his head at the remembrance of this occasion, shortly after their trip to Lake Kinneret.

"Hayyim," Isaac had admonished, "you have become arrogant since attaining the position of my principal disciple."

"Yes, master, but …"

"There is no excuse for this. You also use your status to mock your colleagues. It saddens me to see you ridicule their lack of understanding."

"This is true. But I am impatient for learning and the others slow the pace."

"That is no justification. It is necessary that all my disciples attain the same level at a similar time. That is the only way to bring about the ultimate goal of our existence."

Hayyim nodded. Too often he forgot this basic precept. The rituals and practices that Isaac taught were complex and demanding. They led to a strict regime of contemplative devotion and prayer that would accomplish the repair of defects inherent in Creation. It would be necessary for him to serve a penance to retain his piety.

"You should spend 20 days in fast for your lack of humility and the ridicule you scorn. It will enable you to gain comprehension of this evil inclination and for the necessity of others to acquire my wisdom."

Humbleness. Hayyim had it towards Isaac. In fasting he could contemplate his attitude to others. The gnawing of his stomach would reflect the nagging of his soul. He would be enlightened of their common purpose and need to be bonded as one. This Isaac ordained. This was to become a self-realisation and, as with all that Isaac proclaimed, it was the inner direction provoked that was the main objective.

Now he had to find joy. Not that it was lacking in him. Music and dance uplifted him. He took enjoyment in eating and drinking. And of course the carnal pleasures gave him great delight, but now the misapplication of this act required him to find the joy that went beyond bodily pleasure. As was stated in Psalm 16, the joy was of accomplishment, of attaining the highest reward, of feeling the presence of God in fulfilling his purpose of creation.

Hayyim lifted his eyes during the penance. Perhaps the light would filter through and alleviate the corner of darkness in his soul cast by the shadow of Soniadora. Her presence plagued him. No meditation seemed to assuage his guilt or remove the illicit feelings. What purpose was there in this permanence? Was she his reflection, a spur to his goodness? Could he rationalise this notion and allow himself to end his days with this impurity in his soul?

NOW

11

Safed 1978

I watched them grow out of the congealed mass of seed that lay on the rug. All of Israel. I stepped back to allow their presence as they faced me in their flowing robes, domed hats and straggled beards, their questioning eyes looking at me. This stranger in their midst. I shielded my nakedness as they implored with outstretched arms.

Come to us, come to us clamoured the beseeching voices.

"No, no. I am not ready," I wailed at them in torment born of turmoil within.

Be calm, master, and you will sense the moment. At this they turned and made their way from the house to enter the streets of Safed.

They called me master. What was their belief? Something swelled inside me. An anticipation. An excitement. Something pre-ordained. I raised my arms to the sky and shouted, "I am He".

The proclamation echoed in the room and vanished into the alcoves of infinite blackness. Shivering in my bareness, I awaited the warmth of being clothed in a response.

You must live as Vital. Soniadora's voice repeated what she had first said to me. *Know what he knows. Believe what he believes. Act as he would act.*

The emotion of that statement seared me and I trembled and suppressed a sob. The sublimation became too much and

I was overwhelmed. The floor reached up to me, beckoned, so I sank to the birthplace of my disciples and wept.

That was how Irwin found me. He knelt beside me and waited until I was aware of his presence.

"The night is cold," he said as my face turned towards him, "it is better that you get dressed."

"Where are my robes? I cannot wear these garments." I threw away my jeans and sweatshirt that Irwin had handed to me. "Find me my cloak."

"A cloak?" replied a startled Irwin.

"And clothes like these," I said, pointing at an old print of ancient sages walking the lanes of Safed.

"These will take a while to collect," Irwin replied, continuing to humour me. "I must fetch them from my house."

He backed away silently and returned later with my attire. I slipped on a linen gown of deep beige and tied a black bandana around my waist. From the depths of his wardrobe of ceremonial clothes he had also found a black cloak for me and the domed hat depicted in the drawing.

"Is this the look you desire?" he asked.

"That is not my desire, it is what I am." There was vehemence in my voice. An anger that Irwin had not perceived my being.

"Of course, Peter. And who are you?"

"My disciples do not use my name. They call me master."

The implacable Irwin was startled. The game had taken a new turn.

"Your disciples? Master? What illusions are these?"

"No illusions. They came to me. I am to be with them when I am ready."

"And when will that be?" Irwin's question was coloured with a mix of pandering me and genuine curiosity.

"Soniadora guides me. She tells me to live as Rabbi Vital. And through him I will know the time."

It was obvious to Irwin that he should placate me and go along with my delusion, accompanying me on a journey that was full of intrigue for him and that was potentially revealing.

"And how much do you know of this man?" he asked, leading me into a path of his involvement.

"I feel his emotion and clutch his soul to me, but know little of his mind. This you must tell me."

"So I am to be your teacher."

"That is your destiny."

"I have much to acquaint you with concerning Vital, but first, may I ask, have you done any writing? That may guide our discussions."

Steam from our coffee wafted between us. The aroma of fresh bread heightened our senses. Breakfast was a new beginning. Our relationship was in transition: Irwin was no longer my carer, he was the my link to Soniadora, the conveyor of the guidance.

I clutched my cup, felt its warmth and slowly drank its flavour. The act took me to its essence. Now Irwin was to release his knowledge. But first, my writing. I had not read the scrawl from yesterday. It remained clothed in the envelope. Would it reveal clues?

"It is there, on the table."

I pointed at the envelope. Irwin picked it up, felt the surface of the paper as if trying to interpret it with his fingers, absorb the message through his skin. At last he drew out the single sheet within. I remained silent as he read and avoided any eye contact, trying to see into his mind.

"There is much here to interpret," he said at last. "Do you remember what you have written?"

"What I have written came from inside. It is always there. It is not necessary to remember."

"Surely, Peter. Then I will try and state what you must be feeling. It will help me enter your world and we can progress together."

"**Begin.**" What voice was this that came from me? Irwin had a disconcerted look as he heard a sound that was deeper and seemed from a different age to my own. It took him time to settle before embarking on the insight to my document.

"You have extrapolated your dream and put yourself in a position of power, as a leader to redemption. A transformer of order from chaos."

My mind swelled. I had written from inside. Described how I must act. As Rabbi Vital had acted. Is acting. Irwin entered my world as I asked, "And do they follow?"

"As sheep."

"And are they absolved?"

"As the light follows darkness."

"And are they as one?"

"As the highest essence absorbs their being."

"And what of the living?"

"They are without."

Irwin closed the dialogue by re-inserting my epistle into its concealment. I contemplated the "without". Safed lay outside, its citizens dormant in their houses, waiting for an awakening, without in both its sense of knowledge and its externality. I was to gather its citizens into my coterie, that was clear in my mind. But I must inform them of my authority.

"And what of Rabbi Vital? He will entrust me with his dominion. How is he to help me?"

"Help you?" Irwin seemed puzzled by my question. Had he not seen the logic of my mission? Had he not read it in the intelligence of my words?

"How does he stand behind me? Be with me as I walk out. Be his deliverer."

Irwin reflected. He did not wish to simply humour me. There was something of Vital's character that was being displayed by my mannerisms. Hesitancy. A slight stammer. Nervousness on revealing thoughts. Belief and misbelief shuddered through Irwin. Was I really possessed? Reading of it was one thing, but being confronted with what seemed the actuality was another. Taking a deep breath, he opened the subject.

"What do you know of the Transmigration of Souls?"

My gaze was directed through him. It begged of more, so in silence I responded with no knowledge.

"It is an ancient Kabbalistic belief. Luria and Vital drew on its concepts extensively and its notions were central to their philosophy."

Yes. And.

"The ideas are not dissimilar to the reincarnation beliefs of the Hindus. For Kabbalists there are three types of transmigration and varieties of soul."

Which one am I? Which one am I?

"Straightforward reincarnation, if I can call it that, is when the soul of a deceased person enters a foetus during pregnancy or at birth. This is known as a *gilgul*."

Not I. Not I.

"Many people are familiar with the term *dybbuk*. This is the restless soul of a departed transgressor that enters a living person with evil intent."

I do not seek wickedness. That is not I.

"Which brings us to the concept of *ibbur*. Vital wrote extensively on this, often in great complexity, as he related it to the level that the dead one's soul had reached during their lifetime."

Is this I? I feel the pain.

"As with a *dybbuk*, the soul enters a mature person. But the purpose is very different. The recipient is to fulfil something unaccomplished by the deceased. When this is done, the *ibbur* leaves."

I feel the unease.

"It is said that when an *ibbur* enters a person, there is first a feeling of panic and anxiety."

As after the dream. The dream.

"Luria's disciples believed that he was the messiah, leading them to heal the world in the year 1575. After the Ari's untimely death in 1572, Vital convinced himself that he should assume this mantle. 1575 came and went with the mission unaccomplished."

Oh Hayyim, I have received your soul. I can act as you acted. I will consummate your desire.

"Peter, perhaps I have fed your delusions. Perhaps it is not a delusion. There is a reality in the totality."

"You have concealed the darkness." Soniadora spoke as me.

"The darkness? Of Vital's soul?" Irwin was visibly shaken. He had expounded these theories, saying with his head, questioning with his heart, accepting with his soul. Now he was to debate with … with whom?

"He was arrogant. That was a sin for which he atoned," he continued.

Oh Irwin, you have already alluded to his transgressions.

"I believe he was not pure in his thoughts, conceivably in his deeds. His writings suggest carnal activities that were not allowed."

This is the darkness I feel.

"It is possible that he was troubled by the guilt of this and retained it in a corner of his soul."

"As I have Eva's guilt to remedy." I spoke with my voice the realisation that Soniadora had induced.

I am the ibbur. I am the soul of Hayyim Vital. I wander in search of a body to rectify myself. I seek one with the soul root of Hayyim Vital. I seek one with the guilt of womanly enchantment. I seek one who can redeem the impurity.

I will possess him and guide him to goodness.

That is my purpose.

Till eternity.

12

"Irwin?"

"Yes."

"This is George. How is Peter?"

Irwin had expected the call, but what could he say? That Peter's psychotic state was deepening and that he believed himself to be a sixteenth-century messiah, an incarnation of Hayyim Vital. That he dressed, acted and spoke in this guise and that it was all a delusion.

To say all this would deny his Kabbalistic beliefs, for this episode with Peter had stripped him bare, opened up an intensity of self-questioning.

It had been ten years since he had swapped a tie-dyed T-shirt for the silken coat of a Hasid. Drugs were replaced by the ritual path to spirituality. The mind expansion of LSD had never comforted, had never given him a sense of his own inner reality, whereas meditation and prayer brought him to peace and a sense of his own being. It enabled a connectivity that the chemicals or rational thought had never managed.

He had adopted Hasidism, rather than mainstream Jewish orthodoxy, after reading Martin Buber, who had spun a magic out of this 200-year-old sect that emanated from Eastern Europe. As had Irwin's grandparents. At first he had read the *Tales of Hasidism*, which chronicled stories and legends of Hasidic rabbis and gave a background to the vibrancy and simplicity of their philosophy. To be in touch with God through the intensity of your own life. Through joy and fervour, song and dance. A direct replacement for the rock groups he followed.

And love. The precept "love your neighbour as yourself" was not to be considered a commandment from God, but through it and in it one could meet God. This directness appealed to him. In his book *I and Thou* Buber provided Irwin with a theoretical basis for a relationship with God. It had an intuitive appeal. The words and ideas were complex, but there was a transcendency in the book that could be felt. Again, a directness.

Buber's "Thou" defined an inner space of connectivity with your fellow man as a human entity and not an object, "It" in Buber terms. Irwin perceived the contextual position of "It" and "Thou". The former was set in space and time, the latter eternal. Eternal "Thou" was the surrogate for God.

On this Irwin meditated. For him it gave substance to the formless entity in his prayers. Gradually he was finding himself within the religious and social dimensions of these systems. Kabbalah, being a basic tenet of Hasidism, had also brought to him the aspect of man's purpose within these thoughts and deeds.

At first he had struggled with the maelstrom of ideas and was unable to deal with seeming contradictions and incoherence. Through his art he began the unification process that was to influence his spiritual struggle. His mind of the present drew the symbols representing eternity. He could paint the "Thou" in abstraction. It was how "He" saw it. It was how he interpreted the writings of the sages.

But eternal was a concept of past eternity that always stopped at the present moment. And then moved on with him. With all. With all in the future that was a series of eternities. This was how some Kabbalists saw it. Events without time. Cycles of creation and redemption. The messiah as a metaphor for the end of a cycle. He could feel his place in this perpetuity, could believe in the universe of souls that were bound together in this cosmic pattern.

Now Peter seemed to have made it manifest. No theory could represent the reality of this situation. Was Peter deluded or was he the carrier of Vital's soul? Irwin believed, wanted to believe, the latter. But this made him question the concept of soul.

As an identity for spiritual existence it made sense. It was the physical being in which it resided in order to reflect its presence that puzzled him. He could not equate Peter to Hayyim Vital. Or was he confusing spirituality with religious observance? Was this to be Peter's test? In which case, this episode was a step in Peter's journey to his own spiritual self, his own identity.

There was much to respond to in George's "how".

After his lengthy pause for reflection, Irwin answered with a truth that might satisfy them both: "Peter is in no harm. He is learning to cope with his changed state of being".

"I see. We were all concerned that he would descend into violence. It's not uncommon with psychotics."

Irwin remained silent. He felt it was for George to lead their conversation and he was reluctant to respond to the taunt of psychosis.

George continued, "Can you explain what you mean by changed state of being? Is it anything to do with the voices he was hearing? How is he behaving?" A flurry of questions reflecting George's desire to know how his friend was faring.

"How do I answer you, George? Should I be rational or mystical? Is the outward semblance of Peter's psychosis a manifestation of something deeper within him? Remember, your questioning is directed at someone who leans to the mystical. I repeat, Peter is in no physical danger and he is of no harm to others."

"I comprehend your subtext, Irwin, but you haven't really allayed my fears. Let me accept that these delusions and the voices he hears are all part of Peter's own reality. But you must admit that it is not a reality that will enable him to function in the life he has in England. Do you have a prognosis?"

"I'm not an expert in mental health, George."

"I know that. It was a leading question. Should we get an expert involved?"

"Please allow more time. I feel that Peter is embarking on a journey that should not, at this stage, be curtailed. Allow me to continue my watching brief."

"It is not a question of me allowing you, Irwin. Neither of us has any formal responsibility towards Peter. No one really has. He doesn't seem to have any close living relatives. We are both acting as concerned friends and he chose you as his mentor. It gives you a sort of precedence and I respect your judgment. Please keep me informed."

"I will. It is not my intention to let Peter suffer. If it ever comes to that point I will need your help. Thank you for calling."

"Goodbye, Irwin."

"Goodbye, George."

Irwin mused on what he had said to George. It summarised what he had been feeling for the past few days. He was a fellow voyager on Peter's journey.

As a guide, but Peter defined the direction. As a leader, but he followed where Peter went. As a sage, but Peter had the greater knowledge.

The *Talmud* states that a baby is taught all of the *Torah* during pregnancy from a guiding angel. At birth the angel strikes the baby on the upper lip and causes him/her to forget all of their learning. The rationale is that the baby is not constrained on their path through life to either becoming a righteous or wicked person and (re)learning the *Torah* reveals that which was dormant in the heart. This is what Irwin felt intuitively. He could sense the grandiosity of the cosmic plan and was open to its consciousness. He perceived this in Peter. Both of them being led to spiritual insights, as musicians seeking harmony.

Irwin had succumbed to learning the theory through study. Ritual practices allowed a reproduction of the song of the universe, and then to stand aside and let the purity and concord strike his soul. But could this be achieved without pedantry, with the echo of creation taken directly to one's soul?

Did Peter have this facility? A spirituality without religion? Was this the conflict within him, the overarching trauma triggered by a mystical event? A nagging at the latent knowledge suppressed since birth?

But there was more to cosmic purpose than the personal elevation of the spirit. What of the greater good, Irwin thought, *tikkun olam*, the universal healing. Should he be leading Peter towards this? Opening his mind to the obeyance of the *mitzvoth*, the 613 precepts that Jews must follow to ensure that they are righteous and pure of soul? This was central to the Ari's healing process, for man and the universe. If Peter was to follow the path of Vital, then he must teach him. But then he, Irwin, would enter into Peter's otherworldly existence and risk his own psychosis.

Peter must be left, concluded Irwin, and watched, allowing him his freedom. This was the fateful way. This was the way of predetermination. This is how it must be.

13

I stepped into the light. Dust rose from the patio as my robe brushed the stone flags. Filtered sunbeams shone through the particles, their iridescence lighting my way. I strode through this glade of illumination, leaving these remnants of decay to settle on the slabs from whence they came.

My spirit guide directed my sandaled feet to a well-trodden path. Down the steps alongside the house to the gravel track that led to the synagogue of the Ari.

I was oblivious of the cemetery below. Many of those buried there had yet to die and did not offer their greeting. Some 50 metres away the building loomed. A stone staircase led to the open concourse in front of the entrance. I stopped in front of a towering brick wall alongside the steps that concealed the area for worship and meditation. I could see chandeliers shining through arched windows as framed chariots waiting to ascend on high. Purposefully I climbed the stairway and greeted the assembled congregation within and spoke words that caused wonderment: "I have come."

"I have sensed the moment and am to confirm my readiness." Such statements of conviction caused a stirring and I looked through the puzzlement in their faces.

I declaimed my purpose: "My master calls me to his room."

"And who is your master?" One voice responded for them all.

"Are you not his followers also? Is it not you, my fellow disciples, who have summoned me?" Oblivious of their consternation, I continued, "I am to guide you. But first I must seek the wisdom of Elijah," and I walked towards the chamber where my master communed with the prophet.

Barring my way, they cried in rising terror, "None are allowed to enter the Ari's room."

In surprise at the vehemence of their denial, my insistence grew stronger. "It is ordained. I must go there. I am his disciple. I must complete his work."

Fear shot through the crowd, so I must calm them, reassure them of my presence. "Do you not know me? I am Rabbi Vital."

Gasps of recognition rose from them and they led me to the wooden benches where the congregation sit. I notice a wooden door low in the wall to my left and recognise it as the entrance to the room where my master communes with Elijah.

"He waits for me there," I implore. "You must let me enter."

"Please remain here," they say. "Do you not know it is necessary to pray before your concord?"

I am confused. Why do they not accept me and allow me to perform my role? So I rose and left the synagogue, saying: "I see that you are unprepared. I will talk to all in Safed and tell them of my mission. Then you will accept my presence."

In wonderment they drew back and allowed me to return to the sunlight.

14

There are moments when the past in your current life intersects the present moment and your existence is encapsulated in this fleeting flash. Imagine a concurrence from 400 years, the duality invading your being, your functioning teetering in the scattering of time driven by a reality of purpose. I can now accept that my behaviour was not normal, that is, in the sense of an accepted pattern of interaction. I had my own lucidity prompted by that temporal disassociation.

Irwin let me be Vital. He injected his knowledge of the period, his insights into the personalities of the time, the events from the *Book of Visions*, the legends of the Ari. And as I absorbed this knowledge with intuitive ease, Soniadora confirmed what Irwin had said.

Each night I lay and waited for her to come, to emerge from her darkened chamber and enter the alcove in my mind. And feel her physicality, a breath on my neck, a caress of my thigh, a finger on my lips.

Dreams of expectation that led to a tear, a sob echoing in unheard silence. The curve of the ceiling would descend on me, its whiteness glaring in my closed eyes. I would feel the oppression of the surrounding space and touch the fabric of the air that enclosed me. Writhing in this torment of confinement, Soniadora became Eva and we embraced in our tent once more. And as I lived through Vital and these sirens constructed their allurement, we four were bonded in the cross-currents of time.

So, as night became day I pursued my enlightenment and strove to awaken the dead souls of Safed. My audience observed me in the drama of their involvement, accepting this vision of the past as a reminder of the significance of their dwelling place. They could see the fire in my eyes, hear the flames in my voice, witness the intensity of my motion. And they took me in to their homes to feed me, this stranger who tantalised their convictions and laid bare their beliefs. But I saw through this kindness into the doubt that lay beneath and into the depths of their wickedness, and I had to expel myself from their presence.

"Oh Isaac," I wailed, "do you not see their impurities?" And I felt his shadow. It engulfed me. It closed my eyes and I fought the darkness. I succumbed to the dust and scratched the soil on which he strode. And I crawled through the streets in supplication. And as the steps appeared, I saw the crowd that was all Israel. I raised my head and peered to the sky and saw the outstretched arms against the sun.

"Oh Isaac," was my lament, "are you imploring the heavens for us all?"

And then I slept.

As I slept I dreamt.

In the convulsion of my mind and the confusion of temporal perspective, a piercing light wakened my senses from the somnolence. And muddled their discernment. I heard the hardness of the gravel beneath my feet and touched the shuffling sound of the steps. I looked at the odour of the dust and tasted its dryness. Chanting hammered my soul and with eyes closed the crowd appeared before me.

A hand reached out with quiet voice to introduce two strangers. A kindly face of furrowed eyebrows and pitted skin gazed at my presence. Emanations of sound from the hole that was his mouth create words that embraced my dreaming state.

"*My soul brings me to your presence,*" were the first utterances carried on the gust. And on the second breath came the name that mirrored the ages.

"*It is I, Hayyim Vital. We will confront the darkness together.*" My head spun as I looked on his countenance and succumbed to his imploring.

We looked up into the blackness, beyond the outstretched figure in our mindscape. A figure now frozen in its abeyance, awaiting the divine judgment. Awaiting the good of the multitude.

And I dreamt of my mentor, Irwin. Of the angst in his soul. The sun that was he looked on us both with a beatific smile. Irwin, my attempted healer. My guide. My fellow traveller. Was he the instigator of my dream? Was this his mortal plan? To direct a supernal force and gain a window to that mystic time? And bring him knowledge and insight that his troubled mind felt unable to acquire?

In the haze and bemusement of sleep time, I sublimated the desire to question Vital and bring succour to Irwin.

"*I hear your thoughts,*" said Hayyim, "*they speak louder than the scream in your heart.*" Silence of acknowledgement and my dream partner continued.

"*Your mentor beckons to your soul. He craves its redemption as a substitute for his own.*" I shuddered at this voicing of the evil in Irwin.

"*Appease your master and you both will return. Redeem thy terror.*" And Hayyim spun into the abyss.

Redeem thy terror. Of the agitation in my body.
Redeem the terror. Of the panic in my mind.
Redeem my terror. Of the sanctity of my soul.

Redeem my terror. The words grew large in my head. They shouted their presence to the conscious state that was my awoken body.

The floor from where I slept lifted me up and I cried out his command. *"Redeem thy terror."* It echoed through the lanes and amplified its resonance till I could no longer bear its rejoinder. And my hands went flat to my ears to block this noise. This promulgation to my entirety. And I wept and thought of my madness.

And that was how she found me. Dalia Ahav, artist of Safed, depicter of visions, drawer of dreams. That painting of Irwin's that was reflective of Rachel's dream of Vital's self-aggrandizement. That showed the washer-woman witch. This was the work of Dalia, a woman of perhaps 40. Dark hair, a biblical face, and dressed in a light robe of blue.

"I have seen you in the streets and Irwin has told me of your story," she whispered, and cradled me, taking me to her bosom. My muffled sobs were erased by this comfort. Her stillness communicated my need and was transfused. Limpet-like, the distress within my person attached itself to her and was digested. I calmed and was able to speak.

"Are you my redeemer? Do you come to save me, rescue me from my perdition?" Quavering words, touched by sobs, erupted from me. Beckoning eyes revealed an enticing warmth within. I took in her image, received no word from Soniadora, and succumbed.

"You have the eyes of Ruth," I told her, raising myself from the floor of the alley that was my bed.

A smile emanated beneath her aquiline nose and on standing I perceived her comeliness and the fullness of her figure.

"I will lead you back to your house," came words that rose and climbed through the ether between us. I reached out to touch the face below me, ran a finger down an olive cheek and drew it across moist lips dampened from speaking.

Loose folds enclosed the arm that stirred and directed her hand to mine as she stepped back from me.

"Come," she said, as her turning sandals scuffed the earth beneath us, a melody to accompany our fractured dance as she led me home.

Side-by-side on the carpeted window seat, we sat gazing at the door that separated us from the world beyond. Our stillness did not disturb the air in the room, there was no gust to waken the somnolent witch who resided in the alcoves.

And the hours passed in mutual solitude. There was no sexual frisson between us, purely a psychic understanding. Sensing the moment in our meditative silence, Dalia's gentle tones aroused me, wakened a dormant, rational part of my being.

"Is that what you wish? Redemption? To seek it for your troubled mind?"

But Vital rose through my subconscious and came to the fore anew.

"AND SEEK IT FOR OUR IMPURE SOULS. THE WORLD MUST BE HEALED."

Although she had been warned by Irwin and had also seen me treading the cobbled streets in ancient garb, Dalia was unprepared for this outburst.

She drew breath and steadied herself. Then entered my mystical world as an artist invading her own work.

"Sweet man," for she did not know which name to use, "tell me more of this mission."

"My master, the Ari, leads us. He has taught us his precepts and rules of behaviour. He has divulged the wisdom of his Kabbalistic system, which only I am privileged to fully understand. But he sees our flaws and I am possessed of his troubled mind. The way of our task is pitted." I spoke with Hayyim's passion and belief, transcending my own ego.

Dalia remained quiet and thoughtful. Her succour was now in the balance. Now she had an opportunity to exit, to leave me, Peter the psychotic, the deluded, the possessed, to dwell in this uncertain state.

Compassion, intrigue and a sense of inspiration drove her to stay. Intuition triggered a creative spark, a need to have a visualisation of the personal drama confronting her. That is what she told me afterwards. The process that unfolded was a natural development in the course of my journey of self-discovery.

"Peter, Hayyim," the hesitant uttering of Dalia reached into me, "come, reveal the mysteries of the visions and anxieties that are consuming you."

"I cannot talk of these things." I felt myself retreating, as I had with Irwin. "Leave me now."

And so our first meeting was aborted.

The steps of my dream, the Ma'alot Olei Hagardom, divided Safed. Originally the Jews and the Arabs, but now the Jews and Artists. Differences of religion replaced by distinctions of spiritual ineffability. The majority of artists had been drawn to Safed because of the light and the inspiration that a place with mystical energy can provide. A number of them produced art that was reflective of the history and meaning of Safed and had mystical qualities of meditative insight. Among them was Dalia.

I learnt of her life during our burgeoning relationship. Her parents were from Germany and had settled in Palestine in the 1930s as fulfilment of their Zionist dream. Staunch Communists, they joined the pioneer kibbutz to the south of Lake Kinneret, the Sea of Galilee. Dalia was born and raised in this environment, living from an early age in the children's dormitory. She was unsure what effect this separation from her parents had on her other than a continuous feeling of alienation in her teenage years. Is this what drew me to her, the replication of Eva's persona? The distinction with Dalia was the life-enforcing empathy she drew from it, rather than Eva's self-destruction.

Childless, she was widowed in 1967 when her husband died in the Six-Day War. This trauma triggered the introspection that led to her becoming an artist, seeking solace through morbid drawings of the dead and dying. Unable to picture the souls of her subjects, she turned to the study of Kabbalah for insight.

And so she was drawn to Safed.

Her studio was in the cellar of a nineteenth-century house built after the last earthquake. It was in a narrow winding street and had a terrace that looked out over the roofs of Safed to the cemetery below. Here she would sketch, looking across to Mount Meron, and imagine the spirits ascending to the heavens from the dwellings below.

I had driven her out and now lay alone and desolate in the chamber of my dreams. A gnawing for her company began to grow inside, feeding on some instinctive attraction, so some days later I found myself heading towards Studio Ahav, the place that was to become my sanctuary. Dalia jokingly referred to this as "feetalism" as I had allowed my legs to guide me with an unfettered sense of direction.

I walked in meditation, the houses forming a tunnel as a channel in my mind. Each corner blazed with intensity, the walls and roofs rippling with colour. Sound cascaded through the gulleys of the streets, rushing into my consciousness. Safed the vibrant, propelling me with its mystical coruscation. Stumbling with a secret anticipation, I reached her door and toppled into a waiting gallery, empty of human presence. I stood alone in the centre of a square, white-walled room. The rush matting tethered my feet as I took in the pictures that encompassed me. Their occupants looked down at me from their frames, quizzical in the freshness of their oils and the outmoded nature of their dress.

From each side they penetrated me with their gaze, demanding my penitence. I beseeched them: "What is my sin?" All Israel spoke *"Our master has gone."*

"Am I to blame?" I screeched.

"He told you his secrets, he told you of his death." The crowd grew nearer as they chanted the words.

"No, no, no," my sobbing brought Dalia from her terrace.

Again the stillness of her breast subdued the fire within me.

"What do you see?" she asked when my calmness was perceived by her.

"These are paintings?" I looked around, hurriedly, defying them to demonstrate their animation once more.

"Of the Ari and the legends surrounding him. It is a series I have been working on for some time. The stories are well documented."

Fearfully, I went close to each canvas with an outstretched hand in front of my face protecting me from their inhabitants. Removing this shield I looked into the Chagall-like paintings. Animals and men. Houses and fields. Trees, bushes and leaves as camouflage, shielding the subjects, revealing little by little their soulful story through studied concentration.

"Some have no faces, they cannot be perceived." I looked on at the blankness in the pictures, observing an anonymity that belied their importance in the scene.

"Those are the ones I cannot draw," sighed Dalia, "the Ari, Vital, Ibn Tabul and the other key disciples. There is no pictorial record of them or physical description. I leave it to the beholders of my work to create their own vision of those faces. From the void that I lend them."

"I see them, I am among them, I am one of them. My face is there." I pointed rapidly, stabbing at each painting. Flashbacks to the visualisations in my Camden room came flooding in. I was overwhelmed at being drawn into the settings of my other reality.

"Explain, explain." I was back to screeching.

Dalia was not flustered by my outburst. She assumed an air of tranquillity, which diluted my delirium and enabled her to provide the exegesis I required.

"I cannot explain the deeper meaning within them. The legends have been much interpreted and the symbolism lends itself to as much debate as the *Torah*." Dalia turned towards one of the paintings. "This is called 'The Seven Shepherds Called to the *Torah* Reading'. The Ari intends to summon the seven shepherds, Abraham, Isaac, Jacob, Joseph, Moses, Aaron and David, to the reading of the *Torah* in synagogue. The condition he lays down to his students is that none of them are to laugh at anything they see. One disobeys when he sees David leaping and dancing with the joy of his reading."

I looked upon the synagogue painting and saw the howling. I felt this moment of failure of one of the disciples. Of how it would affect us all. And understood with the intuition of a shared soul.

"I need hear no more," I said in a calmed state, "I am at one with my master."

"Now you must explain," smiled Dalia, entering, as Irwin did, into my world.

"The others must not hear. They accuse me," I answered, once more feeling the sentience of the images, "we must leave this place."

Dalia attempted to lead me to her terrace, to the open, the space, the sky that she hoped would allow me to breathe and escape from my containment.

"I must go," I said, denying her hand, "I am not prepared. There is much I have to do."

And so we parted for the second time, in a common state of perplexity.

I was alone when I began this journey. Solitude begat George, who returned me to Safed. Safed begat Irwin, who reflected my soul's angst and travelled alongside to the boundary of his despair. And brought Dalia to me.

As I lay in the house, hearing the whispers of Soniadora, I pictured Dalia. Her image pulled at me, disturbing the hidden voice, banishing it to the alcoves. Soniadora's job was done and a conviction of purpose was born. I would commit myself to Dalia. She would be an object of my obsession as a depicter of my world. Where Soniadora had guided me, Dalia would lead. Would take me from darkened places and bring me to the light. This I knew and this I must tell her.

And so I made my way back to Studio Ahav, and this time I remained.

My room was sparse and uncluttered. Whitewashed walls, a simple cot against one side. Upon opening the door, the space was invisible as the eye was drawn to the opposite window. To the hills and sky that it framed. For days after I arrived and Dalia had settled me here, this view was my world. I gazed upon it, drawing breath from the landscape, allowing its stillness to inhabit me. Dalia brought me food in silence, in recognition of my need for tranquillity.

This asylum room, this monastic cell, was unbounded in my mind. Its invisibility was my infinite realm.

I registered the changing light of the day, the newborn sun bathing the heights with the softness of its dawn rays. The harshness of noon, striking a brilliance on the sloping ground, illuminating each feature and occupant. The death throes of sunset, inflamed passion lurking between the peaks.

All this I witnessed, these visions reclaiming my convulsive mind.

And then I wandered through the house. To the roof terrace, to become one with the gleam of the day. And observe the working Dalia gain inspiration, sketching the images that descended from the heavens. I remained unblinking for the eternity it took for the figures to form on the paper. Eyes wide open in catatonic trance, looking through the paper being enlivened by Dalia's hand.

My stillness seemed to energise her, my presence undaunting. As each sheet was filled, she took it to her studio and mounted it on the wall facing her easel. The collage grew until a story was told. Dalia came to the roof no more and began the conception of her painting in dialogue with the audience of her imagination. This chamber was private. I was excluded from this creativity.

And still there was silence between us. No mechanism had been found to breach the barrier that was our sublimated voices. She was waiting till I was ready. I stretched time over my psychosis, unwary of my thoughts, letting them linger in the depths of my consciousness.

Alone on the roof, Dalia's materials challenged me. They beckoned, inviting me to display the contents of my mind. Entranced, I approached the sketchbook and sat on Dalia's stool. I felt empowered, as I had done with the automatic writing. Images flowed like the words, uncontrollably, then fanatically until I had filled the page.

I hovered over my mindscape and looked down at it from the clouds. Fluid lines, amorphous shapes, figures of inexactitude in an indeterminate terrain.

Save one, who with outstretched arms, faced into the page, looking at it from my perspective. Or was it I who peered over his shoulder into the barren space beyond our gaze? A space filled with eyes that looked back within hollow faces, gaping with open window-mouths that framed a desolate cosmos inside them.

A breeze; was it me as I descended, ruffled the sheet, animating the images? They spoke and I heard.

"*We are lost,*" they cried, "*can no one save us?*"

Tears dissolved their faces and trickled through the paper. The wetness congealed the drawing, merging my disconsolate figures into a howling whole.

Transfixed with these visions, Dalia emerged onto the terrace to rescue her materials from the rain.

"Peter, come inside. This shower will last the rest of the day." She gathered the pad and pencils, brushing against me in her dryness. I had no awareness of the dampness of my clothes, hair and body. I had cried with my creation and felt only emotion.

"You are wet through. Let us have some tea and you can dry out. And tell me of this." She pointed at the soaking paper that still showed the results of my obsessive work.

What could I explain of this sodden chaos? Enraged, I crumpled the paper and crushed it into a wrinkled ball.

"That's my brain!" I screamed as I threw the ball towards the mountains, hoping it would descend into the cemetery.

With that gesture, I withdrew to my cell, the sanctuary provided for me by Dalia. She became my nurse and ministered to my physical need for nourishment. But she stood back from the disquiet within me, allowed it to follow its own course and remained quiet and non-judgmental, just observing as if it was a scene from one of her paintings. Drawing materials were left out for me, unobtrusively, as a benign reminder of their ability to express my hurt.

I lay on my bed and the voices returned. Sound images, word pictures that etched themselves to the inside of my skull. Cryptic sentences floated inside me and I immersed myself in this world. Gradually the sentences coalesced into separate spheres that formed a pattern, linking themselves in a bravura of activity. I saw the Tree of Life, the *sefirot*, the manifestation of the attributes of God. And then came the flames. They burned and destroyed in the bitterness of their ferocity.

I lay helpless, witness to this spectacle inside me, and shuddered in its heat. The fire subsided and my body calmed, the rage being spent in my somnolence.

And in these moments of relative composure, I felt the need to communicate with Dalia. Uttered words would be uncontrollable, nonsensical. Somehow I wanted to express my abasement. I returned to the paper and drew. The haunted faces I had condemned to the air came back and made a new appearance on the page.

This time I took the drawing to Dalia and offered it to her. Like a small child with a gift for its mother. Like a dog returning with a stick. Like a cat presenting a sacrificial bird.

"Your name, is it Dalia?" I stuttered as I waited for approbation.

"Yes Peter, it is." The anxious face that watched me enter her studio softened into a welcoming countenance.

A shaky voice declared: "I have brought you this" to accompany the proffered drawing in outstretched arms.

A stone floor separated us, with large, smooth flagstones reminiscent of the patio of the house. I looked across the divide and my pulse raced in memory of revelation in that captive room. Perspiring hands dampened the offering once more and I approached Dalia in a simulacrum of my movement to the door of that transcendent chamber.

She looked serene. A queen on her throne as she sat by her easel. All that I desired seemed to be in her person. Something in me had changed, for the energy that fuelled my dissociative state of being was now channelled into a craving for a relationship with Dalia.

She peeled the drawing from my palms, lifting a living layer from me. No words, just motion as she pinned it to her easel. And looked upon it, deep into it, through its surface, neglecting the lack of artistic ability.

I stood in breathless anticipation. Of what? A critique? An explanation? An insight? Motionless, I received her words and was able to breathe again.

"Tell me more of this, Peter. I would like to know what you think the picture represents." Dalia's quiet questioning voice drew me to her. Close enough to touch, to feel her hair and let the strands trickle through my fingers. But I did not. I pointed at my work, jabbed at the faces, prodding them in a wild stabbing motion. My hidden voice lifted, ascended in discord with the gesticulations.

"They cry for me. He does. He does. He does. And him. Him. Him."

Dalia sat unmoved. Her composure overcame my agitation.

"Why do they cry for you?" Dalia asked at last, as the tension in my body eased.

I looked at their faces, requesting them to answer for me. One spoke with my voice.

"He sees the anguish of his master but cannot reveal it. He sees the death of his master but cannot prevent it. He assumes the mantle with guilt he cannot express. He closes his mind and traps the despair. The tears of sublimation transmute to rage. We feel this anger and cry."

"And who is he and who is the master?" asked Dalia, anticipating the answer.

"I am Rabbi Vital and my master is the Ari," I responded in bafflement. An automatic answer. One that was in suspended belief.

Dalia continued, pointing at the figure with outstretched arms, "And who is this?"

"My master, my master," I shrieked, and could take it no longer. I left Dalia in her state of mystery and hurried to my room.

A DREAM UNTOLD

I want to hold it, grasp it, touch it, shape it, mould it, crush it, this furry ball in my mind. It grows and caresses the edge of my wisdom. Takes over and scars with its mane my rightful feelings. The me. And fills the space to become the he. Rotates inside my skull grasping my current sanity, to replace it with the entrant. My possessor. Each time I feel it, but can't prevent it. Its sap rises and fills my living trunk. I know him and talk with his voice of reason. Or reflect on his glory the presence he emits.

I shudder in his cradling, his rebirth manifest. Each sense subsumed to his rectitude. And stride forth in his image. Until I am bereft. I weep for his departure. The ball unravels and clings to the inside of my skull, replete in its hollowness. At last I can rest and witness the withdrawing of disturbance. Contemplate the reality of Peter Paul.

Until his return.

Peter Paul looked within. By gazing at the sky, transparent in its blueness, it cast an image on his body that seeped through to his soul.

The sefirot gleamed on his skin. The left side and the right. On his arms, his legs, his trunk. Each was an aspect of his despair. Each had the power for his redemption. To be sought and revealed.

All the days of his past filtered through them. Each action and event. Reaction and emotion. Success and failure. Truth. Deceit.

He stood on both sides, transcending their power. Abusing it with the indecision of madness. The corruption of his consciousness.

Keter, the Crown, the pinnacle of the Tree, the creator of self. Of self-image. This vessel leaked, the moistness of its emanating tear nourishing the sefirot below. Hokmah, wisdom, and Binah, understanding. The triad of sentience immersed in anguish. And these two grew large from the torment till the swelling caused a rupture and flooded the path to the sefirot below. And blocked the way to his redemption. The healing from the sefirot of Hesed, mercy, and Gevurah, power, acting in conjunction to reveal the beauty, Tifferet, of his self.

So Peter Paul struggled and fought the images that descended upon him. The surrogate madness of violation. And he was rent asunder.

THEN

15

Safed 1571

Early light streamed through the slatted window of Isaac's bedroom. Diffused rays cast his shadow on the white plaster of the wall. He was preparing for his morning devotions. And sobbing, for as the *Zohar* says, *"he who prays and weeps and cries so much that there is no feeling left in his lips – that is the perfect prayer, prayer in the heart and it never returns empty"*.

He completed the blessings to God. For removing the sleep from his eyes and slumber from his eyelids. For returning his soul to him after its nightly ascent. And now he donned his prayer shawl and phylacteries, the leather binding symbolising his tie to God.

In this attire, he walked the short distance from his home to the synagogue to join his disciples for the morning service. Isaac wept again. A tear of despair, for who among his followers was truly righteous? Was pure of soul? Would bring the healing of the world that he so desired? "He" as the conduit – for it could not be his personal ambition, a vaingloriousness that would taint him.

These thoughts were with him as he entered the synagogue. And then they were expunged, for his mind should be clear to focus on the ritual of the service. As was his custom, he closed his eyes during the Eighteen Benedictions and recited them from memory. His left hand lay on his heart and he placed his right hand over it to soften the stricter attributes of the "left side" of the *sefirot*.

In his darkness, the mystical union of the God-head and the divine female presence of the *Shekinah* brought about by the prayer could not be witnessed. He was in fear of gazing at their sexual intimacy for, as Exodus states, *"no man shall see Me and live"*.

It was in this state of meditation that Isaac raised his soul to the highest level. He stood before God and confessed his sins. His life was thrown into the abyss of existence as an ultimate act of submission. Divine mercy and the expiation of his sins would return him from this voluntary, contemplative death, and achieve total purification of his soul. He would be filled with supernal light and become newly created – imbued with new spiritual strength with which to struggle against evil and resist all further sin. He stood ready at the top of the world to hurl himself into the lower regions and rescue the souls of the departed in Gehinnon.

He lifted his arms from his chest and raised them to the sky, to the light beyond the room. And all of Israel looked on. And waited for their redemption.

On the afternoon preceding the Sabbath, Isaac's disciples would meet without him, in a space created for their own thought, to contemplate the past week. But his absence filled their minds as they expressed their adulation.

"He sees our sins," wailed Joseph Arzin.

"Of that we cannot speak, he hears," bemoaned Solomon Sabon.

"And he feels the torment of our souls," lamented Moses Yonah.

A DREAM UNTOLD

"My heart trembles when he speaks," told Isaac Orcha.

"In fear I enter his presence," confessed Jacob Masad.

"My weakness succumbs to his strength," avowed Mordechai Gallico.

"I am darkness to his light," declared Joseph Ahun.

"Are we the undeserving?" cried them all save one. "How can we rise to the task?"

These men, solemn in their own purpose, devout in the ritual of their creed, followers in the path of redemption, took pity on themselves.

Save one.

The meeting room of the Abuhav synagogue repressed the sound of their moans. None of the townspeople of Safed knew of this turmoil. Their hopes remained intact.

"Soon the Messiah will deliver us," they said, placing their destiny in the hands of Isaac and his followers.

Responsibility lay heavy on those within. To be without sin and let their pure souls bring about the healing of the world, this they must do.

"We must be without sin," proclaimed Elijah Falco.

"And open our eyes to the darkness of our deeds," was the response of Shabbatai Menashe.

"Let us tell all that we have done this past week," spoke Ibn Tabul, "and let others judge whether these acts are good or bad. By this we will be shamed out of sinning."

"That is the way," agreed all.

Save one.

"It is not the way," spoke Hayyim, suppressing his silence no longer, "for who would dare reveal his evil deeds to others? Be open to yourselves and upon retiring recall every sin that you have done during the day. Repent each one and confess them all before God, even the most minor of transgressions."

Ibn Tabul disagreed. "Each of us should know the worth of others and place our trust in the honesty of our admissions."

Hayyim did not respond. Isaac had taught him to eschew his arrogance. In his heart he knew the rightness of the practice he had proclaimed and he withdrew from the congregation.

As he left the synagogue, the last rays of the sun became diffused by the clouds and the mountain tops. His pace quickened and his mood darkened in the fading light. The walls of Safed hemmed him in and he raised his head to the sky to free his mind and banish this foul humour. Was he not the principal disciple of the Ari? Did he not have the greater understanding of his system and the manner in which all must behave? And why was he not allowed to exert the authority awarded by these traits? He implored the heavens for guidance. To be able to sublimate these feelings and not subvert the will of his master. In this state of agitation he arrived home. Hannah greeted him.

"You look troubled, Hayyim. You should be joyful to receive the Sabbath. Tell me of your despair." His wife was perceptive and would delay the preparation for the ritual meal in her understanding of his plight. Comfort him by absorbing the troubled words he would speak and make this a union of their consciousness to precede the blessed act of a man and a woman becoming one this night.

"Hannah, as ever you uplift me. Your insight is sufficient to dispel my gloom. Now let us get ready, the time of the evening service approaches and I must return to the synagogue."

A DREAM UNTOLD

But the lifting of his mood had not dislodged the unease within. In an anxious state he prayed and returned again to the sanctum of his home. And that night he dreamt.

> *Of walking down the steps of Safed to the marketplace. Of meeting departed ones who approached from the cemetery.*
>
> *And he walked further to the Jewish quarter where all Israel were gathered. And the sun had set at noontime and there was a thick darkness over the world. And all Israel wept bitterly. And then a stranger came. A dervish in appearance. And this man sang of the Messiah and Redemption. But no one understood or heard this voice save he. And as they approached and spoke, the sun shone once again as before.*

And Hayyim woke in wonderment with but one thought. Who was this stranger of his dream?

A DREAM UNTOLD

One man looks at another in timeless affinity. Their eyes merge as the distance between them cannot be measured. Each brings their own power to the other in a common bond of healing. Recognition is not apparent. That will emerge outside of their lacunate meeting in their conscious awareness, reflecting on their separate realities.

But in these dreams a subconscious exchange takes place, drawing on a primal energy.

The future man is as of the present of the past and so remains discernible to Hayyim. Just a stranger who redeems the darkness of his malaise.

The stranger is unknowing and receives the distress in an unprepared state. Not ready for this burden. Fly away Peter. Come back Paul.

16

Isaac had spent but two years in Safed when the plague descended. The stricken were taken to the woods surrounding the city. To die together, with collective strength, and face the Divine with their affliction. And be nursed and bathed to cleanse their bodies of the expulsions that caused their weakness. From the mouth and their lower parts came the torment of the disease. And death from this flood of their bodies. Young and old. Man and woman. Rich and poor. The righteous and the wicked. The sickness was blind to its receiver.

And so they lay on straw pallets in the darkness of the forest huts. And the healthy took water from the nearby spring and washed the bodies with cloth rinsed in the running brook.

And in the town Isaac suffered.

Each groan that filtered through the shuttered windows was absorbed in his flesh. He grew heavy with their torment, bloated with their excoriation.

Isaac wept, as he saw the leaden souls encased in each suffering body. And took on the burden of guiding them to the heavens for judgment.

Each street in Safed was torn with their cries and Isaac shuffled in his slowness to attend to them all.

Great was his oppression and the filth of the disease rendered a despondency to his being.

Such that he could do no more.

Such that he felt its debasement and unclean nature.

Such that he needed to be purged of this defilement.

Such that immersion in the ritual bath was the way of his purification.

And Isaac made his way to his *mikvah*. That was fed by natural spring waters. That came from the streams above Safed, in the woods of the dying. And the source of their affliction was brought to Isaac as he doused himself in unknowing sanctification.

As Isaac emerged from the coldness of his ablutions he observed the sparrows gathered in the dust of his exit. Twittering. And chattering. Until the sounds they made reflected on his mortality. As he understood them, *"for even the birds of heaven proclaim his dying day"*.

And he felt all the levels of his soul pass into darkness as preparation for his day of judgment. The spiritual death he had practised in his meditations was now but a rehearsal for his physical departure.

He weakened quickly with the onset of the disease. Bodily functions were subject to the trauma of this violation. Control was not possible, so they were subjugated to the spirit that was still alive within him. His presence on this earth moved into the realm of sentient exclusivity.

The high summer sun shone strongly through the shuttered windows of his death chamber. Rays forced their way through the wooden slats and announced a path to on high. Isaac's eyes took in this ladder as a final act of the sun before the great darkness that was to befall him.

His disciples filtered through the rays defining the hollowness that troubled Isaac.

Gasping words alighted on Isaac Kohen.

"Had I found even one completely righteous person among you, I would not be departing this world before my time."

To him he also said, "All, save Hayyim Vital, should desist from studying the wisdom I have taught you. Only he has understood it properly."

And Isaac Kohen replied, "We no longer have hope then."

And more words came borne on struggling breath: "If you are deserving I will come back and teach you again."

With wonder, Isaac Kohen questioned how this would come about.

At this the Ari summoned his final strength to reproach the priest: "You do not understand the mysteries of creation. I shall return, whether it be through dreams, or in your waking state or via other means. Now you must go quickly. You are a Kohen and must not be present at my death."

So Isaac approached his last moment and recited the prayer that proclaimed the oneness of God.

And his rapture began. In the transcendent state between below and above. In the transfer of his righteousness to the Divine light. To have his perfected soul kissed by God as it departed the lifeless flesh that had been its vessel.

And his union was complete.

Hayyim entered the death chamber, saw the wonder in his master's eyes and closed the eyelids so that the sight of the living would not mar this last image.

Hayyim was the first to cast earth on the coffin of Isaac as it lay in its resting place, shielded from the wind that disturbed the trees and bushes lining the cemetery. "All moves with his passing," he thought as the clumps hovered briefly before settling on the wooden lid that separated his master's body from the living.

And with the Ari's departure a darkness was cast over him. Feelings of abandonment, anger and resentment stole into his being at the thought of undone deeds. And with this despair he left his companions at the graveside to seek solace in the hills, making his way along the path that led away from Safed.

"The slope is steeper this side," he mused, looking up at the grassy banks littered with rocks. One stone chose itself, and there he perched between the depths of the cemetery valley and the heavens caressing the brow behind him.

Tiredness slowed his body and the taint of his soul welled anew now that he rested from his physical exertions. Bereft and alone, hunched in grey solitude, he was at one with the end of the day in its gloominess. So it was in the stillness of the twilight that Isaac spoke as he stood by Hayyim's shoulder.

"*Remember that I chose you*," his master whispered, "*now control your evil moods as I have shown you and carry my work forward.*"

And this Hayyim did, expelling his darkness bit by bit on his exhaling breath, and became ready for the task. Enveloped in the cocoon of his breathing, all time became one, past, present and future commingling into a single insight.

In the distance, a figure left the lights of Safed to descend into the burial ground, and from across the valley he looked deep into Hayyim's eyes. And both stood outside their dreams in recognition.

So Hayyim watched as the dervish from his dream approached the grave of Isaac. Above the tomb a flaming candle sat enclosed in a glass lantern, casting the stranger's shadow into the blackness beyond. The penumbra settled on Hayyim; he saw into this man's thoughts and felt the anguish that emanated from one who was a stranger no more. And the turmoil of his soul was great, so Hayyim led him through the ritual practice of unification to aid its recovery.

And his shadow circled the grave till it was transfixed and immobilised. His head drooped and the body wilted as the stiffness of his bones could no longer support him.

So Hayyim guided his flesh to cling to the stone that lay above the physical presence of the Ari and watched a trembling begin, coruscating through outstretched limbs, the rippling tissue vibrating the sanctum of the unknown's mind and goading the emotion of his closed sight.

Peter Paul wept.

And his tears were heard.

NOW

17

Safed 1978

My mind was crazed. In a numinous turmoil. My being expressed a convergence of centuries, a personal collective of the unconscious bounded by specific events and personalities. As Hayyim Vital. As Peter Paul. Connected by a spiritual chain, the ends linking to form a circle. No beginning or end. One subsumed in the other. In each other's psyche, conveyed, revealed in dreams.

I walked the streets of Safed and heard the wailing. Of sickness. Of loss. Of loss of a sublime individual.

One of Dalia's paintings had sparked this humour. It was a moment when I was lucid and had her perpetual calming presence relieving my suffocation. It was an image that evoked both love and death. A featureless body that lay within the darkness of a cave, the blackness supporting the corpse, cradling it. As I looked deeper, a warmth exuded from some hidden space carried on a lightness of breath. My perception changed and the rocks had the form of lips suspended in a glowing backdrop. In a corner of the painting was the inscription from the Song of Songs:

> "Let him kiss me with the kiss of his mouth"

Dalia waited for the moment to enter into my thoughts. "The painting has a name that may disturb you."

"It is the Ari."

"Yes. It represents the death of Luria."

I mourned and looked again. Felt the sight that emanated from the portrayal. "And the kiss?"

"Hayyim Vital describes Luria as having died by a Kiss."

"The 'Kiss of God'?"

"Yes. It places Luria in the pantheon of the most righteous. According to Talmudic tradition, the great prophets Moses, Aaron and Miriam all died by a kiss from God."

I moved away from the painting. From the intensity of grief and joy that it aroused.

Whose eyes did I see this through? Whose anguish was being evoked? In confusion I approached the death scene. Came close to the body. Reached out. Touched it. Placed my fingers on the featureless head. Closed the unseen eyes.

And then I wept. For all.

Dalia drew near. Her outstretched arm rested on my shoulder, anticipating comfort. I drew back.

"Please do not touch me. You are not my wife." Hayyim's voice broke my mould.

A startled Dalia withdrew and then regained her composure. She knew many orthodox Jews in Safed and respected the custom of avoidance of physical contact between male and female other than within marriage.

"Peter. Hayyim. Tell me of your loss, your sadness." Dalia caressed me with her words. The sound touched me in a way that no cleaving could.

"The loss is for all. The sadness is universal. His mission is unfulfilled. Who will lead us to *tikkun olam*, the healing of the world? I must seek the others."

"The others?" Dalia participated in my delusion.

"Jonathan, Joseph, Samuel, Isaac, Judah." I shouted their names, answering and declaiming at the same time.

"Gedaliah, Abraham, Shabbatai, Elijah." I invoked the highest group of the Ari's cubs, my fellow disciples.

At that I stumbled out of the studio and into the cobbled street. The slope propelled me away from the Artists' Quarter, the momentum of my body causing a stumbling, jarring motion. My legs stabbed me with their upward thrusts. Shock waves tremored through my body, reaching my fevered mind.

Left, right. Peter, Hayyim. Left, right. Peter, Hayyim. Left, right.

I stopped. I cried. I saw.

I saw the cemetery below, nestling in the valley, cradled by the hills. On the opposite side I saw a lonely figure on a rock. Desolate in the dusk that was about to fall. I felt a pain as I became one with that figure and walked with him to the cemetery gate, a journey that took us past the entrance to the *mikvah* of the Ari, past his synagogue, past the mound that was his home, past the blue walls of Soniadora's house, and across the dusty path that was the track between the mortal and immortal.

And shuffled downwards past the graves of Cordevero and Karo to await the fall of night. Blackness to be relieved by the sight of three stars to signify a time for empathy with past souls.

I looked at the Ari's grave in the warm glow of candlelight. The lantern above the headstone was already lit, acting as a beacon for those needing to find their way to his resting place.

To appeal to him and share their woes.

An unknown power compelled me to lie upon the tomb. Prone, seeking to mirror the corpse in the coffin below.

There was movement. I grasped the rough stone, its edges chafing my skin till bloody particles dripped onto the soil that had not been disturbed for 400 years. The coldness of the rock that separated us entered my body. I shivered. Trembled. Quivered. My limbs jerked. The lack of physical control was reflected in my mind. My emotions. My essence. My eyes bled tears that sought crevices in the slab that was my sanctum. I stilled as the chill subsided and I felt a radiance emanating from below.

The warmth subsumed me and coursed through my body. To the extremities of my limbs. Searching, finding the fissure of my chafed skin. Mingling with the blood that bore evidence of my turmoil.

And I uttered to the one that I sought to salve my misery. "My soul struggles. I am torn by its uncertainty. I know not who I am." My lips trembled and a voice perched itself on my tongue. It spoke with resolution and acuity.

"All nefesh are uncertain. They reflect the without which concerns itself with your place in the bodily world."

And my tongue spoke for me.

"And if I know not my place in the bodily world? What then?"

"Then you must raise your soul to the next level of ruah."

And the moisture of my tears became vapour and floated as a cloud above the grave. And to this I cleaved my soul and they rose together on high.

A darkness enfolded me and the trance became sleep. And the sleep became dream. And I dreamt of this communion and we looked down on all Israel as one. To drift and glide without turmoil. To succumb to peace. And awake to the glow of a new dawn.

When I did not return, Dalia rushed to find Irwin. "Seeing the painting of Luria's death triggered something in him," she told the concerned Hasid.

"Do you have any idea where he might have gone?"

"He went towards the cemetery, I couldn't stop him. Or didn't want to. I sensed there was something he had to do."

"And you haven't seen him since then?"

"No."

"I think we should look in the cemetery. I've a feeling that's where he may have spent the night."

Together they found me, still prostrate on the Ari's grave. But no longer in tension or tautness of limb.

A light dew covered me in the morning light. Dampness made my clothes cling, the drapes fastening me to the stone. I felt as an outer layer of the tomb, peeling myself from it as I rose.

Irwin was first to speak, addressing me with a concern for my wholeness. And with a desire to reveal the mystery of what I may have experienced. And to test my delusion. And to hear the voice of my response. "Peter, we were worried. Have you been here all night?"

Dalia looked on with tension in her eyes. Silent anticipation. Perhaps guilt to be assuaged as the provider of the catalyst to my venture into a mystical practice.

A DREAM UNTOLD

Stiltingly, I sat upright and looked at my grazed palms. The abrasions were covered in a translucent powder, blue from the grave. Within I saw the trauma of my night and invoked the witnesses that were my hands.

"See these," I said, gesticulating and showing my scars, "they have grasped a truth for me. I am my own reality." No quavering in my voice, just a firmness of conviction. In a tone that resonated with familiarity inside the hollowness of my being.

Dalia and Irwin exchanged puzzled glances, as if wanting to confirm each other's existence. Irwin asked for them both: "Your own reality! What do you mean, Peter?"

I smoothed my hands on my damp raiments, wiping away the vestiges of my struggle, and showed them the cleansed flesh.

"See these, they belong to Peter, they belong to me … not to Vital."

A hush that bridged 400 years circled among us, linking our minds in unasked questions. And in this place where no birds flew, the sound of one was heard and broke the silent bond.

Irwin again asked for them both, Dalia restraining herself from giving me physical comfort, a hug to satisfy us both. "Not Vital. Has he left you?"

"I don't know. Something happened here last night. I suddenly feel a calmness in me."

"We can see that. Perhaps we should leave now, you must be tired."

I looked at them both with new eyes and sank to my knees in exhaustion, making a symbolic gesture to their succour.

No further questions were asked, Dalia and Irwin uncertain of the suddenness of my healing. Each took an arm and they led me back to the cemetery gate, climbing out of the valley to the path that was the other side.

We made our way through the Jewish Quarter. Past the emptiness that was Luria's home. Past his synagogue, now alive with the voices chanting the morning service. Past the entrance to his *mikvah*. Dust and gravel where birds sang no more. Up into the Artists' Quarter and to Dalia's home.

Here they led me to my room, and Dalia spoke her first words since my discovery "You should rest now, we can talk more later."

I lay on my cot and allowed sleep to cradle me and absorb the gentle thoughts prompted by the goading of the night.

Dalia and Irwin sat over their coffee, each cradling the cup, feeling the warmth, taking in the aroma, watching the steam rise.

"What do you think he was doing down there? Did he have a purpose?" Dalia eventually asked.

"Before his attack, if I can call it that, Peter and I had discussions on Kabbalah. He was knowledgeable and very curious. Understandable in the context of his dream experience." Irwin paused and thought carefully before continuing. He had still not resolved the uncertainties thrown up in his own mind by Peter's behaviour. Opening a discussion with Dalia could commit him to questioning his own beliefs.

"Have you heard of the mystical practice called *yihudim* or unification?"

"Vaguely. It's something to do with communion of souls, isn't it? I don't know anything about the rituals or practices surrounding it." Dalia left it open for Irwin to provide an explanation.

"Peter became very interested in this. It was an esoteric practice developed by Luria. Vital wrote extensively on it and described his own experiences."

"What did the practice entail?" Dalia was now extremely curious. Through Peter, she was enmeshed in the disciple of the Ari.

"As you said, a key aspect of the practice is the mystical communion between the practitioner and that of a departed righteous person. It was performed at the graveside of the *tzaddik* at night, as this was the most propitious time." Irwin paused again as the image of how they had found Peter came to him.

"Carry on," entreated Dalia, who was now utterly intrigued.

"As Vital describes it, to perform the *yihudim* you must stretch yourself out on the grave, face down, mirroring the individual who is buried. The purpose of this is to align yourself physically with the corpse and to animate its bones."

"Animate the bones!" Dalia gasped with her interjection.

"Yes, it does seem strange, but for these mystics the body, whether alive or dead, is a vessel for the soul."

"So the *tzaddik* is being brought back from the dead by this practice?"

"Metaphorically. The belief is that the departed one's soul hovers over the grave and that by giving it a corporeal presence then a binding of the two souls can be accomplished."

Dalia's mind raced with this image and her questions gushed.

"Aren't there levels of soul, though? Is there a particular one for this communion? Do they both have to be at the same level? I mean, you couldn't compare Peter's soul to the Ari's."

"I'm not sure you can compare souls in that way," responded Irwin, "but it is the lower soul, or *nefesh*, that makes the connection. Once the souls are cleft the intent is to raise them to the upper realms and potentially elevate them to the higher levels of *ruah* or even *neshamah*."

"All this from just lying on the grave!" Dalia was incredulous.

"Well, there are various prayers and incantations associated with it. The objective is to reach a meditative state and achieve concentration by contemplating the array of divine names, that is, the different spellings of the four-letter name of God."

"Does Vital describe how he felt? It makes me feel creepy just hearing about it."

"In some detail. He tells of how he was overcome with a great dread and trembling all over his body. As I recall, he recounts how his lips began moving at great speed and he began to utter words and short phrases in automatic speech with an unknown voice that seemed as if it was perched on his tongue."

At this Dalia lost all sense of composure. A mystery was unfolding in front of her with the dry, controlled statements of Irwin. She stood up, knocking the table, spilling the coffee, gasping for the right words. "Peter hears Vital's voice, speaks with it. Vital hears voices and speaks with them. Peter lay on the grave as Vital did. He dreams as Vital. He believed he was Vital. Where is all this going? I mean what is really happening to Peter?" Dalia gave way to her emotions, sat down again and wept. "I feel sort of connected to him," she sobbed, "somehow I really feel the need to help him through this."

Irwin wasn't sure how to comfort her or provide explanations. He had read the stories of spirit possession in the time of the Ari and how he and others such as Karo performed exorcisms. Had he discussed this with Peter? He wasn't sure. Was Peter intuitively seeking Luria's help? He responded as best he could, or was willing to reveal. "I can't give you a satisfactory answer. To either question. There does seem to be a greater force at work here, and all we can do is observe. It is a fairly common practice for the devout to undertake *yihudim* when they are troubled and wish to seek the advice of a departed *tzaddik* through this communion. Some artists in Safed have even subjected themselves to the experience in the hope of gaining inspiration for their work."

"Peter was really calm when we found him. It did seem as if something had been released." Dalia regained her self-control at the thought that there may have been a purpose to Peter's ordeal and that it may have triggered something to free him from his fantasies and delusions.

"Dalia, it is good that you seem to have sought each other out. I am sure your presence is an aid to his healing. It will be interesting to see how Peter is when he wakes. I'm afraid I cannot wait with you for this as I have some appointments this morning at my studio. Please call me if you have any concerns or need help later. There is a bond between Peter and I that goes beyond the short time we have known each other. I too wish to see him through this. Goodbye, Dalia, and good luck!"

17

Darkness woke me. Dusk shadows patterned the wall, their movement rousing a sleeping body. As they faded into the night, I rose from my bed in awe. I was between worlds, somehow released from possession but unclear of my identity. The soreness of my hands prompted thoughts of the previous night. A night suspended in time that was both a few hours and 400 years ago.

Silence. I recognised silence. No voices. The awareness startled me. I held my hands to my face. They were mine, they could touch me and I was sensitive to their caress.

Re-emergence of the senses. That was the feeling being transmuted. A re-creation of the self. My self. Formed in twilight, emanating from this crepuscular state.

I pinched myself. Pain. There was pain. It confirmed my physical presence. At birth a midwife counts the fingers and toes of the newborn and pronounces the baby's wholeness. I felt the need to replicate this exercise and examined the flesh that concealed me. I was intact in my corporeal being and soft limbs took me to the window. The hills opposite drove their blackness into the valley below, concealing the place of my return. My heart quickened and I could feel its throbbing rhythm inside my chest. An echo of the Ari's words was carried on the waves of pulsation.

"*You must raise your soul.*"

To perfect my wholeness. To overcome the emptiness of my past.

A DREAM UNTOLD

I had been broken to enact my repair. Frustrated feelings of resentment towards myself as being out of control swept through me. I stood and faced the wall of my room, pressed myself against it with arms outstretched above my head to feel the unyielding nature of the masonry, and cried for help.

When Dalia found me, I had retreated to the floor, back to the wall, hunched and clutching my legs. Much the same position as when I had found Eva and had tried to comfort her. My fingertips were coated in the white residue of the wall, flakes of paint under my fingernails. Hesitantly Dalia moved to the centre of the room, her silence concealing the initial shock of finding me in the foetal position. Stopping, her eyes fixed on the wall behind me and traced my slow descent to the ground from the scratch marks.

Now looking at the huddled figure she had befriended, she exuded an accepting warmth. Comfort and strength emanated from her body as I lifted my eyes to see the softness of her expression.

Light shone through the open door and cast Dalia's shadow over me. It brought me her power and I rose from my cradled posture. She still did not move. The moment was pivotal; I had to approach her. Two, three, four faltering steps and I threw out my arms to grasp her in a hug of hopefulness. Her arms engulfed me and I pressed my face into the accepting space between neck and shoulder and seemed to breathe the first breath of my re-birth. A hand stroked my back, held my head, soothed the turmoil within.

She sensed the trembling in my body and the racing of my heart. Gradually I picked up the rhythm of her breathing and slowed mine till we were as one in the rise and fall of our embrace.

The quietude was a signal for Dalia to say in a hushed tone, "When you are ready."

Her sympathetic words released new tears and she felt my moistness. She held me during those sobs, allowing the catharsis to emerge.

And then I was ready. I released my grip and gently pushed her away. My words fell into the space between us so that I could witness her acceptance of them. Strangulated and increasing in crescendo.

"I cannot explain what has happened, is happening to me. Some sort of journey. A dream. Am I in a dream? Who am I? I AM PETER PAUL LEVI."

Dalia retreated at the sound of my name and began to mouth a question, but held it back. Now is not the time, she must have thought. Instead she regained her serenity and whispered quietly, "Peter, you have been through a traumatic time."

The tone of her voice calmed me and was healing. Trauma hardly described what I had been through. I closed my eyes, looked upwards and allowed myself to say: "I need to find a way back. This journey has taken me to a wall. I can't get beyond it."

As I said it my face froze and I stared fixatedly to the distance.

"Peter, what is it?"

"I, I had a sudden image of a recurring dream I had as a child. It was of an unending smooth wall. I couldn't see over it and was desperate to know what was on the other side.

Bloody dreams!" Anger rose within me and I smashed a fist into the opposite hand.

A startled Dalia finally released her emotion. "I think we had better call Irwin," she cried. "He can help you through this."

I stopped in my rage at the sound of Irwin's name. What Dalia said was true. There was an empathy that penetrated my being and gave me faith that he could release me from my torment.

Dalia continued with her unflustered practicality. "You've slept all day, you must be hungry. It is quite a while since you ate or drank."

I nodded in acquiescence and followed her downstairs to the kitchen for a supper that was breakfast. It sustained me for the briefness of this day before I returned to my room for a sleep of normality.

18

I met Irwin the next day, each of us hesitant in this beginning.

"Would talking about it help?" Irwin opened, "I am a good listener."

"I think so. From our previous discussions you gave me some valuable insights. I trust you and you are aware of what I have been through. I'm not sure I could explain it to anybody else."

Irwin was struck by my calmness and the logic of what I was saying. It was as if the past months, weeks, days had collapsed into a single instant. He would listen and be objective, somehow move beyond the irrationality. That was my hope.

"OK. Shall we have some tea? The samovar is bubbling in my back room. It's also more comfortable there, as you know."

There was silence while Irwin performed his tea ceremony. We sat down and looked at each other across the copper table. Irwin's gaze was fixed at my forehead. It was evident that he needed to be taken to a place beyond this room before my words could be distilled.

I could have become agitated at this time lapse, but succumbed to the stillness and waited for him to be ready.

"Tell me of your night on the grave of the Ari," he said.

I looked across to Irwin. Really looked. To see the question emanate, feel those words as they left him, watch his body soften into an accepting posture. What could I tell him that he did not already know? And his silence begat my answer as the pause gained strength. And I drifted into the space that enveloped me during those dark hours.

"I spoke of the state of my soul." And Irwin heard my voice proclaim of its uncertainty. He waited until the echo of the phrase dissolved into the space between us.

"And what did you say?"

"That I …, it struggles. That I …, it was uncertain. That I knew not who I was." I became agitated as Irwin's pointed questions returned me to the catharsis of the night.

"Take a deep breath," said Irwin, "hold it, then breathe out slowly. Do this with your eyes closed. Repeat this until you feel calm."

This I did and entered a state that transcended the agitation. Irwin took this moment to continue.

"And what happened with your words?" A question in its directness entered the drifting float of my mind.

"They gained a response. I was told that my *nefesh* was like all others in its uncertainty. That it reflected my place in the bodily world."

The emotion of that moment became current and it welled within me. I needed to continue, to force out the words, commit myself to them.

"And I spoke of the vacuum that was my place in the bodily world. And I was told that the remedy was to raise my soul to the next level of *ruah*."

My head dropped and swayed. Sighs emanated from my mouth as an enactment of that journey from the grave. Irwin stood up, walked across to me and placed a comforting hand on my shoulder.

A DREAM UNTOLD

"That is enough for today, Peter. Finish your tea and let's talk of lighter things. Come back tomorrow and we can speak more of your soul."

That night I dreamt. Not of Vital, or as Vital. As Peter Paul. I saw my father mouthing words I could not hear. And then his father, the short bald man from my childhood. And then his father as advised by the dream. An unknown image now, one that drifts into the collective memory. To be replaced by faces that that dissolved into one another with beckoning eyes until the last one froze then turned to look upwards. To the silhouetted figure with outstretched arms who spoke of gathering up the ancestors.

"I was at peace after that dream," I told Irwin the next day, "not anxious or panicky. It gave me a sense of belonging, something I've not had for a long time. If ever."

"Was that last figure the same one from your original dream?" Irwin framed the question that puzzled me. It was the same stance and manner of dress. But an antecedent?

"Symbolically similar, I think. I wouldn't claim to have Luria as an ancestor!" Irwin laughed as we had mooted in previous discussions the possibility of the presence at the top of the steps as being the Ari.

"Well, whatever. I think that what you experienced last night is a step in your healing process."

"Irwin, you said yesterday that we would speak more of my soul. What did you mean by that?" I was anxious to move on. Somehow there was a pace that was being set for me in my transition back to some sort of normalcy.

"I was intrigued by the message you received at the grave. Raising one's soul is central to Kabbalistic doctrine. Ultimately one aspires to reach the level of *neshamah*, the upper soul, which is the platform, or throne for achieving the ultimate absorption into the Divine essence."

"I'm not sure I have that sort of aspiration!" I said jokingly. Wherever I was going, the one direction that I didn't see myself heading was that of being immersed in the rituals and practices of orthodox Jewry and my soul handed over … To what?

"I know," responded Irwin, "but I think there are certain things that can be drawn from these traditions. I broke off our meeting yesterday to give me time to think how I could possibly help you."

"And …"

"Don't rush me! Don't forget this is a new experience and new ground for me. We will learn together."

"I'm sorry. It's just that you have stirred something in me. Might I suggest that we take tea and contemplate the next step?"

"I think you have just taken it. But yes, tea it is."

I cradled the cup, feeling its warmth, watching the steam rise from the surface of the liquid. Irwin observed my stillness and joined me in this reflection. After a while gentle words drifted from him.

"Finish your musing and I can tell you my thoughts. Your ability to meditate will be a great asset."

I became aware of the room again and waited for Irwin to continue.

"You spoke of raising your soul from the level of *nefesh* to that of *ruah*. First you should understand their respective functions as described in the *Zohar*."

"Functions? In a tangible sense?"

"Well, yes. There is an equivalence to body and mind. The *nefesh* is the power that is associated with the bodily processes that sustain life. A sort of watching brief over your physical side."

"And the *ruah*?"

"This is the enabling force for the *nefesh*. It is likened to a breeze that blows over it. The two act in unison, for if *ruah* were withheld from the *nefesh*, it is said that it would bring death in its train."

"Death! So I am to die if I can't raise my soul!"

Irwin smiled at the aghast expression on my face. "Not in the physical sense. It is allusion to the death of the spirit – as you described yourself, the inability to function in the bodily world."

"And the *ruah* acting as the breeze that blows?"

"It is symbolic of the *ruah*'s role as intermediary between *nefesh* and *neshamah*. It is the conduit for the heavenly breath that breathes life into the body."

Irwin had provided me with Kabbalistic insight to the wisdom that had emanated from the grave. An awareness was growing of how he could apply this knowledge and engender the sense of self and identity that was lacking in me.

"You mentioned meditation before. How will that help?"

"As I told you before, there is a limit to my abilities to help you. It is for you to obtain the realisation that propagates the healing. All I can do is introduce you to some techniques that may stimulate the process."

At that Irwin rose from his chair and moved across to the window that overlooked one of the cobbled streets that had remained unchanged since the time of the Ari. He seemed to draw inspiration from this contact with the past. I was still absorbing what he had just said, when he continued: "There is a meditation that the Ari describes called the mystery of the Wings. Its use is to elevate the lower soul to the next level."

"Why Wings?"

"As Luria tells it, through Wings man can fly and ascend on high and take his soul on this journey at the same time as looking down on himself. Paralleling the wings of a bird are the arms of a man."

"I think you need to explain it to me!"

"Well, we have already discussed the *sefirot* as a metaphor for the body, and some Kabbalists imagine the image of it projected on themselves."

"I have felt that during one of my episodes."

"That will make it easier for you to understand and do, then. The right arm is considered to be aligned with *Hesed*, the vessel with the attribute of Love, and your left arm with *Gevurah*, that of judgment."

"And the meditation exercise?"

"The idea is to focus on these two orbs and their hidden qualities. As you expose the concealment, visualise their expansion inside the orb. The pressure exerted causes an oscillation in their effort to free themselves. It will require practice to get to this stage in the meditation, before you can symbolically fly."

"I think I'm with you, but carry on."

"The next step is to concentrate your energy into the vessels so that the vibration increases to such a point that you can imagine your arms fluttering, giving you the ability to be like a bird and fly through the air."

"That's quite a meditation!"

"I know. I am suggesting you try it, even though you are not a practising Kabbalist, as I think the experience could enlighten you, given what occurred when you were on the Ari's grave."

"I have always been open to trying new things. I'll let you know how I get on."

Each day I would use these techniques to escape from my body. So that I could release the emotion that was inhibiting the realisation of my Self. To see myself as whole, feel the actuality of connecting my inner dimension to a common spiritual presence. To that which I could not name. To that which binds humanity. To that which represents our meaning.

And I saw my shadow as it cast its darkness over me. As I flew, the shadow accompanied me, its blackness absorbing my reflections. "*I will always be there,*" it seemed to say, and this I accepted. "*Together we will progress,*" it said of our journey, and this became my truth.

And the realisation brought peace and I was ready to establish my existence, to move on.

Irwin observed the change in me, but was curious about one thing. "Do you still hear voices?" he asked.

"They will always be with me," I replied, "but now I know they come from within and can be my companions."

We spoke more of my past and it cleft itself unto me. Through all this I became united with myself. I had begun to reclaim my wholeness.

Dalia kept the world from me as I was enclosed in my room for these days of contemplation. We spoke little, mainly pleasantries over the evening meal until, sensing a change in me, she suggested that I now exercise my body as well as my mind. So began my walks with her. Around Safed and into the deep recesses of our imagination. I looked at places for a third time. First I saw them as a stranger. And then as Vital. And now I saw them refreshed. The synagogue, the steps, the house. Dalia took me back to the house. I walked around it, observing the encroachment of vine onto the blue plastered wall that bounded it. Fingers from the ground grasping the stucco, binding this place to the soil of Safed's foundation.

"How do you feel?" she asked. "What does this place mean to you now?"

Where my meditations were releasing my inner Self, these questions addressed my ability to function. Would standing in the presence of the house take me back to that troubled state? It was a chance that Dalia took, but I think we both realised the importance of this step.

"I still feel the presence that this place exudes. That will not go. It is for all time. I don't fear it now. I am convinced that this was the home of Soniadora and that her spirit guided me as she did Vital. I can find some comfort in this and in that deepness lies the dream."

"Yes. Your dream. We have not spoken much of that. I am intrigued by what you just said about the dream lying in the deepness of comfort."

"How do you explain a feeling, a sensation or rationalise a mystical experience?"

"Is that how you see the dream?"

"As the catalyst for a mystical journey, I see it as such."

My mind went back to George's questioning. He sought the rational explanation and desired to unveil the symbolism contained in the dream. But where his questioning was directed at the objective reality, Dalia was more concerned with the subjective emanation. She was leading to the inevitable, probing self-inquiry.

We walked back along the gravel path above the cemetery that led to the Ari's synagogue. These steps were silent, as both of us were submerged in thought. As the high wall of the temple loomed before us, Dalia spoke. It was the question I had anticipated.

"Why do you think you had the dream?"

I turned away and walked over to the fence that bounded the path. I looked down across the valley, my gaze flitting over the graves, seeking the answer. But eventually it came from within.

"I said it was a catalyst. What I sort of believe has a logic within an implausible scenario. Many in Safed have dreams that provide them with spiritual inspiration. I'm sure that if I had been deeply religious then I might have reacted quite differently. But then I might not have had the dream. I think I was in a position to receive something, though

"... I'm not sure how much Irwin has told you about my background."

"Nothing, really. He's quite discrete."

"Well, there have been a number of traumas in my life, particularly with a girl I was very close to. We lived together and probably would have got married. She died ... suicide."

The sound of that last word bounced back from the cemetery, as that form of death is rejected for burial. I felt the impact and gasped as an asthmatic clutching for breath.

"You don't have to tell me any more if you don't want to." Dalia stood by me and whispered the words along the fence.

"That's OK. I think it would help me to talk."

We leant on the railing and I spoke uninterrupted for the next half hour. I told her of my life with Eva, the alienation I have always felt and the isolation of being an only child orphaned by my early twenties. It all built to answering her question, my question.

"This was my state when I came to Safed. A lost and troubled soul, you might say."

"And do you think those feelings charged the atmosphere in the house that night?"

"Yes. And the lingering energy from Vital was captured by my emanations in the form of his dream. A more fanciful idea is that his *ibbur*, or transient soul, entered me. Whichever or what you wish to believe is not as important as the consequence."

"What consequence?"

"It triggered investigations and insights building to the cathartic moment in the house when I was filmed." I stopped talking and realised the significance of that moment.

"The episode that followed," I continued, "gave me an opportunity to experience the nature of reality and to be focused on what I truly was."

"And now?"

"There is no switch. It is not that the realisation that I had delusions and heard voices, and that I am now able to function, means that I am cured. I will always carry the adventure, for that is how I see it, and it will continue prodding, guiding and goading me."

We turned to look at each other and Dalia's understanding deepened. There was more to be said, but the day was getting cool and we made our way back to her house in the Artists' Quarter – the other side of the Steps.

We sat in Dalia's living room, a place that had evaded me in my stay with her so far. I think she had excluded me as the Peter Paul she had experienced would have been an intrusion into this private space. But now we could relax in the glow of a brisk uphill walk back. And wine was poured, not Irwin's tea. An atmosphere of conviviality, not exploration.

One wall was lined with old black-and-white photos in dark wooden frames. Mostly people, singly or in groups, with some shots of buildings.

I stood up, glass in hand, and approached the wall. Dalia came and stood by me.

"These are from Berlin. My parents brought them when they came to Palestine in 1933." Dalia had pre-empted my question.

"Tell me about them; they are extremely evocative. What little I know of my father's family is that some of them came from Berlin."

"These are my parents – Leo and Jenny Niemann. They left Berlin after Kristallnacht along with many other Zionist-inspired Jews."

"You were born here, then?"

"Yes, in 1938. On a kibbutz."

"And who is this?" I pointed to a distinguished figure in a formal portrait. Frock coat and top hat, standing in front of a city landscape.

"That is my maternal grandfather, Aaron Levi."

"Levi? With an 'I'?"

"Yes."

"That's my surname!"

"I know. When you shouted out your name the day after we found you at Luria's grave, I was going to ask you about it, but the time did not seem right."

"My father told me that I was named after one of his German cousins, Paul Levi. I believe he was a prominent Communist."

Dalia gasped and drew my attention to another photo. "This is my mother with her brother Paul. He was Rosa Luxemburg's lawyer and succeeded her as leader of the German Communist Party after her murder. Perhaps we are talking about the same Paul!"

An expectation suddenly rose in me. I looked at Dalia with different eyes, searching for a familial link. Excitement drove my response.

"That story sounds familiar. Did Aaron have any brothers?"

"Two, Jacob and Isaac. A biblical family!"

"Is there a picture of Jacob? That was my grandfather's name."

"Not among these, but I have a family album. It may be in there."

Dalia ran upstairs while I gazed at the mixture of portraits and snapshots, projecting myself into them, hoping to become part of them.

A breathless Dalia returned with a red and gilt leather-bound album, her finger marking one of its pages.

"Here," she said, opening the book, "here is Jacob with his children."

She showed me a photo of a youngish man with receding hair. Seated on a stool by his side was a boy of perhaps eight, with two older girls standing beside him.

"I have this photo at home," I shrieked in recognition. "That is my father on the stool and those are his two sisters Naomi and Rachel!"

"Then we are cousins."

Dalia dropped the book and we hugged until the tears flowed.

19

"My mother lives in Eilat, by the Red Sea. I'm sure she would be thrilled to meet you." Dalia paused as we continued to look through the photos.

"How old is she?" It was difficult for me to think that anyone of her generation was still alive. My aunts had both died quite young, well before I was born. An unknown cause, well, unknown to me. The nature of their deaths had never been spoken about.

"She'll be 87 next month. She's quite independent and still full of life."

"A birthday visit, then?"

"Of course. I was planning to drive down in a couple of weeks and spend some time with her. Her flat has a spare room where I normally sleep."

"Would there be somewhere for me to stay?"

"She has a sofa-bed in the lounge. She is used to lots of visitors."

"Great!"

Suddenly I was into the normality of living arrangements. A far cry from sixteenth-century mysticism and one that seemed to fulfil a need in me.

"I must telephone her first and prepare her for the shock. I'm not sure when she last heard from your father. I don't recall anything, so it may have even have been before they came to Israel."

"Other than the story of Paul Levi, my father never really spoke of his family."

"Did you ever ask him?"

"Well, no. As a teenager you don't really think about it. And when I was interested in knowing about the family it was too late. As I told you, he died when I was 21."

"I'm sorry."

We exchanged glances and she reached out and squeezed my hands. Keeping hold, she continued: "You haven't spoken much about your mother."

"My mother!" I wasn't anticipating that question. There was a darkness in my memory to which she'd been confined. Hidden away and not thought of. Dalia maintained her grasp and waited for my response.

"She died when I was a teenager. Of breast cancer."

"Yes, you said. You seem to have experienced many close deaths for someone your age. Actually I don't know how old you are."

"Thirty-two."

"Look, I shouldn't pry. It's just that I want to know all about you. Apart from my mother, you're my only relative."

"That's OK. It just came as a bit of a shock. No one has asked me about her for a long time. I'd sort of hidden it away."

What could I tell Dalia? The truth. I continued. "She was aloof and remote. I always felt that my father and I never met her aspirations. She made him feel that she had married beneath her. And as for me, I was too much of a rebel. She ran the home efficiently, but without warmth. Eventually I withdrew and didn't make an effort to relate to her."

Dalia did not need to speak. Her eyes were a deep well of compassion and she absorbed the renewal of despair that flowed through me.

And enabled me to confront my past.

This time my exit from Safed was not an escape. It was drawn from expectation, not panic. Knowing, not unknowing. Calmness, not anxiety. And I knew I was to return, that there was a permanence that was Dalia. London would continue to be my physical home, but Dalia provided a comfort, a sanctuary, a place of belonging.

We drove down the winding road away from that hilltop town. My eyes were open to the surroundings. I took in the trees that sheltered us from the sheerness of the drop alongside us. They were a life force, symbolic of much I had experienced. I was uplifted.

"I need to drop some paintings off at a gallery in Tel Aviv," Dalia had told me. It meant that the route would be the same as last time, along the coast road south of Haifa.

As we approached it my mind drifted back to the thoughts and feelings of the drive with George. The antithesis was complete. Where before I had looked through the face in the driver's seat, seeing it with blurred vision in a transcendent state, gazing at infinity, now I saw the profile of Dalia.

And I could look within and see the tranquillity contained there. And feel the reflected stillness born of our connection.

So the journey progressed, with us communicating in silence, deepening the attachment between us.

"It'll be a long day's drive," Dalia said as we left Tel Aviv, "but I'd rather go straight to Eilat than stay overnight somewhere, if that's OK."

"Fine. You're doing the driving, so it's really up to you and how you feel."

"Once we are past Beer Sheva there are only a few settlements along the way, so it'll pretty much be an uninterrupted drive and little traffic."

"I've not been to this part of Israel before, are there any particular points of interest along the way?"

"We'll be going through the Negev Desert. The highlight is the Ramon Crater. It's Israel's equivalent of the Grand Canyon. We can stop there for a bit if you like."

"Fine."

Beer Sheva was the last we saw of the greenness. The 50 miles to the viewpoint was a drive through increasingly arid land. A light wind ruffled the landscape and stirred the sand, and we progressed through a gallery of dust shielding the sun from our view. The road started to climb and I had a first glimpse of the hollow torn from the earth hundreds of millions of years previously. Jagged chunks of quartzite stood in serried ranks populating the crater's edge, witnesses to the history of this country.

"The best view is from here," Dalia said as we stopped at the observation point that looked westward across its 25-mile length.

We had left Safed soon after dawn, so it was still midday when I got out of the car to take in this place born out of the primordial ocean. Dalia watched as I crossed the road, pursued by a shrunken shadow that dissolved into the blackness of the asphalt and then disappeared as the sun went behind a cloud.

Time was suspended as my history coalesced with each stride. My eyes closed with the re-emergence of the sun and my mind was filled with the striated light of its brilliance, gleaming through protective lids. Each breath was new and in the comfort of shared solitude I paused to behold my future.

Peter Paul the Levite approaches the edge of the crater. He stands before it and looks west to the land whence he came.

He hovers on the brink, his trials behind him and surveys the risk of the world before him.

His arms rise and become outstretched to encompass all.

And the sun shone.

Hayyim Vital
Damascus 1610

Acknowledgements

Personal

First I must recognise my debt to Hayyim Vital for writing his *Book of Visions*, for without the discovery of our shared dream this novel would never have been written. The fact that this is a work of fiction rather than autobiography is down to Miriam Halahmy, who suggested I try this approach after my early attempts at a factual narrative. For the experience of being filmed in Safed I must thank Roy Ackerman of Diverse Production and my daughter Natalie Spanier for making the initial introduction. The documentary was screened in 1998 as part of the series "In Your Dreams".

My initial reluctance to be filmed was overcome by the late Marianne Jacoby, who introduced Jungian training to the UK. Her comment that "your dream wants to become famous" was a convincing argument. Our friendship and discussions provided me with many insights and I hope her critical eye would have looked kindly on this book.

I am grateful to my readers Jack Chalkley, Tony Feldman, Monique Morris, Maureen Rissick and Neville Shack for their feedback and encouragement and to the members of my Creative Writing Groups who have commented on extracts from the novel at many sessions. Ros Horton and Sue Ecob of the Cambridge Editorial Partnership have been both thoughtful and efficient in supporting the production of this book.

My family have travelled with me on this journey since that fateful night in Safed when they awoke to a frantic father and husband. So thanks to my children Natalie and Daniel for being there and to my wife Ros, who has been a vital sounding board and has provided unquestioning and continuing support.

Sources

Over the past thirty years I have read many books and articles on Kabbalah and the lives of Jewish mystics but must especially mention the Louis Jacobs book *Jewish Mystical Testimonies*, where

A DREAM UNTOLD

I first encountered the dream. Subsequently I have used the full English translation of Vital's *Book of Visions* by Morris Faerstein, called *Jewish Mystical Autobiographies*. For the life of Isaac Luria and Hayyim Vital, my prime reference has been Lawrence Fine's monumental work *Physician of the Soul, Healer of the Cosmos – Isaac Luria and his Kabbalistic Fellowship*. His earlier book *Safed Spirituality* was also of great use. In addition to Morris Faerstein's book, for original material I used the translation by Yitzchak Bar Chaim of Luria and Vital's volume *The Gates of Reincarnation*. J H Chajes' book *Between Worlds – Dybbuks, Exorcists and Early Modern Judaism* was invaluable in writing about Caleb's possession and exorcism. Kabbalistic theory has been drawn from many sources, but in particular Gershom Scholem's work *Kabbalah* and the Aryeh Kaplan books *Jewish Meditation* and *Meditation and Kabbalah*. Extracts and commentary on the *Zohar* have been drawn principally from two books – *Zohar, the Book of Enlightenment* by Daniel Matt and *The Wisdom of the Zohar* by Isaiah Tishby. For sociological background I mainly used *To Come to the Land: Immigration and Settlement in Sixteenth-Century Eretz-Israel* by Abraham David and Stanford Shaw's *The Jews of the Ottoman Empire*. Stories and legends of Luria and Vital have also been drawn from Aryeh Wineman's *Beyond Appearances*, Dovid Rossoff's *Safed: The Mystical City*, Solomon Schechter's *Safed in the Sixteenth Century* and the landmark book on the mythology of Judaism, *Tree of Souls*, by Howard Schwartz, whose wife Tsila kindly agreed to the use of her diagram of "The Ten Sefirot".

The fact sheets from Rethink (formerly the National Schizophrenia Fellowship) provided a clear background to psychosis and their daughter website www.voicesforum.org.uk (The National Perceptions Forum) provided valuable anecdotal material. *Psychosis and Spirituality*, edited by Isabel Clarke, gave an understanding of the theoretical basis. I would also like to thank those mental health professionals who have provided me with advice and feedback during the course of my writing.

Michael Berg
London 2008

Glossary

Binah	The third *sefirah* Understanding
Converso	Spanish or Portuguese Jew converted under duress
Cortijo	Spanish-style country house
Dybbuk	The soul that enters a living person with evil intent
Ein Sof	The endless or infinite; the ultimate reality of God
Gematria	Assigning a numerical value to words for further interpretation
Gevurah	The fifth *sefirah* Power
Gilgul	Reincarnation
Halakah	The legal side of Judaism
Hesed	The fourth *sefirah* Grace
Hod	The eighth *sefirah* Glory
Hokmah	The second *sefirah* Wisdom
Ibbur	The soul that impregnates a mature person with the purpose of rectifying past transgressions or fulfilment of an unaccomplished task
Kabbalah	The esoteric wisdom of the Torah, literally "receiving"
Keter	The first *sefirah* Crown
Khan	Hostelry or inn
Malkhut	The tenth *sefirah* Kingship
Metoposcopy	The art of discerning the meaning of signs on the forehead
Midrash	The written method of investigation into the Scriptures
Mikvah	Ritual bath used for purification
Minyan	The quorum of 10 males over the age 13 required for communal prayer reading
Mitzvah	An injunction of the *Torah* which can be positive or negative, plural *mitzvoth*
Nefesh	The first level of soul

Neshamah	The third level of soul
Netzah	The seventh *sefirah* Eternity
Peot	The sidelocks of hair which cannot be removed
Rosh Hodesh	Beginning of the lunar calendar month
Ruah	The second level of soul
Sefirah	One of the ten aspects or emanations of God, plural *sefirot*
Shekinah	The female Divine Presence associated with the tenth *sefirah* Malkhut
Shofar	Animal horn, usually from a ram, blown at *Rosh Hashanah* (New Year)
Shul	A synagogue
Talmud	Anthology of Jewish teachings
Tetragrammaton	The four-letter name of God
Tifferet	The sixth *sefirah* Splendour
Tikkun	Restoration, healing or repair
Tikkun olam	The healing of the world
Torah	The five books of Moses, i.e. the first five books of the Old Testament
Tzaddik	Righteous one
Tzimtzum	The contraction of Infinite Light allowing a finite world to be created
Tzizit	The fringes on the corners of garments dictated by the edict in the *Torah*
Yesod	The ninth *sefirah* Foundation
Yihudim	The practice of unification or communion with the souls of the dead
Zohar	"Illumination" or "Brightness", the classical work of Kabbalah originated in the second century by Rabbi Shimon ben Yohai